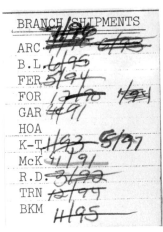

D1603554

EKA 2

MYS   West, Charles.
              Funnelweb / Charles West. -- New York :
           Walker, 1989, c1988.
              206 p. ; 22 cm.
              Reprint. Originally published: London :
           Collins, 1988.
              ISBN 0-8027-5738-3

        I. Title.

                                                89-9096

FUNNELWEB

FUNNELWEB

Charles West

Walker and Company
New York

Published in the United States of America in 1989
by Walker Publishing Company, Inc.

Library of Congress Cataloging-in-Publication Data

West, Charles.
Funnelweb.
Reprint. Originally published: London : Collins, 1988.
I. Title.
PR6073.E7624F86   1989   823'.914   89-9096
ISBN: 0-8027-5738-3

Printed in the United States of America

10 9 8 7 6 5 4 3 2 1

PROLOGUE

She wished she could accept the idea of dying.

Most of the time, her mind was so fogged, so full of dark, slow-moving monsters, like snakes writhing in mud, that she couldn't bring any thought into focus, about death, or anything else. She cried a lot, without understanding why she was crying; and sometimes, with the tears still dripping ·from her face, she would suddenly bray with meaningless laughter.

But every now and then her mind would clear, and she would become shockingly aware of what they had done to her. Through the throbbing in her head, the foul-tasting mucus in the back of her throat, the leaden heaviness of her body, she felt a worse pain: the pain of impotent hatred.

They were going to kill her. They *had* to kill her, now. If only Frank were here, he would tear them apart with his bare hands, he would go berserk, he would do such things . . . Her pulse quickened, and her jaw tightened at the thought of what Frank would do.

The glow faded. Frank was dead. Perhaps that was why she was here, *because* he was dead. She was getting confused again: she felt a hot resentment at Frank for dying and leaving her alone to face this horror, this *unfairness*.

'I hate bullies,' she said aloud. It was no more than a hoarse whisper, but it was immediately answered by a warning growl from one of the dogs outside. Her flesh crawled; she loathed that sound.

Where was she? The room was unfamiliar, and stiflingly hot. Her frock, filthy and spotted with bloodstains and food, clung damply to her as she stood up. Out of habit, she tugged against the chain with her left foot; then looked down, startled. The chain had gone. The raw marks circled her ankle, but the iron loop was gone. She was no longer chained up like one of their bloody dogs.

She looked slowly round the room. A new place. Was that

good or bad? She discarded the question. Everything was bad. Bad, and unjust and meaningless.

The room was bare, as the other room had been. An iron-framed bed, bolted to the wall. A thin mattress, two blankets and a pillow. A solid wooden table against another wall, with a bucket on it and a bucket underneath it. On the table beside the bucket were a tin mug, a dirty towel, a piece of soap and a roll of cheap toilet paper. There was nothing else in the room at all: not even an electric light. Not even a light-socket.

She moved unsteadily to the window. The dogs stirred, fidgeted, settled again. It was uncannily still. There was a distant, whirring sound, that stuttered intermittently like a faulty engine; insects whined and droned in the oppressive heat; and somewhere there was a raucous whistling and a snapping sound like the breaking of dry sticks. Outside the window was a railed verandah, and beyond that a strip of dark, marshy-looking ground, studded with blue flowers. Then a wall of trees, so tightly packed together that their tops interlaced into a thick, glossy green ceiling. Tall ferns seemed to float in the darkness under the trees, and thick lumpy vines hung from the topmost branches. Rain forest. But that told her nothing: they could have moved her a hundred miles, two hundred, a thousand.

She had been driven away in the big Range Rover, which had the caged-off part at the back for the dogs. She had slept most of the time. She remembered the smell of the dogs. She ought to have got used to it, but she hadn't; every time she woke, it was there, thick, musky. There had been a lot of jolting, which had made her grunt. She couldn't control the grunting, which settled into a rhythm—like a musical pig, she thought. She had laughed out loud, and hiccupped. And slept.

They had stopped somewhere, in the middle of the night, and she had hobbled from the car and squatted in a grove of tall trees. They—no, it was just one, the stocky one, who called her 'ma'— watched her. He was smoking one of his thin cigars. It was bitterly cold. Logically, she should have been beyond shame, but she was not. Like a mongrel bitch straining in a gutter, she thought acridly. She felt betrayed by her own body.

She staggered drunkenly on the way back to the car, but he made no attempt to help her. She felt overwhelmed by so much evil, so much contempt, so much hatred; it seemed incredible that the stars could be so beautiful, and the air, threaded with the scents of eucalyptus and cigar smoke, so sweet.

He had grinned at her, relishing her hatred. 'I reckon you'll be ready for these now, ma.' He pressed the brightly-coloured capsules into the palm of her hand, and wrapped her fingers round them. She was shivering uncontrollably; terrified that she might drop the capsules, she scrambled them awkwardly into her mouth, using both hands. He uncapped a plastic bottle and gave it to her. The water was warm and tasted musty; a lot of it dribbled from her chin on to the front of her dress. He held open the door for her, mockingly polite. She lay on the back seat, and waited numbly for the tablets to drag her back into sweet oblivion.

How long had she been in the car? One night? Two nights? She could no longer keep track of time; in the last weeks, whole days seemed to have got lost. She fell asleep in darkness and woke in darkness, not knowing whether one hour had passed or a whole day. Between the lucid spells, the hours were filled with starkly hideous nightmares, so sharp and vivid that her waking mind would refuse to accept the real world. Wide-awake, she would paw at her arms and legs, brushing off armies of imaginary spiders; or she would talk to the shadows in her room, seeing friends, relatives long since dead, watching unsurprised as they wavered and changed shape like images in a distorting mirror. Frank appeared often. She would hold out her arms to him, but he always drooped and turned away, his flesh hanging like wet clay from his skull.

She shook her head violently, as if to dislodge the horrors by force. She wasn't hallucinating now. She felt weak and ill, but she knew who she was, and why they had done these things to her.

Soon, they would have to kill her. They couldn't let her

7

go, after all this. If only she could get away! I want to *live*, she thought. Oh God, oh sweet Christ, I'm not a religious woman, I've only begged once before, when Frank was dying; you wouldn't give me that, please give me this. Please, *please* let me live, just long enough to kill those two young bastards.

She could make a run for it, right now. She wasn't chained up, there was no one in sight, she could slip past the dogs—

She slumped against the window-frame. In her present state, she couldn't bear even to think about the dogs, let alone face them. They were almost as terrible as their masters.

The dogs heard the car first, and erupted into a riot of hysterical barking and snarling. A minute later, the Range Rover shot into view, trailing dust, and skidded to a halt under her window. She could only see the top half of it. The stocky one got out, grinning round his cigar, and ambled towards the house. The barking subsided into anxious yelps. The slim one, wearing his baseball hat as usual, lifted something from the back seat, and carried it indoors.

They came straight to her room. 'Little surprise for you, ma,' the stocky one said. His companion dropped the thing he was carrying on the bed. It was her suitcase. 'There you are, my darlin',' he said.

Her legs felt weak. It was despicable to be so afraid of these men, but she couldn't help it. She knew—she just *knew* this was a trap, another way to hurt her. She stared at the suitcase as if it were a bomb. They watched her, apparently relaxed, but she sensed a tension between them, a shiver of excitement under the casual air.

The pale man in the baseball hat snapped open the locks of the case, and threw back the lid. 'Don't you recognize it?'

She couldn't meet his eyes any more. She knew his face too well—the pale waxy skin; the narrow band of freckles that smudged a crude W across his cheeks and over the bridge of his nose; the tiny ears, pressed close to the head; the deep lines each side of the nose, triangulating with the thin-lipped mouth. Even if she came out of this alive, that face would haunt her for ever.

Worst of all she dreaded his eyes. They were the colour of the sky at midday—a blue so pale as to be almost non-existent. And they were as empty of emotion as of colour. She had looked into those eyes a thousand times, searching—begging—for a sign of something—*anything*—that might reveal a trace of humanity. She had found nothing. There was nothing to find but a brutishness beyond her comprehension. This man had tortured her for forty-eight hours, using the crudest of methods. Later, she realized that he could have broken her in half an hour, if he had wanted to. He had made it last.

'She doesn't understand, the stupid old tart,' the stocky one sniggered. He laughed a lot, that one; his mouth was always on the fidget. 'You don't understand, do you, ma?' The perpetual grin was sly and wet, like a dog's, and was framed by a thin, scruffy beard. His hair, by contrast, was not scruffy: it was glossy and black, and curled forward over his brow like a breaking wave. 'They're all your things, ma. Your clothes. You left them behind, remember?'

She shook her head. 'Why—?'

'Because you're going home, ma. The party's over. We got what we want, now you can have what you want. You do want to go home, don't you?'

'Yes.' But it was a trick, she could tell. They couldn't hurt her while she had no hope, so they gave her hope in order to break her heart all over again. She backed away sullenly, trying not to look towards the bed.

Of course, it was the slim one who knew where to slip in the knife: 'There's some shampoo in the bag, darlin',' he said softly. 'I bet you'd love to wash your hair.'

'Oh God!' She slid down the wall, her arms wrapped clumsily round her head. 'Why don't you just lock me in a cage and prod me with sticks?' The bitterness burned in her throat.

'Here.' The pale-faced man stood over her, offering something in the palm of his hand. More pills. But these were different. These were blue. Three pretty blue tablets. 'A change of medicine, darlin'. Make you feel better.'

She snatched them hurriedly, and swallowed them before he could change his mind. She needed a pill. Badly.

'Right!' He spoke with exaggerated patience, as if instructing a backward child. 'Through that door, first left, there's a shower room. In the bag there's all your stuff—clean clothes, soap, hairbrush—all you need. What you're going to do, darlin', is to clean youself up, put on some pretty clothes, a bit of lipstick, a dab of scent to make yourself smell nice, 'cos right now you smell like a sheep's arse at crutching-time—' his partner snorted with laughter—'and then we'll send you on your merry way.'

'But . . .' She picked herself up, and moved unsteadily towards the bed. 'But . . .'

As usual, he read her mind. 'But where's the catch, you mean?'

'Yes,' she whispered.

The topmost dress was new. Yellow silk. She had never even worn it. She reached out to touch it, and then drew back as if stung. She had forgotten how filthy her hands were, how cracked and torn her nails.

He was watching her intently. 'You think we can't let you go, right?'

'Yes.'

'Because you will go straight to the police?'

'Yes.'

'It's a problem, isn't it? If we kill you, we might get done for murder; if we let you go, you're gonna snitch on us.'

She was suddenly very alert. This was the first time either of them had even hinted at the possibility of failure. Was that why they had moved her? Was somebody at last getting suspicious?

He went on: 'Anyway, I think we've cracked it. Here's what we'll do. We're going to dump you in the middle of nowhere. You'll have your car, and some petrol, but not much. Not enough to be careless. Pick the wrong direction, and you'll wind up in the desert, with the dingoes and kites for company. And it'll be dark, so you'll need to watch out.

10

The point is, you're going to give us a head start. If we're very unlucky, you may get to civilization and start getting someone to listen to you, in about twelve hours; but I doubt that. And long before then, we'll be away and gone. Another country, another life: the life of Reilly. And all on your money, my darlin'. Don't think we're not grateful.'

It was plausible. It was even possible. She was fumbling in the case for her sponge-bag before they were properly out of the room.

The water in the shower was cold, but the relief of using real shampoo, the luxury of perfumed soap, was like being reprieved from Hell. She scrubbed the dirt and dead skin from her body until her arms ached.

She left the soiled dress in the shower room. She couldn't bear to touch it. The underwear in her case presented a problem: it was too small. Had she put on weight in her captivity? It didn't seem possible. She shrugged. Conventional decency was the least of her problems. The cotton dress she chose was badly creased, but blessedly clean. Out of some bizarre sense of delicacy, she crammed her filthy pants into her sponge-bag.

To her surprise, they made her eat something before they set off. She could only manage some breakfast cereal and a piece of fruit; and that only out of a fear of upsetting them. She felt light-headed and full of energy; her headache and all the other pains had disappeared completely.

She half expected them to blindfold her once they were in the Range Rover, but they obviously hadn't even considered it. She sat in the front passenger seat; the bearded man drove and the other sat behind them, with her suitcase. The dogs were already in their cage, restless and bad-tempered in the heat.

As soon as they set out, she realized that his warnings about getting lost were well-founded. The way through the forest was hardly recognizable as a track at all. It twisted and turned bewilderingly; one minute they would be squelching through axle-deep mud, and the next straining at impossibly steep gradients, treacherous with loose stones. They jolted through clearings, carefully skirting the fallen logs, and squeezed between narrow banks, where thick vines with vicious curved tendrils clawed at the sides of the car.

The way gradually improved, from rutted path to dirt road to narrow bitumen track. They went fast, heading straight into the sun, the road pointing like an arrow to a range of blue hills. There was a little traffic here: mainly farm trucks and camping trailers, a couple of tankers. But in twenty minutes, she saw no more than a dozen vehicles. Mile after mile of drab, olive-grey bush; and then the road began to climb and twist, and they were back in the forest again.

Somewhere in the hills, they turned on to another dirt road. They passed through an open gate: there was a sign on it in red letters, but they were travelling too fast for her to make it out. The sun was quite low by now; from the crest of each rise they plunged from dazzling brilliance into tunnels of gloomy, blue-tinted shadow.

They turned on to another barely distinguishable track and jolted slowly down a steep incline.

'This'll do,' the man in the back said sharply.

'It's okay.' The driver chuckled. 'Just a bit further.'

'I said this'll do!' There was a tightness in his voice that startled her. Was he afraid of something?

She felt curiously detached from the proceedings, and unalarmed, as if it was all happening to someone else. Perhaps they were going to kill her after all. But if so, why all the charade of the bath and the clean clothes? To persuade her to come without a struggle? That was ridiculous: they could just knock her out with dope, like the last time. Maybe they just didn't like to murder dirty women. The thought struck her as funny, and she had to suppress a giggle. Mustn't be rude, she thought. The driver looked sideways at her, and grinned knowingly, as if he shared the joke. However, perhaps in deference to his partner, he slowed to a crawl, pulled off the track, and parked on a piece of flat ground studded with mounds of tussocky grass.

It seemed very quiet, here. Magpies fluted in the distance, and mosquitoes, excited by the evening's coolness, whined in at the open window. Her euphoria slowly evaporated. Her car was nowhere to be seen.

The driver got out. 'Come on, ma.' He lifted her case from the back seat. The slim man leaned out of the open door, and peered suspiciously at the ground. 'I tell you, it's okay,' the stocky one said. 'But you can stay there if you want to.'

The woman moved nervously round the front of the Range Rover. Then, unable to prevent herself, she cried out aloud in relief. She could see her car.

At right-angles to their track another path plunged steeply downhill between thick hedges of lantana. Her car was in a small clearing, near a grove of palm and huge carribin.

Scattered in the clearing were several irregular-shaped mounds of red clay, two or three feet high, looking like giant sandcastles eroded by the wind.

'Here.' The driver put her case down and pulled her car keys from his jeans pocket. 'Take it easy now, ma.'

The case was heavy, but she didn't mind. She didn't mind anything. She started down the track, her heart thumping wildly.

The pale-faced man fidgeted angrily, slapping his hand against the front seat. 'Come on!'

'No hurry.' Black-beard lit a cigar and showed his teeth. 'We'll wait till she gets to the clearing.'

'Why?'

'I'll tell you later.' He reached down by the front seat, and came up holding a whip like an oversized riding crop. Without haste, he walked round to the back of the Range Rover.

Half way to her car, it occurred to the woman that it was silly to carry the case any further. She could drive the car to the case. Suddenly she wanted to run, to find herself safely behind the wheel.

The man in the Range Rover said, 'She's dropped the bloody case! She's running!'

'Shit!' The stocky one banged open the rear doors. The two dogs slid swiftly and noiselessly to the ground. One of them tried to nip his ankle, but saw the whip in time, and cringed away, eyes rolling. He spoke to them softly, and they crouched close to the ground, circling warily, like black sharks.

'For Christ's sake, hurry it up!' Panic squeezed the slim man's voice into a despairing treble.

The other threw away his cigar and moistened his lips. Slowly he walked backwards to the spot where he had dropped the suitcase. The dogs followed him, weaving from side to side, their eyes flicking from the whip to his face and back again. He whistled once: a long, low note. Their ears went back, and they tossed their heads like horses. The bitch who had tried to bite him barked once impatiently. Her teeth looked like yellow knives. The man trailed the whip on the ground, drawing it backwards; they crowded to the spot, heads down, eager. He whistled again, a sharp, upward-curving phrase. Holding the whip close to his side, he made a short chopping movement with his other hand. A split second of quivering hesitation, and the dogs were off, moving over the ground like racing shadows.

The woman had almost reached the car when the leading dog struck. It sank its teeth into her wrist, and pulled her round, off balance. The second dog circled her, snarling, and leapt at her throat. She tried to fend it off, but the weight of its attack toppled her to the ground. She started to scream.

Black-beard was already lighting another cigar. 'I heard a cat make that noise once,' he said, snickering. 'I was skinning its tail at the time.'

The pale-faced man had overcome his reluctance to get out of the car. He walked slowly down the lantana track, as if mesmerized.

'Don't get too close,' Black-beard called. 'Let 'em finish. They're not too particular, once they get excited.'

'But it's getting so dark. I can't *see*.' The slim man's voice whined like a petulant child's.

The screaming changed abruptly to a series of short, deep, unrhythmical grunts, followed by a spaced coughing, like a stalled engine. Finally, an obscene slobbering sound, which was somehow worse than all the rest.

Between the banks of orange-yellow blossom the slim man stood like a statue. And yet not quite like a statue; not absolutely still. Staring intently down at the clearing, oblivious of the rest of the world, the man in the red baseball cap was contentedly sucking his thumb.

CHAPTER 1

'I'll show you what I want you to do,' the director said. He led the way up the slope, taking the path the technical crew had used, up the dry bed of a small creek. Tom Grant followed, picking his way carefully. It was treacherous going in the half-light: boulders rocked underfoot, and their shoes skidded on unexpected patches of slimy mud. But at least it was still cool, and the flies hadn't yet built up to battalion strength. Behind them both, the director's PA, an efficient young woman in dungarees and climbing-boots, trailed along carrying her clipboard and radio intercom. The creek became narrower and less clearly defined as they climbed higher, and finally disappeared in an untidy tangle of ferns and scrub. But the way forward was clearly marked by the thick black cables that snaked up the hillside. At the top, where the ground levelled out, the crew had erected a platform of planks and scaffolding, and the angular hoist for the camera was already in place. Dozens of men were still toiling on and around the platform in ceaseless, and apparently quite arbitrary activity. The director cast a knowledgeable glance in their direction. 'Couple of hours yet,' he observed.

Tom nodded without comment. In his limited experience of location filming, the technical set-up always took twice as long as the director estimated, and the current shot was always the most important one of the picture.

They were high up, here: not above the tree-line, but on a bare, rocky knoll that crowned the wooden hill like a tonsure. The light was improving minute by minute. On the eastern horizon, the rich layers of colour—orange, yellow, green, mauve—paled rapidly, and were punched aside by the golden rim of the sun.

Nikos, the director, turned his back on the sunrise, and pointed. 'That's where I want you to run. See the camera?'

Tom looked. 'No.'

'That's good. They've got to keep it camouflaged from this angle until you're past the half-way mark. But it's there —just to the left of that rock that sticks out like a thumb. Use that rock as your mark from here.'

The rock he was pointing to looked to be about six hundred yards away, and some hundred feet higher than the plateau where they stood. Tom grunted. 'It's going to be a tough run.'

To his credit, Nikos didn't remind him that that was what he was being paid for. He said enthusiastically, 'That's the idea. In many ways, this is the most important shot of the whole movie. It's a race, see: a contest, like the tennis match, only this time the stakes are for real. Life and death stuff. Hell, you've read the script.'

Tom had. He didn't think he could stand a paraphrase. 'Okay,' he said quickly. 'Just tell me what I have to do.'

'Simple. Just run from here to that rock as fast as you can.'

Tom examined the terrain attentively. 'That's pretty rough going. It's not going to be fast.'

'Oh, come on! You'll cover the ground like a gazelle.' Nikos snickered unpleasantly. 'At any rate, you'd be faster than Lewis.'

Tom raised another objection. 'I'll have to watch my feet all the time. I won't be able to clock that bloody marker while I'm running.'

''Course you will.'

'You want me to break my leg? Before we do the tennis sequence?'

'I'm not crazy about that tennis stuff anyway,' Nikos said thoughtlessly. He considered the problem with manifest lack of patience. 'Look, this has got to be for real. You're going to look like you're doing it for the first time, because you *will* be doing it for the first time. I've got three cameras on it: we can cover you every inch of the way.'

'You're hoping to get this in one take?'

'Sure. That's the only way it's gonna work. True realism.

18

If you slip, you pick yourself up and battle on. When you fight your way up that final slope, the audience is gonna see real sweat, man, real pain.'

'Thanks a lot,' Tom said drily. He thought of all the technical hazards: power-failure, inferior film stock, hair-in-the-gate, not to mention the potential for human error—and he guessed that he would be doing this run, or at least parts of it, half a dozen times.

Tom studied the territory ahead with some care. If the director wouldn't allow him to reconnoitre, he had better glean what information he could. There was no clear path between the spot where he stood and the marker. Immediately ahead, the land sloped gently downwards for about fifty yards through widely-spaced trees and scrub, then levelled off until the last two hundred yards, which featured a long, curving climb to the thumb-shaped boulder. The level stretch was bare, except for a few stunted and wind-tortured trees; and here the land to the south fell away sharply in steep slopes of loose scree interrupted by jutting headlands of rock. Nikos pointed to the ridge. 'I want you to keep as close to that edge as you can. I've got a tracking camera at the bottom of the hill, shooting you in silhouette against the sun.'

'What happens where the ridge joins up with the hill?' Tom asked. 'From here, it looks as if I run straight into that bluff. I can't see any path at all.'

'It's narrow,' Nikos admitted, 'but only for a few yards. It's safe, I swear. On my mother's grave.'

Nikos's mother was alive and well and living in Florida, but Tom didn't think it was worth quibbling about. He said, 'I'm not a stunt man, Nikos. Be sure you're not trampling on any union rules, here.'

Nikos didn't bother to hide his exasperation. 'Stunt men I got like a mongrel has fleas. This is the job you were hired for. This and the tennis. If I can't get in close, I lose tension and credibility. You want to ruin my picture? No, don't answer that. Go get some breakfast and report to Wardrobe and Make-up. I'll need you back up here in ninety minutes.'

19

The director's assistant, who had been hovering at a discreet distance, gave Tom a meaningful smile. 'I'll call you when we're ready, Mr Grant,' she said.

The clutter of vehicles at the bottom of the hill—cars, trucks, trailers, caravans—gave the site a fairground air. Tom picked up a mug of coffee at the chuck-wagon, and went over to the temporary hut that served as a dressing-room. His dresser for the day, a painfully thin, middle-aged man with skin the colour of weathered teak, was setting out his clothes, referring frequently to a group of Polaroid photographs he had pinned to the wall. ''Morning, sir,' he said. 'Got the place to ourselves today, very nice. Not what you'd call over-elaborate, costume-wise, as you can see. One pair dark trousers, rather dusty; one tattered shirt, tastefully decorated with bloodstains and mud; one pair cotton socks with funny patterns up the sides; and one pair shoes.'

Tom sipped his coffee. 'Let me see the shoes, Alfie. And the socks.'

Alfie held them out for examination, and studied Tom's face with some anxiety. Actors were so unpredictable. If there was a row this early in the morning, he'd have an all-day migraine: he knew it.

'I can't run in these,' Tom said mildly. 'I'd break my bloody neck. There's a pair of joggers in my bag. See if Wardrobe can break them down to look like these. And I need a thick pair of socks.'

'They got the thin ones specially. Thought they'd be cooler.'

'Thick, short, woollen socks, Alfie. Those rocks are hard.'

'Yes, sir. Of course.'

'If they can't disguise my own shoes, they'll have to get me some others. Thick, flexible soles, with a good grip. Tell 'em I've got to run half a mile over a sodding mountainside.'

'Yes, sir. Half a mile over a sodden mountainside. I'll tell them.' Alfie escaped, thankful it had been no worse.

Tom put on the tattered shirt and the dusty trousers, and wandered over to the Make-up cabin. There was only one girl on duty. In deference to Tom's grimace, she turned down her transistor radio a few decibels, but not below the pain threshold. She waved Tom to a chair, wrapped a plastic bib around his neck, and began to apply make-up to his face with a small sponge. Tom closed his eyes, and tried to ignore the noise. There was a little relief from the pop music while the disc jockey reviewed some item of local news, his voice quacking implausibly up and down the scale like some species of operatic duck.

'They're still fussing about that dingo business,' the make-up girl shouted. The pop music started again, and she jiggled to the rhythm, bumping Tom's arm with her hip.

'What dingo business?' Tom asked, in spite of himself. He didn't really want to conduct a conversation at full bellow, but his curiosity got the better of his caution.

'That woman who died in the desert,' she yelled. 'Some people say dingoes killed her, others say they couldn't've. All sorts of people are getting real het up about it.'

'Wasn't there an inquest? What did the coroner say?'

'Accidental death.' The girl lost interest. Her favourite commercial came on, and she sang along happily with the jingle, stepping back and surveying Tom's face in the mirror. 'Okay. Time for the wiggie.'

Even now, Tom could never get used to the transformation the wig made. It was partly the colour—the dark hair certainly framed his face more dramatically than his own sandy crew-cut; but it was mainly to do with the shape, and the line of the brow. He still looked tough, but it was a gentler, more romantic toughness. He looked, in fact, exactly like Lewis Goring.

Tom leaned closer to the mirror. 'It's slightly different.'

'A few more grey hairs,' the girl shouted. 'Mr Grigoros is a stickler for realism. Oh Lord, I nearly forgot—' She found a brush and a pot of paint, and sketched in faint shadows under his eyes, blending the colours in with her thumb.

Tom's mouth twitched. 'Lewis will go mad.'

'Mr Grigoros *insisted*. He came down specially and *insisted*.' The girl rolled her eyes in mock terror. 'He's a stickler.'

The cabin rocked slightly, and a vision appeared in the doorway. Immensely tall and deeply tanned, the vision had shoulder-length blond hair and tiny, twinkly blue eyes. He wore a chauffeur's cap, a black satin shirt open in a wide V that extended down to his navel, and white leather trousers of a truly incredible tightness. The bulge at his crotch had the size, if not the symmetry, of a Rennaissance codpiece. There were heavy gold chains around his neck and at his wrists. He was broader than Tom, and taller, although it was not easy to determine his height exactly, on account of the immense heels on his white, patent-leather cowboy boots. His face ought to have been square-jawed, Nordic, severe: but in fact it was round, soft and motherly. He was Lewis Goring's dresser, valet, chauffeur, secretary and general slave.

The vision stretched out a contemptuous hand and extinguished the din from the transistor. 'Madame says, will you call in when you've finished in this tart's parlour,' he drawled languidly. 'And who put those fucking bags under your eyes? Mother will go mad.'

'Mr Grigoros *insisted*,' the make-up girl shouted. She seemed unaware that the music had been turned off.

'Okay, Brian, I'll be along in a minute,' Tom said. 'I've got to find Alfie and see if he's fixed my shoes yet.'

'You leave that scrawny little palome to me, my precious,' Brian said. 'I'll see to the foot-clobber. You hurry along and comfort the Queen Bee. She's going bananas about those script changes.'

'I didn't know he was working today,' Tom said, surprised. 'How is he?'

Brian eyed him coldly. 'Mother is in perfect health. She will live forever.' It was a rebuke, and Tom acknowledged it with a nod. He should have known better than to raise the subject.

He walked to Lewis Goring's caravan, parked in the quietest corner of the site. Lewis didn't appear to be going bananas. He was sitting on a couch by the window, with his feet up, cushions at his back, reading an illustrated book on modern art. He greeted Tom with obvious pleasure.

'Hi, General,' he said. He laid the book aside. 'There's a Nicholson coming up for sale next month. I was wondering if I could afford it. Who put those fucking bags under your eyes?'

'Apparently it was Nikos's idea.'

Lewis scowled. 'I think I hate that kid. Every day he finds a new way of telling me I'm getting old.'

'The make-up girl says he's a stickler for realism.'

'A pain in the ass is what he is. What's the big idea, paintin' up my double to look like Methuselah? Hey, you look terrific in that wig, you know that?'

He does look older, Tom thought: every day a little older. But that voice still works its magic: that twangy, mid-West drawl that was even more famous than his face.

Thousands tried to imitate that voice: a few could manage the throaty resonance, but no one at all could get near the style, the timing. Tom had admired Lewis Goring's films before he had even met the man; now, though he counted him as probably his closest friend, he was still a fan. 'I didn't know you were working today, Lew?' he said.

'It ain't likely. But that vain sumbitch thinks he's gonna clear that running scene by three o'clock. General, have you seen the new pages of script?'

'No.'

'You're a lucky man.'

'I don't need to see any script, come to that.'

'Hey, that's right. Have you ever spoken a single word in any picture?'

'You know I haven't. I don't have a career in this business. I'm only here because I look like you.'

'Make no mistake, General,' Lewis said seriously, '*I'm* only here because you look like me. If it weren't for you I would've been finished three years ago.'

'Moonshine. How are you feeling, anyhow? Brian told me you were going to live forever.'

'He hopes I will. Who else is gonna put up with that freak? Hell, I'm okay. These new pills don't make me as dopey as the others, but I have to throw up every once in a while. How about you? How're *you* feelin'?

'Fine.'

'How's the tennis coming along?'

'I have no idea. It's got to be the most boring activity ever invented. And the coach is the most evil-tempered maniac I've ever met.'

The van rocked like a boat in a heavy swell, and suddenly Brian dwarfed the narrow room. 'Here's your shoes, beautybum,' he lisped. 'I hope to God they're all right. Wardrobe is foaming at the mouth, and Alfie has retired to her tent with a headache.'

They were Tom's own shoes, painted over with black dye. Tom was relieved to see them: that was one problem out of the way. 'Well, put them on, honey-child,' Brian said pettishly. 'I'll take your shoes back to your dressing-room. God knows I don't want to stay here. You two lookalike wallabies give me the creeps.'

Lewis yawned, and settled himself comfortably on his cushion. He regarded Tom with some concern. 'We were talking about how you feel?'

'I told you, I feel fine.'

'The last time I saw you, you were looking a little broody.'

'Broody?'

'Is that what I mean? Moody, maybe. Not overflowing with happiness. Homesick?'

Tom shrugged. 'I guess so. A little.'

'How long you been out here?'

'Three years and seven months.'

'Why don't you go home to England?'

'Scotland. Maybe I will.'

'Oh, I see.' Lewis nodded wisely. 'Woman trouble.'

Tom stared at him in some confusion. 'You mean you don't know about it?'

'How should I?'

'Well—God, there aren't any secrets in this business. Everybody knows everything about everybody.'

'Except me. Well, I don't wanna hear it if it's nasty.'

'It's not particularly nasty,' Tom said, 'just ordinary. I had a messy divorce, and after a while, it seemed a good idea to get out of the country.'

24

'Trying to forget, huh?'

'Not exactly. It became a bit embarrassing. You see—'

Brian had lingered, to eavesdrop brazenly on this exchange. 'My God, you are an ignorant fairy!' he exclaimed, waving a bejewelled finger at Lewis. 'You are probably the most ignorant fairy in the whole twinkling universe. You must be the only periwinkle this side of the Black Stump who doesn't know who Tom's ex-wife is.'

'Thank you, Jeeves,' Lewis said blandly, 'you are truly a treasure. So, General, who is your ex-wife?'

'Maria d'Abrolhos,' Tom said. 'Of course, she wasn't called that when she was married to me.'

'Maria d'Abrolhos? The opera singer?'

Brian snorted. 'Opera singer! Only the greatest prima donna in the whole damn world!'

'I think I read that in *Time* magazine,' Lewis commented. 'So I guess it has to be true.'

'She *is* pretty famous,' Tom said. 'And every time she hit the headlines, I was fair game for the news media. That was one of the reasons I got out.' He was uncomfortable with this conversation; he wished he could find a way to change the subject.

'Weren't you—' Lewis began, but he was interrupted by a knock on the door. An anxious-looking youth poked his head inside. He was one of the gophers on the film, nicknamed the Artful Dodger because of his ability to disappear when heavy work was in the offing. 'Mr Grant?' he said. 'Mr Grigoros asked me to call you. We're ready now.'

'Okay, Dodge. Just coming.' Tom escaped thankfully.

Brian had obviously changed his mind about leaving. He sat down, his tiny eyes twinkling like stars, bursting with information. 'That's less than half the story. Our Thomasina used to be one of London's finest.' The masculine gender never featured in Brian's vocabulary. He simply refused to acknowledge its existence. Understanding him was largely a matter of intuition and guesswork.

'You mean a cop?' Even Lewis resorted to a glossary from time to time.

'Yes, of course. Doing well—Detective-Superintendent, no less.'

'Is that good?'

'It's impressive, at her age. But then, my dear, domestic bliss turned to ashes, and she shot right off her trolley. She bopped a journalist.'

'Tom did?'

'Broke the creature's jaw. For hinting, in some greasy gossip column, that Tom's lovely wife, the ambitious young opera singer, was making a special kind of music with a rich French banker. Now, when you think about it, bopping people is not the way to shrink out of the limelight. The Press crucified that poor, cuckolded person. Firstly, the news item was true, which broke Tom's heart; and secondly, in his fury, he bopped the wrong news-hound. Or should that be news-bitch? Anyway, the embarrassment was simply too ghastly to bear; so Thomasina ran off to the Colonies. To forget.'

'My, oh my.' Lewis shook his head. 'He doesn't look the impulsive type, does he?'

'She looks like you.'

'Only with that wig on. Hey, do you think he's still in love with his Maria? In her photos she's some handsome broad.'

'We may have a chance to find out.' Brian chuckled. 'She's coming to sing at the Opera House in a couple of months.'

CHAPTER 2

Tom went through his sequence of loosening-up exercises while the director had his say. Nikos, like so many young directors, got wound-up and nervous before the first take of a new sequence, and he wasn't yet experienced enough to conceal it. 'All you have to think about is staying on line and running like hell. There's no sound to worry about—this whole sequence is covered by music and wild-track. But

26

remember the drama here. Lew has *got* to get to that helicopter before the bad guys.'

'Or it's the end of civilization as we know it,' Tom said, straight-faced.

Nikos was affronted. 'There's a lot of symbolism here. Wait till you see the picture. Now, I may want to give you instructions while you're on the move—'

'What kind of instructions?'

'How the hell do I know? Spontaneity is the name of the game, here. If it gets dull, I may want some variety. Jumping over poisonous snakes, maybe: something like that.'

'How many poisonous snakes do you have out there?'

'The snakes we can put in later. If I want you to jump, I'll tell you.'

'Tell me, how?'

'That's what I'm trying to tell you!' Nikos's voice climbed shrilly, and the crew on the camera platform cackled in appreciation. Nikos frowned, and lowered his voice. 'From here to the ridge, I'll use the loudhailer, if I need to. My assistants with the other crews also have loudhailers, and we're on a separate radio channel. So, I can control you over the whole run. Just be alert, and do what I say.'

'Yes, sir.' Tom suppressed a grin. Nikos was annoyed, because he hadn't been able to pass on his nervousness. Film directors only came in two kinds, in Tom's experience: either they were so laid-back you wondered if they were awake, or they hopped around like popcorn on a hot pan.

'Good,' Nikos said. 'We'll go in ten minutes.'

Two hours later, everything seemed to be ready. Communications had been tested, a fault in the camera hoist had been fixed, arguments with the cameramen about wasted film had been settled, the first announcement on the loudhailer, 'This is a take!' had echoed down the valley, scaring crowds of birds into the air; and the director was clutching the intercom microphone as if he thought someone was going to steal it.

'Okay, everybody,' he breathed. 'Here we go. Turn over!'

The intercom crackled: 'Camera one—rolling!'

'Camera two—rolling!'

'Camera three—rolling!'

'Speed?' inquired Nikos.

'Speed one!'

'Speed two!'

'Speed three!'

'Mark it!' The answers squawked back on the intercom.

'Okay.' Nikos raised his arm. 'Action! Go, man, go!'

Tom ran. He covered fifteen yards, caught his foot in a root, and hopped wildly through the bush, windmilling his arms to keep his balance. Behind him the camera crew shrieked and hooted with laughter, pummelling each other in their joy.

'Cut! Cut!' shouted Nikos, ignoring the intercom.

As Tom trailed back up the slope, the second cameraman came on the air: 'Still rolling. Got a lot of footage of empty hillside, here.'

'Cut! Cut!' Nikos yelled into his mike.

'Take it easy,' the voice protested. 'You damn near blew my ear off.'

'We'll go again as soon as everyone's ready,' Nikos said. For the first time that day, he sounded relaxed. To his PA he added in an undertone, 'I want that. Print it.'

Somewhat belatedly, people began to wonder whether Tom had hurt himself; but in spite of their very real concern, giggles kept bubbling to the surface and erupting like marsh gas. Tom bore it all stoically. He was actually very relieved: he could easily have sprained his ankle, or worse; but in fact he had escaped unhurt. And certainly, everyone was a lot more cheerful.

In due course they went through the whole process again, and this time Tom got off without mishap. Behind him, Nikos urged him on: 'Faster! Go! Go!'

There was a breeze up here, but it was still damnably hot, and the sun had warmed up the rocks of the bare ridge. Tom shook the sweat away from his eyes and concentrated on his footing. This stretch looked level from above, but the rock actually sloped slightly to his left, and occasional loose boulders littered the route. He heard a shout from below: 'Get as close to the edge as you can!' He ignored it. He was as close as he wanted to be. Another shout: 'Pull up short! Stop dead!' He did as he was told. 'Now, back a few paces, run and jump—there's a snake in your path!' Tom backed off and jumped over the imaginary snake. He landed on a loose stone, which flew up and hit him on the arm. 'Run! Run!'

Tom ran. Jumping over non-existent snakes was earning him ten times what he earned as a policeman. Funny world.

He was nearing the end of the ridge, and in range of camera three. Not far to go, but it was all uphill. The pain in his side began to make itself felt, but it wasn't going to be a problem. He was more than half way there. He pushed himself harder.

Now that he was closer, he could see that the next part of the route, where the ridge abutted on to the next hill, was going to be a scramble. Nikos had admitted that the path was narrow: Tom could see no path at all. There was firmer ground higher up the hill, but to reach it, Tom had to clamber round a pyramid of loose shale and rock that looked ominously like a recent fall. Worse, the slope to his left was getting steeper and steeper, falling away abruptly in places to leave a ragged cliff-edge.

He made the best speed he could, slipping and sliding on the shifting stones. Up ahead, the loudhailer urged him on: 'Move! Move!' In places he had to go like a cat, on all fours. The stitch in his side stabbed harder: he gritted his teeth and pushed himself to run through the pain.

He nearly made it. He could hear the stones still shifting after he had passed: an ominous grinding sound, the smaller pebbles pinging like glass. But he was still finding enough purchase to move forward. He rounded the outer bulge of the rock-pile, and saw firmer ground just ahead. He jumped.

He was conscious of applause and cheers from the crew, now less than a hundred yards in front. He registered with some satisfaction that he was still where the director wanted him to be. Then, with a heart-sickening lurch, the ground fell away from under his feet.

He threw himself forward, face down, instinctively grabbing for a handhold. His fingers scrabbled through thin soil,

29

scraped on rock. The ground underneath him crumbled away, unstable as sand. Tom began to slide inexorably down the hill.

As yet, he had no sense of danger. He was still concentrating on the job in hand: to finish the run. The director had said that if he fell, he was to pick himself up and run on.

He rolled sideways and grabbed for a jutting shoulder of rock. It slowed him for a moment, but the handhold was too shallow, too smooth. Underneath him the thin soil-cover shredded like cotton-wool, and the sliding shale gripped at his clothes, pulling him down. The angle of the slope increased sharply, and Tom at last began to realize that he was in trouble. He could see nothing but shifting, sharp-edged stones and clouds of grey dust. He wasn't hurt yet, but he was sliding faster and faster, out of control. He had no idea what lay below. This headlong slide might gradually level out, and prove to be no more dangerous than a gentle toboggan ride. On the other hand, the slope, even steeper now, might suddenly turn into a vertical drop.

Out of the corner of his eye, Tom saw a plant. It was a tiny, thin-stemmed flower, its head not much bigger than a peppercorn. But what interested Tom was that he was sliding past it. It was not moving down with the rest of the hillside! He grabbed at it; the roots clung to the rock with surprising tenacity, gave him momentary purchase. There were more flowers: a whole clump of them. He clutched at them like a drowning man at a rope; they couldn't stop his fall, but they slowed it, gave him just enough of a hold to pull clear of the tumbling avalanche of stones. He was no longer being carried along by the moving tide of rock, but he was still falling, the slope now so steep as to be almost vertical. He clawed at the cliff face with bleeding fingers, trying to slow down his descent. Somehow, he gained control. With a wrench that jolted every bone in his body, his hands closed round a spur of rock that held his weight. His feet explored the territory below, found toeholds that would take his weight, ease the strain on his arms. He pressed close to the rock face, panting and dizzy, grateful for the coolness of the stone.

30

The dizziness passed, and the frantic beating of his heart steadied enough for him to begin to take stock. The roar of the rock-slide stopped as abruptly as it had begun. He could hear shouting, but it sounded a long way off. It seemed strangely dark, somehow. He was, of course, on the south side of the hill, but at this time of day the shade wasn't usually so deep. He twisted his head round. There were trees behind him: a forest of massive ghost-gums and other tall trees he couldn't identify. The nearest branches seemed almost close enough to touch. It was a reassuring sight; he was below the level of the tree-tops, so this slope must bottom out soon. He tried to look down, but his shoulders were pulled too high to see very far. There was a solid-looking ledge only a few feet below, and to his right. Moving slowly, and testing every toehold before he transferred his weight, he inched down to it. For the first time he felt secure, and could look down properly.

His troubles were not over. Twenty feet below, a jumble of loose rocks and scree stretched out to meet the ragged edge of the forest; but although he leaned outwards as far as he dared, he couldn't see the rock-face beneath the ledge at all. He was on an overhang; but how firm it was, or how far it extended, he had no means of knowing. A few pebbles and fine gravel showered around his head, discouraging him from attempting the upward climb.

Below, and to his left, he could see some dark patches on the rock that looked like moss or lichen. The rock formation at the base of the cliff ballooned out in smooth, bulbous shapes, like a heap of partly-inflated gigantic footballs.

It looked the most promising option. He shuffled his way along the ledge, checking every now and then to see if he had reached the end of the overhang.

He negotiated carefully round a jutting buttress of rock and suddenly saw that it was going to be easy, after all. There was another, wider ledge, only ten feet below him. It looked a comparatively simple matter to lower himself on to that ledge and, with luck, drop from there to the base of the cliff. His biggest danger was of overbalancing, if he slipped and hit the lower ledge awkwardly. But the descent was furnished with a few possible footholds, as far as he could see. It was worth a risk.

He lowered himself carefully over the edge, and tested his weight on the likeliest-looking foothold, a knuckle-shaped stub of rock about four feet down. He made good progress, clinging like a fly to the cliff-face, and in a few minutes, he realized that his feet were only inches above the wide shelf he had seen from above. With a sense of relief, he felt the tips of his toes touch the ledge, and he was able to let go, and ease the tension on his aching arms.

The ledge crumbled under his feet, and collapsed with a dry, rasping sound, like gravel tipping from a truck. Tom fell with it, grey dust enveloping him like a fog. His hands grabbed wildly at the ledge as he fell; it crumbled like dry bread under his hands. The dust blinded him, invaded his mouth and nose, bringing an instant of total panic: this was worse than drowning.

The landing drove the breath out of his body, but it could have been worse. His feet jarred, then skidded on the loose, fine scree, pitching him sideways to roll helplessly down the steep slope. He finished on all fours, coughing and spluttering, clawing the dust from his eyes, cut and bruised, glad to be alive.

He could hear the shouting from above and below, but he couldn't make out any of the words. It would be several minutes before he could get his own voice to work. He spat out dust, and waited for his heart to stop hammering. Finally he felt fit enough to look around and take stock.

The rescuers below were having trouble getting through to him. Tom could hear them cursing and yelping with anger and frustration. They had encountered a dense thicket of lawyer-vine, trickier and more dangerous than a barbed-wire entanglement. Up above, they seemed to be better organized, but occasional showers of pebbles and dust showed that they were having difficulties, too. Tom stood up unsteadily. The slope had deposited him almost at the very edge of the forest; flies were already leaving the shelter of the ferns to investigate this new source of moisture. The shouting from above became increasingly anxious. Tom wanted to reassure them, but he could achieve nothing louder than a strangled croak.

Nikos's voice, young and strangely unconfident, reached him: 'Hang in there, Tom. We're sending someone down as soon as we can get a rope.'

It was shadowy and cool down here, trapped between the trees and the steep hillside; harshly beautiful, except . . .

Tom found his voice. 'Just get the bloody rope,' he shouted. 'And fast. And phone for the police. There's a goddam corpse down here!'

CHAPTER 3

The tall, well-dressed woman waited impatiently in the phone-box, the receiver to her ear, one hand pressing down on the hook. The phone rang, making her jump, although she was expecting it. She lifted her hand and began speaking immediately. 'I hate this,' she said. 'Are you sure it's necessary?'

'Yes,' the man said bluntly. He went on, flattening any argument: 'Nobody told me the man Chiswick was shot.'

The woman felt a trickle of fear at the nape of her neck. 'It was the safest way.'

'Safe? Now there'll be a murder inquiry. It's only one step from those two crazies to me.'

'Relax. Nobody's going to make the connection.'

'What about the gun?'

'At the bottom of the ocean,' she lied easily.

'Sure?'

'Of course. Look, you've been safe for seven years. You're still safe.'

'Maybe. That Surfers' Paradise business made me edgy. It could happen again.'

'Not if you're careful.'

'Careful?' The man's voice crackled with vicious anger; she was grateful for the miles that separated them. 'Jesus Christ, I can't live like a hermit.'

'Nobody's asking you to. Look, it was a million-to-one shot. And we took care of it, right?'

'What about the detective?'

'Ex-detective. No problem. He's a lush. What with the guilt and the juice, he's practically imbecile. Anyway, we have him watched.'

'Watched? What the hell good is that? What do you think this is, a TV show?'

'Brumby is taking care of it. Don't worry, the guy's harmless. He's drinking himself into an early grave.'

The man was silent, thinking. Finally, he said, 'I got this feeling. In my gut, you know?'

She forced herself to keep the exasperation out of her voice. 'What feeling?'

'I just got this feeling that everything is coming unglued up there. Maybe I should come and check it out for myself.'

'You know we'd love to see you,' she said evenly.

'Both of you?' The man cackled.

'Of course. Just be careful.' She lowered her voice and spoke hurriedly: 'Look, there's people waiting to use this box. I'd better go, before they get too nosey.'

'Wait!' the man said sharply. 'I want to know about the other business.'

This time she didn't bother to hide her exasperation. 'It was *necessary*. We didn't know how much the girl told her, but we couldn't take chances.'

'And you didn't want to miss the chance of a fat profit.' He chuckled. 'It's okay. Everybody likes to kill two birds with one shot. But I'd feel safer if you had taken out the cop as well.'

'Is that what you want?'

'As a favour. Not like the woman, though.'

'Of course not! We're not stupid.' She realized that she was in danger of going too far, and hastened to placate him. 'I'll get Brumby and Red on to it. Right away.'

CHAPTER 4

'Okay.' The coach, Alvin Hurley, glared over the net. 'We'll play a coupla games.'

Tom Grant sighed. Why was tennis such a bad-tempered affair? His hands were still sore, and he was bored. 'Do we have to?' he asked mildly.

Alvin swore fluently, and hammered his forehead with the heel of his hand. 'Hell's teeth, man, that's what all this is about! Competing, winning, knocking holy hell out of your opponent.'

'That's hardly necessary in this case,' Tom said reasonably. 'We both know you're better than me.'

'What *I* know, is that you're the most aggravating wally I've ever come across.'

This seemed a little harsh. Tom protested, without heat: 'I hate wasting your time, but I have to make some sort of fist of this. It's part of my job, you see. Can't you just teach me a few more tricks?'

'Tricks!' Alvin grasped his racquet with both hands, as if he was planning to make an assault with it. 'I will teach you strokes, sonny, or even shots. I will teach you—I have taught you—how to volley, smash, lob, chop, serve and swerve. What I will *not* teach you is bloody tricks. What do you think I am, a bloody monkey?' His voice had risen interestingly, and the few other people on the courts stopped to listen. Tom looked round in some embarrassment. Alvin turned up the volume even higher. 'And it's no use goggling around like a frog in a bog. She ain't here today.'

'Miss Legs?' Tom asked eagerly. 'Did you find out who she is?'

'I'll tell you this much, just to ruin your day: she's out of your league, sonny. An heiress, no less.'

'But what's her name?'

'What difference does it make? Easterbrook.'

'First name?'

35

Alvin regarded him evilly. 'Miss.' He twirled his racquet. 'Or was it Mrs? Not that it matters. She's not gonna give you the time of day, sonny. Hell, here comes the brass. The Pommie twit and the Yankee shit.'

The Briton thus inelegantly described was the head of publicity on the picture, a tall, tentpole-thin character called Julian. He was dressed in neatly-pressed white trousers, striped blazer and a yellow straw hat. He looked like a left-over from some musical comedy of the 'twenties, and his voice, a high, nasal bray, reinforced that impression.

His companion, grossly fat, and fully a foot shorter, was Sam Sabran, the film's producer. Sam was one of nature's stereotypes. A snappy dresser, he wore baggy purple shorts, rope sandals, and an eyeball-blasting shirt of many colours. His round, smiling face would have looked naked without a cigar.

'Hi, Teach!' Sam called out. 'How's our boy doin'?'

Alvin shrugged. 'You want a clumsy ox for your picture, you're home and hosed.'

'You're kidding!' Sam sounded confident, but then he always did. 'He's never let us down yet.'

'Ah, but this is rather different,' Julian drawled. 'This isn't just your brute strength, runnin' and jumpin' lark. Tennis requires a modicum of skill. If he can't go some way to matchin' Zee Miller, we'll have bought ourselves a whole cartload of aggravation for nothin'.'

The comment was meant principally for Tom's ears. Zee Miller was one of a familiar breed: a wild man of the movies, known for his temper and irresponsibility. Tom had never met him, but he had heard the stories—the drunken brawling, the storms of violent rage, the pitiless bullying of lesser-ranking actors. It was said of him that he was never satisfied with his day's work until he had wrecked the set and reduced the director to snivelling hysteria. It might be thought strange that he was employed at all: but in fact his employers secretly enjoyed his conduct, as if they thought it a proof of genius. Tom knew he was in for a bumpy ride.

To underline the point, Julian said heavily, 'You know

that Miller thought of becoming a tennis pro before he turned to acting?'

'That's according to his press agent,' Sam said. 'I never heard a word about that before we booked him.'

Alvin listened to this exchange with considerable interest. 'Looks like we've got to sharpen you up, sonny. This Zee character's gonna make monkey out of you, else.'

Tom winced. 'It's only a movie, Alvin. A fiction. A fairytale. The good guy has to win.'

Alvin stared at his feet, troubled. There was something deeply unsatisfactory here, if only he could find the words to express it. He gave up the effort. 'Here—' He flicked the balls expertly over the net. 'Serve, sonny.'

Tom served and moved instinctively to counter Alvin's cross-court return. He wished, for his instructor's sake, that he could work up more enthusiasm for the game. The trouble was, it seemed so repetitive: going through the same repertoire of movements, over and over, covering the same limited battlefield time and time again. Well, he was being paid a lot of money to do this job: it was only fair to do his best. In spite of Julian's forebodings Tom didn't expect too much trouble from Zee Miller. It was the director's job to control the scene: if he couldn't manage it, or if Lewis didn't like the finished product, the scene would be cut, and that was the end of it. Tom played a fluid backhand shot which was rather pleasing. He hoped Alvin noticed that he had assimilated some of his coaching rather well . . .

Tom became aware that Alvin was shouting at him. And not merely shouting: he was literally dancing with rage. Tom, who had never seen this phenomenon before, observed it with considerable interest.

'Why didn't you kill it?' Alvin yelled.

'Kill what?'

'I was out of position,' Alvin spoke with exaggerated patience. 'The court was at your mercy. The object of the game is to hit the ball out of my reach, not place it conveniently to my forehand.'

'Ah. Yes. I guess I wasn't thinking. As a matter of fact,' Tom confided, 'I was quite enjoying it. We seemed to be keeping it going rather well.' Alvin's apoplectic gurgling warned Tom that he had said the wrong thing. He hastened to apologize. 'I'm sorry. I guess I'm just not very good at this game.'

'You are probably,' Alvin said flatly, 'the most naturally gifted ball-player I have ever taught. If I'd had your talent twenty-five years ago, I'd be a bloody millionaire now. I'd own this stinking hotel instead of coaching dunderheaded wallies who aren't even interested in the game.'

There was a depth of bitterness in his tone that shocked Tom into silence. Alvin stooped to pick up a ball. 'My serve, I think. Change ends.' He walked stiffly to the baseline.

Tom never saw the first serve at all. He felt the wind of it past his ear, and saw the scar on the clay where the ball had pitched, but that was all. Alvin shuffled to his left, and took a ball out of his pocket. Tom crossed over, and prudently stood a yard further back.

It made no perceptible difference. Alvin served three more times, and Tom was not able to lay a racquet on any of them. Outside the court, Julian brayed with laughter. Wordlessly, Alvin flicked the balls down to Tom's end.

Tom served, and lost every point of the next game. But imperceptibly, and without even being aware of it, he moved into a higher gear. He realized he was being taught a different kind of lesson, and for once, he wasn't bored. Alvin was doing new tricks, making the ball swerve, and kick and stop. It was interesting. There were subtle differences in the way Alvin set himself up for each serve: the position of the feet, the loop of the racquet, the balletic arc of the body; and each difference produced a different result: the change of pace, the unexpected bounce. Tom's attention was caught, and his brain registered everything.

It was not until the fifth game that Tom actually managed to return one of Alvin's serves. His shot was not well placed, and Alvin's volley left him stranded; but it was progress of a sort. Julian sniggered, and clapped his hands slowly in ironic applause.

Tom's concentration enclosed him completely, like a glass globe. He had experienced this sensation before, at different

38

times and under different pressures: playing chess, taking exams—a moment of total certainty, total clarity. He never questioned the certainty, when it came: and it never occurred to him that it didn't come to everyone.

The next serve found him prepared and in position. The ball kicked viciously, just as he expected: he swept it down the line, and noted Alvin's hurried change of stroke with detached amusement.

There was another thing, so obvious, that Tom was surprised he hadn't thought of it before: Alvin couldn't possibly keep up this pace. The anger that had psyched him up to this superhuman effort couldn't sustain him for ever. Two long, tough rallies would take the sting out of his game. Tom waited, confident now, that he could read Alvin's service, and genuinely curious to test out his theory. He thumped the return of service back at Alvin's feet, concentrated hard on keeping the ball in play, hitting as close to the baseline as he could, moving it smoothly from wing to wing. Alvin ran, and side-stepped, and back-tracked. His knees began to ache. Tom watched him grow tired. He felt no particular elation, just the mild satisfaction of a problem solved. His next return was short, and Alvin pounced on it gratefully and hammered it out of Tom's reach. Tom held up his arms in mock surrender. 'Okay, coach. You've made your point.'

Alvin glared. 'You wanna quit?'

'That's right. But I'd like you to teach me a few more tricks. Tomorrow?' Behind him, Tom heard Julian complaining to Sam: 'But he didn't win a single point! Miller will crucify him.' And Sam's patient reply: 'That's Nikos's worry. It ain't Forest Hills, it's a film, Julian.' Mimicking Tom, he added, 'A fairytale. The good guy gets to win.'

Alvin was trying to catch his breath without being too obvious about it. 'Tricks! That's all it means to you. Just bloody tricks. You must be the coldest fish I've ever met. You think you had me beat just now, didn't you?'

Tom avoided the question. 'I think you're a great coach. If you can teach me, you can teach anybody. Tomorrow?'

'Seven o'clock. If you can tear yourself out of bed.'

39

Alvin stalked away, grateful to have had the last word. Sam and Julian waited for Tom to pick up his gear, and the three men walked up the path to the hotel. Tom expected Sam to interrogate him on his progress at tennis—the whole production team was keyed-up to fever pitch about the imminent arrival of the temperamental Zee Miller—but in fact he had other preoccupations on his mind. 'They identified that body you found, did you hear? The media boys'll be swarming round again.'

'I've organized a Press Conference for six o'clock tonight,' Julian said. 'They want to talk to you and Nikos. Again. Great publicity for the picture.'

'Will Lewis be there?' Tom asked.

Sam shook his head gloomily. 'Lewis ain't feeling too good. Best if we keep him out of this, maybe.'

'You say they've identified the body?'

'Name of Chiswick. Customs official, went missing about seven years ago, in suspicious circumstances. The police assumed he'd done a bunk. In his locker at the sports club they found a packet of uncut heroin, plus about ten thousand dollars in cash. A naughty lad.' Julian was sweating profusely. He marched towards the comfort of his air-conditioned suite with the single-minded purpose of a gun-dog on the scent.

'What the hell was he doing on that mountainside?'

Julian chortled. 'Running away from other naughty fellows, presumably. He was shot in the back.'

The Press Conference was a pain. Julian and Nikos had fixed up a huge video screen, and rushed up a lot of footage from the movie, showing Tom's fall and subsequent rescue, with some gruesome shots of the uncovered skeleton. Then the questions; and the reporters' tedious, persistent game of squeezing out the answers they wanted to hear. It would be nice, Tom thought, if just once they would write their headlines after the interview and not before. He found himself getting more and more depressed. A man died; and the manner of his death filled column inches, programme schedules, air-time. It even publicized a film that had not even been thought of when the man was alive. We are all vultures round a long-dead corpse, he thought.

Afterwards, he needed a drink badly. Luckily, the bar was not crowded, and he found a quiet corner where he could sip his malt whisky and relax. He leaned back and closed his eyes, willing the tensions out of his mind and body.

A heavy hand fell on his shoulder. 'Now then, sonny. Thought you'd got away with it, didn't you? Hard lines, sunshine: you're nicked!'

CHAPTER 5

The man was massive; and as heavy-shouldered as a prize bull. His face was square and knobbly, as if it had been shaped by an adze; and his thick mop of hair was streaked with grey. His fingers dug with alarming strength into Tom's shoulder. 'Gotcha!' he said, swaying slightly. He was grinning like a monkey.

In spite of the shock, Tom recognized him immediately. He remembered the man's job, where he lived, the fact that he had a wife and two kids. What he couldn't remember was his name. The stranger chuckled, recognizing the dilemma. 'Ned Caton,' he said.

'Of course!' Tom shook his hand warmly. 'Sergeant Caton! It's good to see you after all this time.'

'Superintendent, if you don't mind, son. Or rather, ex-Superintendent. I retired last year.'

'Retired? I didn't know you were that old?'

'I'm not. I quit early.'

'What are you doing out here?'

'In Australia? I live here, like you. Same sort of reason.'

'Oh.' Tom suddenly had a mental picture of Ned's wife —small, dark, bosomy. 'Are you and Florrie—?'

'Connie. Yeah, we split up. Year ago. Let me get you a drink.'

'I have one, thanks.'

But Caton bought two large Scotches at the bar and carried them over to the table. 'I heard about you and Mary. That was a damn shame.'

'Occupational hazard,' Tom said bleakly. 'I'm told that some cops manage to stay married, but I'm damned if I know how they manage it.'

'Too right.' Ned gulped down one of the glasses of whisky, and absently-mindedly reached for the other. 'Gee, you're looking well, Scottie. The actor's life suits you.'

'Och, I'm not really an actor. Nor yet a stunt man, as the papers have it. It's a one-off kind of job, but it's fine while it lasts.'

'Better than fingering collars, eh?'

'I was never very good at that. I only did it for the money.'

'We've all said that, in our time. I wonder how true it is?'

Tom changed the subject. 'Do you live here in Brisbane?'

'Got a flat in Surfers' Paradise.' Ned looked round the near-deserted bar critically and somewhat apprehensively, Tom thought. 'I'm not used to drinking in these chintzy places. Look, I'd like to talk to you, Scottie. Can we go somewhere else?'

'Sure. Where would you like to go?' Belatedly, Tom realized that Caton was several drinks ahead. He was not exactly drunk yet, but the whisky had loosened him up, put a certain slackness into the lumpy contours of his face.

Caton looked round again. 'I've got a bottle in the car. Why don't I bring it up to your room? We can be more comfortable there.'

Tom wished he could refuse. Drunken reminiscences about the past he could do without. But he had no excuses ready; and besides, he sensed that there was more urgency in Ned's appeal than appeared on the surface. There was a tension in the man that had nothing to do with drink. 'Sounds like a good idea,' he said, with as much sincerity as he could muster.

Caton's glass was empty, and he was eager to move. 'Good. I'll see you up there. Room 503, right? No hurry. You finish your drink.' He left quickly. He seemed to know the hotel layout quite well: he took a side exit to the car park, rather than go round by the foyer.

Tom viewed the encounter with mixed feelings. Caton might turn out to be a drunken bore, or he might have some interesting and amusing bits of gossip from back home. On the other hand, the alternative to Caton's company was a lonely supper and an early bed. As he sipped the last of his whisky, a tiny bat-squeak of apprehension sounded at the back of his mind. It was unreasonable, unprovoked and uncalled-for. He ignored it.

Caton knocked on the door only seconds after Tom had let himself in. He shambled into the room, and looked around with obvious relief. 'That's better,' he said. He found two glass tumblers in the bathroom, and, without bothering to remove the paper wrapping from the bottle, filled them almost to the brim. Tom watched him in some dismay. The man was already half-drunk; he seemed determined to go the rest of the way as fast as possible. The whisky was very rough, rasping the back of his throat.

Ned slumped into a chair. He had said he wanted to talk, but now he was here, he seemed to have nothing to say. He stared vaguely into his glass with a slightly puzzled air, like a man waking up in unfamiliar surroundings. Finally, he said, 'Do you like this country, Tom?'

'It's okay. Takes some getting used to, but it's okay. Don't you?'

'It scares me to death.' Ned held up his half-empty glass. 'Do you think I'm drinking too much?'

'It looks like it.'

'That's 'cause I'm scared. I'm so scared of dying, I'm drinking myself to death. There's a word for that, but I've forgotten what it is. Did you ever see a funnelweb, Scottie?'

'A funnelweb spider? No, I never have. I've heard about them, of course.'

'Vicki showed me one, once. Its web was a dirty scrap of white material, hanging lop-sided on the face of an old stone wall. We crouched and watched it for a while, quite close. It was a cool day, for a change, and it seemed to get colder as we watched. Graveyard cold.' Ned shivered at the memory. 'Nothing happened for a long time. Everything was still, dead. Then a big, fat bug ambled along at the base of the wall, hugging the shade; and suddenly, like a pantomime demon out of a trapdoor, old funnelweb was there, black and evil as sin. It looked clumsy, but it was as fast and deadly as a shark. It reared up, dancing on its hind legs, and struck downwards with its whole body. Chop. Finish. Dead. Vicki told me that its fangs are like curved swords, and its poison can kill a man in hours.' Ned's hands were trembling, and he set his glass down carefully. He studied his hands curiously for a moment, and then leaned his head back against the chair. He murmured, so quietly that Tom had to strain to hear him, 'I'm afraid, because I think—I *know*—he's going to kill me, Scottie. Old Funnelweb.'

It was not just drunken rambling: Caton was obviously deeply troubled. 'Who's old Funnelweb, Ned?' Tom asked, gently. 'Why should he want to kill you?'

Ned massaged his forehead with the tips of his fingers. 'I don't know. Maybe I'm wrong. Maybe I'm crazy. I'm sure as hell confused.'

'The booze can't he helping,' Tom pointed out.

'It helps to keep the bugaboos out of my head. Sometimes. Hell, I'm sorry. I thought if I could talk—to an old friend —I might get it out of my system, somehow. But this is only making it worse. I'd better go.'

'Sit down,' Tom said. 'Talk, relax. You've only just got here, man. We've got years to catch up on. Who's Vicki?'

Ned sat silent for a few moments. 'She was my girl,' he said finally.

'Was?'

'She's dead.'

'Is that what you want to talk about?'

Ned drew a long, shuddering breath. 'That's part of it. I've been pretty lonely, these last few months. I want to talk, but I've lost the habit.' He paused, then launched into another subject: 'Do you remember, about twelve years ago, the Yard sent two of its top bananas over here to look into allegations of police corruption?'

'I remember hearing about it. The State Government invited them over, I believe. I can't remember anything coming of the investigation.'

'Well, you wouldn't, would you? I mean, something like that has *got* to be dealt with internally. Drag it all out in court, and the public might lose confidence in their public guardians. Anyway, about two years ago, they repeated the exercise. The local papers were getting agitated, so the politicians asked the Yard to send over another brace of coppers.'

'Why were the papers getting agitated?'

'There had been a lot of complaints from the public about their police. Allegations of excessive violence towards minor offenders—coupled with persistent rumours that some police were on the take, from prostitutes and drug-pushers. One paper even ran a story about two junior detectives who were said to be running their own marijuana farm, up-country.'

'Was it true?'

'Sure. But they had resigned, and burnt the evidence before we even arrived.'

'We? You mean, you were one of the detectives the Yard sent over?'

'Yes. The first time they had sent two very bright boys from the A10 Division, but this time, they sussed that it was just a cosmetic exercise, so they sent someone they could spare. Me.' Now that he was into his story, Ned had lost some of his haunted look. He was even neglecting his whisky.

Tom prompted him: 'So when you were over here, you decided to stay?'

'No, it wasn't quite like that. I sort of volunteered for the job. Connie and I weren't getting on too well, and I thought a two-month break might be good for both of us. It looked like a doddle—more of a holiday than a job.'

'And then you met Vicki?'

'By accident. There was a complaint that a plain-clothes cop was taking kick-backs from massage parlours in Surfers' Paradise. I went down there to snoop around. Vicki was working in one of the parlours.' Ned suddenly remembered

45

his whisky, and drank half of it in one swallow. 'It's hard to understand, if it's never happened to you. I mean, you look at a person, and that's it, bam, like being struck by lightning, you just know that you're stuck with wanting her for the rest of your life. And the impossible happens, and she likes you, and the wanting turns to loving, and nothing can ever be the same again.'

'You're a romantic, Ned. I never would have guessed it,' Tom said, smiling.

'That's me. A fifty-five-year-old, overweight, sentimental slob. With a weakness for whisky.'

'What happened? You said that Vicki died.'

'I was too happy. I should have realized it couldn't last. Then, it all went bad. For a start, somebody sent an anonymous letter to Connie. There was no need: I was going to tell her myself at the end of the tour of duty. I just didn't want to *write* it. So, I had to go home early, to face the music. Connie insisted on a divorce; the Met gave me early retirement without any argument; the legal tidying-up went on for weeks. I rang Vicki most days: she knew I was coming back to her, she was counting the hours, she said. Then—' Abruptly, Ned got up and refilled his glass, the liquor slopping over his hand. 'Then she died. Less than a week before I was due back here, she took an overdose of sleeping pills. She died in her sleep. Barbiturate poisoning.' Ned had forgotten his fear. Bitterness crackled in his voice like moving ice. 'I came back here anyway. I arranged the funeral. Her relatives stayed away. She left all her property to me: Including her flat.'

'She had made a will? Isn't that unusual for a young girl?'

'She wasn't all that young,' Caton said defensively. 'But yes, I suppose it was a bit strange. As if she had a pren— premonition, or something.' Ned frowned as he tripped over the word: at last the effects of the drink were beginning to show. He blinked several times, as if to refocus his eyes, and swallowed hard. A fat tear ran down the side of his nose. He seemed unaware of it. 'And now they want to kill me.'

'"They"? Who are "they"? And why do they want to kill you?'

'I don't know why.' The fear had begun to creep back into Ned's face. His head lolled against the back of the chair. 'A gang of kids—teenagers. About three months ago, they started following me. I kept seeing one or other of them everywhere I went—in the shops, the pub, at the beach. They'd sit in a beat-up old jalopy in the street outside my flat. For hours. They bump into me on the pavement, or try to trip me up. They don't say anything. They just grin and watch.' Unsteadily, he gulped down the rest of his drink, gasping and thumping feebly at his chest as the liquor scraped his throat.

'What makes you think they're going to kill you?'

'Phone calls. "Why don't you go like Vicki went? Save us the trouble." Things like that.'

'Have you been to the police?' Tom asked.

Ned grinned crookedly. 'They came to me. Two detectives called at the flat to say that some kids had laid a complaint against me. Threatening behaviour.'

'Detectives?' Tom frowned. 'That's pretty heavy artillery for that kind of offence. Did you know them?'

'Know them?' Ned pulled a face, in an effort to understand the question.

'You had been investigating the police. Had you come across these officers in your inquiry? They must surely have known about you.'

'I never thought of that. No, I didn't recognize them. Remember their names, though. Kilkee and Erwin.'

'Did you tell these officers that the kids had been harassing you? And about the phone calls?'

'Tried to.'

'What do you mean?'

Ned yawned. 'They din' wanna listen. Who's gonna b'lieve a confused old lush? Wassa point?' He yawned again, hiccuped, and closed his eyes. 'Wassa point of it all? I better go home. Sorry, ole son. Truly sorry.' He dropped the glass on the carpet, and began to mumble incoherently.

Tom shook him awake. 'I'm taking you home. You can't drive in this condition. Where's your car?'

47

'No car. Bus. Put me on a bus.'

'I'm taking you home.' Tom consulted a list by the telephone, and rang one of the Assistant Directors. 'Tom Grant here. Look, do you have a car I could borrow for a couple of hours? Right now?'

'Sure. White Renault, parked near the palm trees. I'll send the keys down to Reception directly.'

Tom hauled Caton to his feet. 'Can you walk?'

'Sure. Christ, this is nothing. You should see me when I'm really drunk. Where's the car?'

'Car park. Come on!'

'No.' Ned was swaying on his feet, but there was no mistaking his determination. 'Check outside door first. Go down separately. Mustn't be seen together. Don't want you involved.'

Tom knew better than to argue with a drunken man. The corridor was empty: he let them both out, and pushed Ned towards the lift. 'You go first, then. The car's parked by the palm trees.'

On the drive to Surfers', Ned went to sleep, his head resting against the side window. Tom had to wake him when they arrived on the long promenade, to get directions. Ned lived on the third floor of a white-painted apartment block well back from the beach. The décor of the flat was very feminine: all pink and gold materials and spindly white furniture. Ned looked as out of place as a prizefighter in a Wendy house. But he clearly didn't feel out of place: he was home. He looked around proudly, the effects of the drink hardly apparent at all. All the same, he didn't want Tom to leave right away. 'Let me get you a—' he changed his mind. 'Let me get you something to eat. You must be starving. I know I am.'

It wasn't an ambitious meal: hamburgers and mixed salad, and great chunks of wholemeal bread; but Caton was quite right: they were both ravenous. Ned chatted constantly while he was preparing it, as relaxed and sober as if he had never even looked at a drink all day. Tom sat and listened and marvelled at the change. It was as if the frightened, maudlin character who had drunk himself into a stupor in

48

his hotel room had never existed, or had existed in some other age, some other dimension.

Ned talked about Vicki. He spoke of her with extraordinary pride, as if she had been a prizewinner, a great and famous artist. When they had eaten, he got out Vicki's scrapbooks and Press cuttings. She had been in musicals, in cabaret, entertained on cruise ships. She had been to America, danced in clubs in Los Angeles, Las Vegas. There were photographs of her with famous people in restaurants, and even more photographs of her with not-so-famous people, all of them plump and prosperous-looking. She was pretty and she had been a dancer, that much Tom was able to work out. She had come back to Australia in '73. And somewhere along the line she had become a whore.

Tom was glad to leave, and felt guilty at being glad. He made insincere promises to keep in touch, laughed too heartily at memories of 'the old days', and at last let himself into his car, feeling unaccountably sad and cheap.

The air was warm and heavy. A few fat drops of rain fell on the windscreen. Thunder muttered in the distance, as vague and indistinct as the rattle of dry leaves. A thin youth in bathing-trunks and a tank-top ambled past, stooping to peer in at Tom through the side window. He grinned, straightened up, and walked on. Tom started the car, picked his way through the side streets back to the highway, and drove back towards Brisbane. The rain increased, blowing in gusts on a freshening wind. Tom turned on the radio, and hunted around the dial for something other than pop music and inane chatter. The only thing on offer was an operatic soprano singing Puccini. Tom turned it off quickly. The last thing he wanted right then was to be reminded of Mary.

There was something niggling at the back of his mind: something he had seen or heard tonight had started some ghost of memory, but of what, he had no idea. The harder he tried to pin it down, the more elusive it became. It would come back to him later; it could hardly be important. He put it from his mind, and concentrated on driving through the storm, which was increasing in strength minute by minute.

The gusts of wind rocked and pushed at the car, and the rain hammered on the roof, ran in wide ripples down the windscreen, defeating the efforts of the wipers. The sound of the thunder came and went, sometimes close and then distant, its rumbling muffled by the nearer clatter of the rain. Soon Tom found himself in a slow-moving queue of traffic, grinding painfully northward, back to the city. It was a long, dreary, unreal time, varied only by sudden buffets of wind that cracked over the car like a whiplash. The speedometer needle flickered, but there was hardly any sensation of movement. Behind him headlights bobbed and dazzled; in front, rearlights glinted through the spray, which ballooned up from the road in white pillows of fog. Now, he could hear nothing but the rain and the swish of the tyres. He followed blindly, trusting that somebody up front knew the road well enough to stay on it.

It was well after midnight by the time he got back to the hotel. The rain had steadied now to a sullen downpour, undramatic and seemingly endless. The thunder had long since passed over. Tom cruised up and down between the glistening, close-packed ranks of cars in the parking lot, looking for a space. In the end, he had to turn off into what was called the overflow car park, a rough piece of ground behind a screen of bushes, near the utility outbuildings. There were several cars here, too, and Tom drove to the far end of the row, glumly contemplating the long, wet trek back to the main building. He parked the car, and with a sense of relief, switched off the engine. A high, clear voice cut through the thrumming of the rain. 'Help! I'm sorry to be dramatic about this. But—help!'

The girl was sitting behind the wheel of the car next to his. In spite of the darkness and the rain-smeared windows, he recognized her at once: the girl with the great legs and the fabulous smile. The heiress, Alvin had said. Tom leaped out of his car, and scuttled round to her side. 'What's the trouble?'

She grimaced apologetically. 'This is so silly. My seat-

50

belt's jammed. I can't move. And to make things worse, I've dropped my car keys under the seat. I've been shouting and sounding the horn for the last half-hour, but I seem to be marooned by this damned rain. Do you think you can help?'

'Let's see.' Tom opened the rear door and slid on to the back seat. He found the cause of the trouble quite quickly: the case of the seat-coupling had cracked, and a tiny wedge of plastic had slipped down inside, jamming the locking mechanism. It took him rather longer than might be expected to hook the piece of plastic free with a bent hairpin; but in that time he learned a great deal about her. Her name was Alison, and she was living at the hotel temporarily, until the lawyers said she could take possession of a house that she had just inherited. She gasped with relief when the belt-catch finally came free. 'Thank you: I had visions of sitting there all night.'

They trotted up to the hotel entrance together, holding Alison's raincoat over their heads as shelter against the rain. In the foyer, Tom tried to prolong the moment, but his small-talk wasn't up to it. 'Haven't I seen you down at the tennis courts?'

She smiled, devastatingly. 'I've seen *you*. You're in danger of becoming a tourist attraction. The girls on the Reception desk are practically at fever-pitch about the film-star with the fabulous legs.' Her eyes twinkled wickedly for a moment; then she turned and walked away.

Tom collected his key, avoiding the receptionist's eyes. A sharp, uninvited memory of Ned Caton's loneliness invaded his mind. And Ned's voice: 'It's hard to understand, if it's never happened to you.'

Tom thought he was beginning to understand.

CHAPTER 6

The rain passed over during the night. The next morning was bright and sparkling, the sky completely cloudless. Tom read through the call sheet someone had pushed under his door during the night. It made fascinating reading. The main business of the day, it stated, was to familiarize the heads of departments and the actors involved with the location of the Tennis Club scene, and the special problems involved with that particular location.

The Venn Country Club [the memo ran], is the swankiest set-up of its kind hereabouts. It's a huge complex, catering for golf, tennis, squash, swimming and a score of other sports. Only the cream of local society is admitted as members. Although we are paying a hefty fee to use some of the Club facilities, we are there very much on sufferance. On the filming days the Club will be open as usual to its own members, and that means there will be problems. Be polite and patient at all times, no matter how rude or crass some members might be. Remember that although they think they're tin gods, to us they're only unpaid extras.

The centrepiece of today's activities will be an alfresco drinks party and buffet lunch, so that the members can meet us. Be charming; make a good impression; don't get too drunk. We're going to need all the cooperation we can get, when we actually film up there.

There followed a lengthy transport schedule, and some instructions about how much equipment the technical crew could take. Then a final paragraph: 'NB. Dress—casual, but not sloppy. Do *not*, repeat *not*, wear a dark blue blazer and white slacks. This uniform is reserved strictly for Club servants. Identifying badges will be issued on arrival.'

So that was today's hard labour: a drinks party. Thoughtfully, Tom examined his limited wardrobe. Tracksuits were out, he decided: they probably counted as sloppy. It looked like an occasion for the Blazer.

The Blazer was in the registered colours of a Rugby club for expatriate Scots, called The Macaroons. The Club was no longer in existence; but for a few dozen ex-members the Blazer was a treasured memento, worn only on special occasions, and then only when one's courage was up to it.

The tartan material had been specially designed and the unsubtle blending of purple, green, orange, and pink stripes on a mustard-yellow background had to be seen to be believed. In fact, most people who had seen it refused to believe it. Tom knew that wearing it would expose him to ribald and ignorant comment; but by now he was used to the envy that the Blazer provoked. He decided that the Venn Country Club probably deserved it.

According to the schedule, Tom was to travel to the location in an Austin Rover, along with an assistant cameraman and one of the actresses, a decorative young woman of limited vocabulary. The car clearly indicated his status: producers, directors and stars travelled in Rolls-Royces; lesser luminaries got Bentleys or Cadillacs; *hoi polloi* travelled in a fleet of Rovers. No egalitarian nonsense in the world of showbusiness.

The young actress was tactfully silent on the subject of Tom's blazer, although she may have winced inwardly; but the second cameraman guffawed without shame. 'What have you come as? The Glencoe massacre? That's not a coat, it's an animated rainbow!'

Tom could recognize jealousy when he heard it; he responded only with a condescending smile and a gracious wave of the hand. He settled himself in the back seat of the car, and resigned himself to the inevitable delay. They had to wait for the whole convoy to be assembled, since Julian had decreed that they should all arrive together. Mercifully, small-talk was not required: the actress pointedly buried her head in a film magazine, and the cameraman was soon immersed in a well-thumbed paperback. Experienced professionals both, equipped against the day-to-day boredom of film-making.

At last everyone was accounted for, and the convoy set off, rather in the manner of a funeral procession.

The drive took nearly two hours, and culminated in a steep climb through a forest of tall eucalyptus. Where the road levelled off, a discreet sign pointed them towards the entrance of the Club. A hardtop track between an avenue of ornamental shrubs led to a pair of massive wrought-iron gates set in stone pillars. To either side of the gates, high metal fencing topped with barbed wire stretched as far as the eye could see. A uniformed guard opened the gates for them, and two blue-blazered Club servants checked each car and its occupants. One of them held a clipboard and consulted a typewritten list as each car passed; the other stood a couple of paces behind him, keeping tight control over a tough-looking black guard-dog. Security was obviously a high priority at the Venn Country Club.

The grounds were magnificent. A long drive curved gracefully through sculptured parkland with carefully-tended stands of oak and birch. Wide expanses of lawn, green and fresh after the recent rain, showed between banks of wattle and tall clumps of wild hibiscus. In the distance, brightly-shirted golfers drove canopied golf-buggies to and fro.

To the east, beyond the metal fence, the land fell away steeply, in a series of narrow terraces, to a flat, matted carpet of mangrove and salt scrub. Farther distant, just discernible through the heat-haze, the sea shone like old silver.

They drove to the centre of the sports complex, where the Club buildings were laid out like an American campus in miniature. One by one, the cars offloaded their passengers; and Julian began fussing around like a headmaster in charge of a school outing. He groaned aloud at the sight of Tom's blazer. 'Is that your idea of fashionable chic? Who asked you to come as a ruddy firework display?'

'You said to come casual,' Tom protested.

'I suppose we should be grateful that you didn't wear a fright wig and stick a red ping-pong ball on your nose,' Julian said bitterly. 'The party's down by the swimming-pool. Follow the signs.'

Paths, lined with ornamental trees, radiated out from this centre; and multi-armed signposts pointed the way to a bewildering diversity of activities: golf, tennis, swimming, badminton, bowls, squash, shooting, archery, gymnastics—the list seemed endless. The young actress who had travelled with Tom studied the signs carefully, and then spoke for the first time that morning. 'No croquet?' she commented, deadpan. 'Now that's what I call cheap.'

By the swimming-pool, a handsome, verandah-ed pavilion housed the changing-rooms for both the pool and the nearby tennis courts. A temporary bar had been set up on one of the verandahs, and a small crowd of club members had already assembled. Even from a distance, it was easy to tell that champagne was the most popular tipple: corks popped like volleys of rifle fire.

The Blazer received its customary social recognition.

Nikos said: 'Ye gods, I've had nightmares like that.'

Sam said: 'Man, that's not a coat, it's a lethal weapon.'

A Club member left hurriedly, claiming that his hangover was worse than he thought.

But Lewis was enchanted. 'It's beautiful; a work of art. I covet this glorious, life-enhancing thing. Brian, get me one exactly like it. Immediately.'

Brian raised his eyes heavenward in genuine horror. 'She's delirious,' he explained to some invisible deity. 'She's not feeling at all well.'

This last remark might well be true, Tom thought. 'Are you really up to all this?' he asked Lewis.

'I'll be okay if I don't throw up. Shan't stay long, anyway.'

'You certainly won't, missy,' Brian said severely. 'A gracious saunter round the local gentry, and then momma's going to whisk you home to beddy-byes.'

'You're just trying to make me vomit before my time, you disgusting slag,' Lewis said candidly. 'I'd sell you and buy a real monkey, if you had any trade-in value.'

Tom left them cheerfully insulting each other, and strolled up to the bar. The Club was impressive, he had to admit. The lawns were manicured, the flowerbeds looked like pictures from seed-catalogues. Blue-blazered Club servants were discreet, but ever-present, serving drinks, delivering messages, running errands. 'It's certainly luxurious,' he commented to Sam. 'The membership fees must be astronomical.'

'Sure they are. But the place doesn't pay for itself. Not yet. And it won't, until they get a licence to run a casino here. When that happens, the place will be a goldmine.'

'*When* that happens? You mean it's a certainty?'

Sam shrugged. 'It's a political decision. This company's being helped out by some of the best politicians money can buy.'

'What company's that?'

'It's an outfit called Venn Holdings. Used to be Venn Trucking and Transport. Owned by a sharp character called Mike Venn. Came up from nothing in less than ten years.' Sam held out his empty glass, and a waiter was by his side in a flash, pouring champagne and murmuring apologies for not anticipating the wish. 'As a matter of fact,' Sam confided, 'Venn offered to put some money into the picture. I didn't take it.'

'Why not?'

Surprisingly, Sam had no ready answer. He thought about the question very seriously. Finally, he said, 'Even a whore draws the line somewhere.' He looked embarrassed. 'Forget I said that.'

Glass in hand, Tom strolled around the pool towards the tennis courts. Several of the Club members greeted him enthusiastically, mistaking him for Lewis; but their animation shaded off into indifference, when they realized their error. Mindful of Julian's strictures, Tom was smilingly polite, even to the most boorish and blatant head-hunters.

There were eight tennis courts, he discovered, generously laid out in an irregular pattern and divided by hedges and herbaceous borders. One of the courts had a small, covered stand for spectators: and a group of technicians from the lighting and sound staff were wandering about nonchalantly in that area, taking notes, drawing maps and making sketches.

Tom stood in the shade of a clump of palm-trees and thoughtfully sipped his champagne. All morning he had resisted the temptation to daydream about Alison Easterbrook: but now that he was alone, it seemed silly to go on resisting. He had seen her only three times, and spoken to her only once; but the memory of her made his pulse race. That fantastic smile, the shine on her long, blonde hair, that subtle perfume . . .

Another perfume enveloped him. Not subtle, this, but

heavy, sensual. The woman stood only a couple of paces away, watching him, amused. She was tall, full-bodied, dark-haired, dark-eyed. 'That jacket is really wild,' she said. She had a husky voice, with a pleasant American accent.

'I'm glad you like it.'

'I didn't say I liked it, I said it was wild. Here, let me top you up.' She was carrying an almost full bottle of champagne with a proprietorial air, as if she had brought it to the party herself. 'You were lost in thought then, weren't you? Didn't even know I was there.'

'I'm sorry.'

'Don't apologize. I'm the one who's intruding. But I wanted to talk to you. I'm Francesca, by the way; and I know who you are, of course.' She raised her glass in a silent toast. A diamond the size of a cherry-stone flashed blue fire from a ring on her finger. She was also wearing a wedding-ring, Tom noticed. He said awkwardly, 'I hope you're not mistaking me for—'

'Lewis Goring? No. I missed him. He's gone home. Not feeling well, I gather. You're Tom Grant. I saw you on TV.'

She had a raffish air, and her dark eyes looked very intently into his, as if making some unspoken challenge. Tom wondered if she was drunk. He was interested in spite of himself. She was a very good-looking woman. And the way she moved her body told him she was aware of his interest.

He pulled himself together. 'You want to talk to *me*?' It wasn't much of a conversational gambit, but it was better than blurting out what was uppermost in his mind.

'You're an interesting man. Chasing round the bush, finding seven-year-old corpses.'

'I don't make a habit of it.'

'Those TV interviews were so tantalizing. They always stopped just as they were getting really interesting. Are you really a stunt man?'

'No.' Reluctantly, Tom allowed himself to be drawn into describing the incident in some detail. Francesca was thrilled. 'How wonderfully macabre! And I read somewhere that the poor man was murdered?'

'Shot in the back.'

'But how can they tell a thing like that! After all this time?'

'Forensic scientists are very clever.'

'Do you think they found the bullet?' she asked eagerly.

'It's possible, but they might not want to advertise the fact. There's an outside chance that they may find the gun.'

It seemed a curious conversation to be having, while drinking champagne in the shade of the palm trees, but parties, Tom reflected, were often like that. He still wasn't quite sure what the real conversation was about. He didn't need an interpreter of body-language to realize that she was giving out strong sexual signals, but he was unsure how to interpret them. They might be automatic—part of her social armoury; but on the other hand, the unspoken message might be the real one, and all this chat about unsolved murders mere camouflage.

She smiled slyly as if she read his uncertainty, but continued innocently enough: 'I read somewhere that you used to be a detective?'

'Yes.'

'Did you give it up to be an actor?'

'I'm no actor. No, I quit and came to Australia, because —' His mind veered on to an unexpected tack, and he hesitated in mid-sentence. 'Well, for personal reasons,' he finished lamely. 'All very ordinary and undramatic.'

She poured more champagne. 'I think you're fascinating,' she murmured huskily. 'But what does your detective instinct tell you about the Murder In The Bush?' Her tone supplied the capital letters.

'Nothing. I don't have enough information. The victim was a Customs official. He may have been involved in drug-trafficking, which can be a dangerous business. But without knowing more facts, I would hesitate even to call it murder.'

'You're very cautious,' she said ambiguously. 'Do you always play so safe?'

Tom met her gaze directly. 'Not always.'

'Oh, good. However, the tall, thin fellow who is pounding

58

towards us with the speed and subtlety of a dinosaur is my husband.' She turned to greet the advancing figure. 'Hi, darling!'

'So this is where you're hiding yourself.' The tall man had a deep, musically sonorous voice, rather like a stage parson. His whole manner struck Tom as rather stagey. He looked fit and athletic, in his Italian slacks and sports shirt; but he had a heaviness of tread and a sombreness of manner that seemed quaintly artificial. His after-shave completely swamped his wife's perfume.

'Hardly hiding, darling,' Francesca said, 'since there isn't a scrap of decent cover within a hundred yards. Mr Grant, this is my husband, Jeremy. Jeremy Clays. Darling, this is Tom Grant.'

'Ah.' The tall man did not offer to shake hands. He spoke across Tom, ignoring him completely: 'Look, I merely came to tell you that I'm leaving in a few minutes. I think I had better take your car. Dawson will take you home in the Rolls when you're ready.'

Francesca protested. 'Hey, are you implying that I'm too drunk to drive?'

'I'm not implying it, my dear, I'm stating it. I'm going back to the office before I die of boredom here. If you would be so good as to let me have the keys?'

'I'm damned if I will!' She clutched Tom's arm with surprising strength. 'Mr Grant, you'll drive me home, won't you? Observe, Jeremy, Mr Grant is sober as a judge. I shall be perfectly safe under his wing.' Her dark eyes glinted with mischief.

Clays said coldly, 'It is unfair of you to blackmail a perfect stranger, Francesca. I must—'

'Tom!' The high, clear voice took them all by surprise. 'There you are!' Alison, carrying a long canvas sports bag hurried towards them, smiling with relief. 'Jeremy, Francesca, how nice to see you! Tom, I thought you'd forgotten all about me.'

'I could never do that,' Tom said truthfully. 'But—'

'Tom very kindly offered to give me a lift back to the hotel,' Alison explained brightly. 'But it was all arranged in such a rush, last night, I was afraid he might have forgotten.'

'No, no.' Tom hastily covered his confusion. 'I hadn't forgotten. I was waiting for you.' In a sense, that was true, he thought.

Francesca looked puzzled. 'I thought you had hired a car, Alison?'

'Not a very reliable one, I'm afraid. Tom had to rescue me last night.'

'Ah.' Jeremy's mouth twisted sardonically. 'Well, that seems to settle the matter. Mr Grant, talented as he may be, can hardly be in two places at once. Francesca?'

'The keys are in the car,' she said sulkily.

'The safest place for them, no doubt. I'll see you this evening, my dear. Alison, you look as charming as ever.'

Alison was looking rather pink, but whether it was on account of the compliment, or some other cause, was hard to tell. 'Thank you. And thank you for introducing me to the Club.'

'My pleasure.' He nodded formally to Tom, and strode away, heavy-footed and confident.

'He's such a thoughtful man,' Alison said. 'And so clever. You must be very proud of him, Francesca.'

'Oh sure. He's perfect, in a chilly sort of way. Which is more than I can say for this champagne. I detest warm champagne. Much as I adore your company, the craving for properly-chilled Veuve Clicquot is becoming more than I can bear. Au revoir, both.'

She turned to leave, but looked back after a couple of paces. 'Next time we meet,' she said silkily, 'you must tell me all about your wonderful wife. I've been a fan of hers for years.' Swinging her hips, she walked off towards the bar.

CHAPTER 7

'Ex-wife,' Tom said automatically. He looked thoughtful. 'Now, that *is* odd.'

'Just catty. She was miffed because I popped up and

rescued you in the nick of time.' Alison suddenly looked dismayed. 'Oh my God, I've just thought: perhaps you didn't want to be rescued?'

'Of course I did. It had all the makings of an embarrassing situation. You were wonderful. No, what was odd, was that she knew a lot more about me than she pretended.'

'What do you mean?'

'Well, firstly she said that she had read somewhere that I had once been a policeman. Now, she couldn't have read it anywhere over here, because it's not a fact that's been released to the media. Then again, it seems that she knows all about my ex-wife; but I know for sure that *that* item has never appeared in the Australian Press.'

'Is she an actress, your ex?' Alison grimaced at her own gaucheness. 'Sorry. None of my business.'

'She's an opera singer.'

'Famous?'

'Maria d'Abrolhos.'

'Good God! *That* famous?'

'Most of her fame arrived after she left me. The two events may not have been unconnected.'

'Isn't she coming over here? To sing at the Opera House?'

'The Sydney Opera House, yes.'

She whistled. 'No wonder you want to keep a low profile. If the media found out, you'd have reporters round you like bush flies. How do you suppose Francesca found out?'

'I don't know. I don't even know who she is. I've never met her, or her po-faced husband before in my life.' He took the sports bag from her hand, and they began to walk along one of the tree-lined paths.

'He *is* a stick, isn't he?' Alison said. 'He's my lawyer. Or rather, he's my aunt's lawyer: the executor of her will. His manner *is* quite off-putting, but he's been kind and helpful to me.'

'Have you known him long?'

'Less than a month. I only arrived back in the country four weeks ago.'

'Back from where?'

'India.' They strolled and chatted with easy familiarity,

as if they had been friends for years. It slowly dawned on Tom that she was as lonely as he was, and that she actually enjoyed his company. He learned that she was a nurse, and had been overseas for nearly four years, working in medical missions in Africa and India; that her parents had died in a car accident when she was seven, and that she had been brought up by her Aunt Clare and her Uncle Frank. 'They had a house in Melbourne, then; they only moved up here about three years ago, soon after they discovered how ill Frank really was.'

'They moved north for the sake of his health?' Tom asked.

'Nothing so sensible. For the sake of his money. Frank was a self-made man. Made a fortune in the warehousing business. When he was sure he was dying, he sold his company, and moved up here. You see, there are no death duties in Queensland.'

An heiress, Alvin had said, jeering. Out of your class, Tom. Alison went on: 'Clare never wanted to move. Her real home, all her friends, were down south. I can't help thinking: if she had stayed in Melbourne, she might be alive right now.' She mopped her eyes matter-of-factly, and blew her nose on a large white handkerchief. 'By the way, where are we?'

'We seem to have arrived at the golf course,' Tom said, surprised.

'So I see. Where are we going?'

'Anywhere you like. I was just carrying your bag.'

'I was just following you. At least, I thought I was.'

They both seemed to find this much funnier than it actually was, and laughed a lot. They began to retrace their steps. 'By the way,' Tom asked, 'were you serious about wanting a lift back to the hotel? It's no problem, but I'd have to mention it to the transport director. Everyone on a film unit is very touchy about protocol.'

'No, in fact I do have a car here. Not the one I had last night. I took that back to the car-hire place and swapped it.'

'So—' Tom was delighted—'you fibbed to Francesca?'

'To save you from a fate worse than death, yes. But I did

have another motive. I wanted to ask you to introduce me to Lewis Goring.'

'Ah.' Tom struggled to conceal his disappointment. 'I'm afraid he's not here. He had to go home early.'

'Oh, I wouldn't dream of tackling him about this at a party. I wanted to ask his advice. It is true that he's an expert on art, isn't it? On paintings, I mean?'

'He's very knowledgeable, like most serious art collectors. I suppose it's fair to call him an expert.'

'Well, I'm no expert, and I have a problem.' She touched him lightly on the arm. 'If I told you, would you mention it to him? To tell you the truth, I'm a bit shy of approaching him myself.'

'If it's about pictures, you can be sure he'll be interested. What's the problem?'

She hesitated, collecting her thoughts. 'I've just inherited an art collection. To be specific, thirty-two paintings, mainly by Australian artists. I'm told this collection is very valuable: the probate value is over two million dollars.'

Tom stopped in his tracks. 'That's a problem?'

'I'm being serious, Tom. Yes, it's a very real dilemma to me. You see, Jeremy keeps telling me how *important*—his word—this collection is. He thinks I should loan it to one of the State galleries, as a sort of memorial to my aunt.'

'It was her collection?'

'She bought the pictures, yes.'

'So there was some sense in the move to Queensland, after all. The estate duty on that lot would be pretty hefty.'

Alison shrugged, dismissing the side-issue. 'Jeremy keeps hinting that Clare would have wanted the collection kept together, and on permanent exhibition to the public.'

'And you don't agree?'

'I just can't imagine Aunt Clare being that pompous. No, my real problem is my own ignorance, my own lack of response. Jeremy says the collection is *important*, and I simply can't understand what he means. To me, they're just pictures. Some of them please me—but even the most pleasing is only a picture. Look, there's no way I can say this without sounding like a Philistine or a prig. For more than three years, I've worked overseas in underfunded missions, nursing people whose sickness ought never have been allowed to happen. People dying of scurvy, rickets, *measles*, for God's sake! People poisoned by the very water they drink. When I look at those pictures—my responsibility—I can't help seeing two million dollars' worth of medical supplies, food and clean water. Can you understand what I mean?'

'I can also see that you've made up your mind. I can tell you now what Lewis will say—follow your own instincts. Be true to yourself.'

'No, that's not enough. Even I can understand that I could have the wrong perspective on this. I don't want to be remembered as the woman who carved up a masterpiece, out of sheer ignorance. I mean, if by some miracle, I had inherited the original manuscript copy of *King Lear*, my attitude would be totally different, because my personal response to literature is stronger than my response to paintings.'

'So you want an expert to tell you whether this collection is the visual equivalent of a Shakespeare manuscript?'

'Well, that's a bit extreme, but—something like that, yes.'

'Okay. I'll talk to Lewis about it.'

Their apparently aimless wandering had unconsciously discovered a purpose: without planning to, they had arrived at the car park. 'We could go back to the party, if you like?' Tom suggested, without enthusiasm.

'I should hate it. I loathe that kind of mindless milling about. And I really would rather not bump into Francesca again, right now.' Alison smiled dazzlingly. 'What you *could* do is to take me somewhere civilized for lunch. If you like, that is.'

They took Alison's car, and headed for the coast. A 40-mile drive brought them to the beach road near Macoola, blessedly and surprisingly uncrowded. They had lunch in a taverna-style restaurant on the beach, sitting in the shade of a canvas awning, watching the Pacific rollers booming in. They ate and talked; and from time to time were comfortably silent. It was a good day: the best Tom could remember for years. Everything looked good: the sea, the sky, the long expanse of pale, sandy beach. A few youngsters playing volley-ball; groups of surfies lounged in the sun, their boards like tall gravestones thrust upright in the sand. Couples walked at the sea's edge, hand in hand.

Inconsequentially, Tom thought of Ned Caton. Had he wandered along this beach with his girl? What was her name?—Vicki. Young enough to be his daughter. A memory clicked into place like a spring-loaded ratchet, taking him by surprise.

Alison noticed his change of expression. 'Is something the matter?'

'It's not important. Something's been hovering at the edge of my mind, and I just couldn't identify it. It came to me just now, when I wasn't thinking about it.'

They both agreed that that was what often happened, and the conversation drifted pleasantly to other things. The moment passed; the memory was caught, stored away under problems solved. He must mention it to Ned sometime. Right now, the important thing was—he admitted it cheerfully to himself—the business of falling in love.

He was not to know it until much later, but if he hadn't chosen that moment to be distracted, he might have prevented half a dozen murders.

CHAPTER 8

Arranging for Lewis to have a private viewing of Alison's pictures took some time. The pictures were stored in a bank vault, for safe-keeping; and Jeremy Clays was reluctant to have them uncrated, examined and then locked up again, merely to gratify his client's whim. He made no secret of the fact that he considered it a waste of time and money. He undertook to make the arrangements with tight-lipped disapproval.

Meanwhile Tom continued his daily tennis lessons with Alvin Hurley, and in his spare time, cultivated every opportunity of getting to know Alison Easterbrook better. As Alvin sourly remarked, 'If you worked as hard on your game as you do in chasing Miss Legs, you'd be a bloody world champion.' But he was finding it more and more difficult to conceal his pleasure at Tom's progress.

One morning, Alison came down to the courts, and watched the last few minutes of his lesson. Tom was pleased: she had never done that before. This was a real step forward.

His delight evaporated when he took a closer look at her face. 'What's the matter?'

''I've had a letter,' she whispered. She was shivering, as if afflicted with cold. 'I've had a letter.'

'What do you mean? A threatening letter?'

'No. Please—' She looked round blindly. 'I must sit down.'

He led her to a bench, and sat with her, holding both her hands. 'Tell me about it.'

She looked grey, sick. 'I've had a letter from Clare.'

'Your aunt?'

'Yes. It arrived this morning. She wrote it three months ago.'

'And it's taken all this time to catch up with you?'

'She sent it to the wrong address. It's been all around India; it's a miracle it reached me at all.'

Some miracles one can do without, Tom reflected. He couldn't think of anything adequate to say. But although he regretted her pain, he was absurdly pleased that she had brought her trouble to him. Alison tried to smile. 'This is the second time in a week I've wept all over you; you must think I'm a terrible whinger. Look, are you sure you don't mind my bothering you with all this? It's your own fault, really: you're very . . . sympathetic.'

'Talk,' Tom said simply. 'You'll feel better.'

'Clare's letters were always long, messy affairs, written over several days, like a diary; full of gossip about clothes, diets, the garden, family. This last one was like that, right up to the last two pages. And then—' Alison pulled the letter from her handbag. 'Here, let me show you.'

She thrust a couple of handwritten pages at him, 'What do you make of this?'

The writing was large and shaky, and in places totally illegible.

'Darling, I've opened this again, because the weirdest thing has happened, and I must talk about it, or go mad! I wish you were here! I'm shaking like a leaf; I don't know what to do. I had a letter this morning—right out of the blue—from someone who says he's Frank's son!! He says his name's Clark, and he was born in '64—the year before I met Frank—and his mother was a barmaid at the pub near the Drummoyne warehouse. He says he's got letters to prove it.' The next couple of lines defeated Tom: the anguished, jagged strokes of the pen slashed formlessly across the page. Then, a few words clearly decipherable: *'—cruel trick, to get money out of me. He says he's—'* The writing disintegrated again, for several lines, this time. Then: *'—face to face. Then I'll do whatever is necessary. You mustn't worry about me, darling: I'm all right. Shaking, but more with anger now, than shock. Write soon! Your ever-loving aunt, Clare.'*

Alison looked anxiously into his face. 'What do you make of it?'

'I can't really decipher much of this last page at all. Can you?'

'No, but the gist is clear. She thought she was being conned, and she was determined to meet this boy, Clark.'

'Face to face, yes. And "do whatever is necessary". I wonder what she meant by that. Has this Clark attempted to get in touch with you?'

'No.' Alison was still trembling, preoccupied with the letter she held in her hand. Tom realized that she hadn't understood the point of his question. He tried again: 'If Clark believes he is related to your aunt, he may also believe he is entitled to benefit from her estate.'

Alison considered this. 'No.' The effort of concentration made her visibly calmer. 'Even if he's not a cheat, he's a bastard, by his own admission,' she said brutally.

'All the same, it seems strange that he's not been in touch. If he felt he had a moral claim on your aunt, he might feel he had the same moral claim on you. Perhaps he hasn't heard of your aunt's death.'

'I don't see how he could have missed it. It made headlines all over the world. They even interviewed *me*—the TV cameras were waiting at the airport. As if I could tell them anything.' Alison became aware of Tom's bemused expression. 'I'm sorry—you don't know what I'm talking about, do you? Clare died in an accident up-country about ten weeks ago. Her car ran out of petrol in a wild and lonely part of the bush—it seemed that she had strayed into a restricted area: War Department territory, out of bounds to the public. It had been used as a tank-training area, and it's off-limits because of the danger of unexploded shells.'

'The Dingo Killing!' Tom exclaimed. 'I remember reading about it.'

Alison sighed. 'That's what the papers called it. And that's really what stirred up all the publicity. At the inquest, there was forensic evidence of dog-bites on the body, and the pathologist said that he believed they had been inflicted before death. That's what caused the uproar. The wild Dog Preservation Society put its own lawyer into court, to cross-examine the pathologist and to challenge any suggestion that Clare might have been killed by dingoes. The Society was worried that if the dingo was branded a killer, the species might well be wiped out altogether by trigger-happy farmers. The media carried the debate to the general public, and in the end, the inquest seemed to be more about wild dogs than about Clare Yelverton.'

'But in the end, the verdict was accidental death, wasn't it?' Tom asked. 'I think I remember that, somewhere.'

'Yes. A stupid, unnecessary accident.' Alison was silent for a moment, sad, but no longer wildly agitated. 'Thank you for being patient. Would you like to read the rest of it?' She held out the other pages. 'This gives you a better idea of what she was really like.'

Tom read the letter to please the niece, rather than out of interest in the aunt. Clare had obviously loved her garden, and wrote a great deal about plants and flowers, communicating her affection with force and humour. There was no mention of local friends, but she wrote of old friends and acquaintances in Melbourne, with whom she kept up a lively correspondence, apparently. She also took an interest in the welfare of her husband's ex-employees.

Do you remember—no, you won't, because you never met him; so I'll have to introduce him: old Dick Trowell, who was a depot manager at Richmond till the new management closed the place down. I say 'old', but really he's barely sixty—faced with retirement at fifty-seven, poor sod. Now, they tell me, he and his wife Victoria are drinking themselves to death in a one-bedroomed flat down by the jam factory. The neighbours say the curtains at their front window have never once been opened, all year. Well, anyway, Mrs T, in a rare sober moment, sent me a postcard, saying that her daughter had moved up to Q'land, and giving me her phone number. I was curious, because I never knew the Trowells had a daughter, so I rang her up and invited her to tea. My lor! She was an eyeball-stretcher. Mini-skirt so small it was hardly worth wearing; gipsy blouse in loose-knitted silk, with her nipples poking through; heels like stilts; and enough paint to smother the Harbour Bridge. And underneath it all, a simple-minded, moon-faced child with more romantic fancies than you could shake a stick at. Perhaps 'romantic' is stretching it a bit. Over the Earl Grey and cucumber sandwiches, I asked her what she did for a living. 'Well,' she said demurely, in her little girl voice, 'I used to be a dancer, but now, I suppose you'd say I'm a hooker.' She had to explain what she meant; and when I'd finished spluttering crumbs all over the place, she said, 'But my boyfriend's making me give it up!' Allie, she's a dream; I've fallen for her completely. I begged her to call again, soon; but she said that would depend on when her boyfriend got back. I hope she calls; I'm itching to phone her again, but I don't want to be an old pest.'

Alison was watching his face. 'You're reading about the girl? Doesn't that tell you the kind of person Clare was?'

'Yes.' Tom looked at the postmark on the envelope. It had been posted on July 9th, sixteen weeks earlier. He finished reading the letter. 'That's odd.'

'What is?'

Tom reconsidered. 'Perhaps it isn't. I didn't know your aunt, of course; I've only seen her through your eyes. But the bit about the art sale struck me as strange.' Tom read it aloud: '*Somebody sent me the catalogue of the Ruisdel auction today. V. impressive. The most important sale of Aussie art for yonks.*'

'What's strange about that? She collected Australian paintings.'

'Two million dollars' worth, I know. But the tone seems strangely offhand, for a serious collector. I wonder why she didn't send for the catalogue herself?'

'Because someone else sent it to her.' The coolness in Alison's tone warned him off the subject. But it still bothered him that Clare Yelverton should have written so much about her garden, and nothing at all about her art collection.

CHAPTER 9

Jeremy Clays made quite a ceremony out of exhibiting the Australian paintings for Lewis's benefit. He had them displayed in the Board Room of the Brisbane bank which held them in store, and laid on sherry and dry biscuits in an attempt, apparently, to enliven the proceedings. Except for the packing material stacked in one corner of the room, and the security guards stationed ostentatiously outside the door, it might have been a private viewing at an up-market commercial gallery.

Tom arrived early, and found Alison and Jeremy deep in conversation. She greeted him cheerfully. 'Oh, good, you're wearing your blazer again,' she said. 'How very cheering.' There seemed to be no irony in the remark; perhaps she really meant it. 'Jeremy and I were just talking about this Clark thing,' she went on. 'He's sure it was a hoax.'

'I said so at the time,' Jeremy said. If he remembered

snubbing Tom at the Club, he showed no sign of it. 'Mrs Yelverton showed me the letter, of course. She was most distressed. I have often wondered, since, whether her distress was a contributory cause of her accident.'

'Do you think we ought to do something about this hoaxer, if that's what he is?' Alison asked. 'Hire a private detective to find him—something like that?'

Jeremy wrinkled his long nose. 'To what purpose? Even if you find him, what then? As far as I can see, he has committed no crime.'

Alison would have argued the point, but they were interrupted by the arrival of Lewis, accompanied as usual by Brian; and the serious work of the morning began. Jeremy had prepared an elegantly-bound folder, containing descriptions and historical details of all the paintings on show. He handed copies to everyone, and made as if to conduct them round on a guided tour.

Lewis ignored him. He sat down and read through the notes as slowly and carefully as if he was memorizing them. He laid the folder down. 'Who wrote this stuff?'

Jeremy wore a pained, patient expression. 'A Mr Bartholomew.'

'The auctioneer?'

'Exactly. A sound man. An expert in his field.'

'Sure,' Lewis said. He stood up and began to examine the pictures, taking his time over each one, studying them from a distance, and putting on huge, black-rimmed spectacles to look at details. Occasionally he took out a magnifying glass, and went over the canvas inch by inch. Brian nudged Tom in the ribs. 'She's enjoying herself,' he whispered. 'Beats acting any day, in her book.'

At last Lewis was finished. He sat down, looking tired and abstracted. 'I forget—' he began, and then stopped, shaking his head angrily. 'Brian?'

'Yes? Oh God!' Brian thrust a large handkerchief into Lewis's hand, and lifted him to his feet. ''Scuse us folks. Just a little local difficulty. Where's the john?' He called one of the security guards, and the two men half-carried Lewis from the room.

71

'What's wrong?' Alison made to follow them. 'Is it an attack? I'm a nurse, maybe I can help.'

Tom tried to reassure her: 'I think it's only a side-effect from the pills he has to take. Brian knows how to cope. With luck, he'll be over it in a minute.'

Brian appeared at the doorway. 'Tom?'

'Coming.' Tom walked out into the corridor. 'Is it the pills?'

'That, and the air-conditioning. It's like an ice-box in there. She'll be all right in a minute, but the poor cow has chundered all over her jacket. Can she borrow yours?'

'This?' Tom was taken aback. Nobody had ever offered to borrow his blazer before.

'Beggars can't be choosers,' Brian said tactlessly. 'I don't want the Queen Bee to freeze to death.'

'Well, sure.' Tom transferred his wallet to his hip pocket, and handed over the coat. 'But it's just a loan, mind.'

Brian curled his lip derisively, and disappeared.

Jeremy was visibly impatient. 'I should like to get these pictures re-packed and back in store, Alison. This whole exercise is taking up expensive time, and to be honest, appears to me quite pointless.'

'It's my whim, Jeremy, and I'm happy to pay for it. There is really no need for you to stay.'

But Jeremy stayed; and after about ten minutes Lewis returned, looking wan and hollow-faced. 'Sorry about that. Truth is, it was just a ruse to sneak off with Tom's coat. What I was going to say, before that untimely interruption, was that I've forgotten the exact purpose of this viewing?'

'I wanted to ask your advice, Mr Goring,' Alison said.

'About what?'

'These pictures—my aunt's collection . . . it has been suggested that, because of their importance, they should be made available to the public on permanent exhibition. I know less than nothing about art. I'd value your opinion.'

Lewis looked at her quizzically. 'I take it you want me to be absolutely honest?'

'Absolutely.'

'Well, lady—' that famous half-smile haunted his face—

72

'there's no doubt in my mind that you're the finest work of art in this room.'

Goddam, Tom thought, why can't I say things like that? And in that voice?

Lewis went on: 'As for the paintings, well, they're pretty, too. Pretty fair. Actually, they're good paintings, all of them, individually. But together, they're a mish-mash. A special exhibition ought to fit together in some way. This doesn't. There are technical reasons for that, which I won't bore you with; but I can tell you its fatal defect: it has no heart.'

Alison looked slightly dazed. 'Well, I asked for honesty, didn't I? Are you always this direct?'

'Only when it really matters.'

Jeremy interrupted tetchily. 'Well, that *is* only one person's opinion. I know that Mrs Yelverton particularly wanted this collection kept together—'

'You never told me that!' Alison said sharply.

Jeremy was suddenly cautious. 'That was her *private* desire. Naturally, she wouldn't have wished to tie your hands in any way.'

Lewis, with innate and impeccable timing, waited a beat before he dropped the bombshell. 'There is just one complication I ought to mention,' he said mildly. 'Two of the pictures are fakes.'

CHAPTER 10

The woman waited exactly half an hour, then went into the phone-box and dialled a number. The man answered immediately. 'Trouble?'

The woman crossed her fingers. 'Not serious.' She explained briefly.

'Careless.' The man sounded exasperated, but not alarmed. 'Give the money back.'

'That's been arranged.'

'Then what the hell are you bothering me for? It's goddam cold out here, you know that?'

'I'm sorry.'

'Anything else?'

'Well—he's badly shaken.'

'Panicking? Again?'

'I can handle him.'

'Be sure.' It was a threat.

'I am sure. That's not the problem. There's a delay over the other thing. One of the dogs is sick.'

'I said not to use the dogs again.'

'It's not that. One of the guys won't leave the farm until the dog gets better. Couple of days' delay, is all.'

'That's too long. I told you this cockamanny thing was too complicated. Now you're losing your sense of priorities. I want something done, *now*.'

CHAPTER 11

Alison sounded relieved when he finally answered the phone. 'Tom? I nearly gave up: I thought you must be out.'

'I was in the shower.'

'Oh, sorry. I'll ring back later.'

'It's okay. I'm all through. Just attending to a few damp patches right now. What's on your mind?'

'Are you busy?'

'Nope. Free as air.'

'What about your tennis lesson?'

'I just had it.'

'This early? God, how Spartan. Look, I know I'm a pest: I'm yelling for help again.'

'You are not a pest. I can say, on expert authority, that you are a work of art. What's the trouble?'

'It's not trouble, exactly. It's—well, today, I officially take possession of Clare's house, and I just don't think I can face going over there on my own. I've never been there before.'

'I can be ready in ten minutes.'

'You're wonderful. See you in the foyer.'

They took Alison's car, and headed downtown. Alison explained that they had to call at her lawyer's office to sign papers and pick up the keys to the house. Also, she said, Lewis had expressed a wish to see the provenance of the pictures he had examined, and she was going to ask Jeremy for them. 'To be honest, I don't even know what a provenance is,' she said.

'It's the documentation that goes with a picture, to prove it is what it claims to be. It usually lists all the previous owners, right back to the first person who bought it, or commissioned it. If there's a gap in the records, the provenance might include some expert's authentication.'

'So, if the picture's a fake, the provenance must also be a fake?'

'Not necessarily. An expert might authenticate a painting in good faith, only to be proved wrong years later by new scientific techniques.'

'Jeremy was terribly miffed over Lewis calling those pictures fakes. He's insisting on an "independent evaluation", as he calls it. My money's on Lewis.'

She drove to a quiet, cobbled square near the Government buildings. The square had an atmosphere of confidently-understated prosperity. The pavements were clean and un-littered, the slim trunks of the ornamental trees were encircled with elegant wrought-iron guards. The brass plates on the Georgian-fronted houses were discreet, and uniform in size and style. Jeremy's offices occupied the whole of one of the Georgian houses. The brass plate on the door said simply, *Clays, Chance and Cross*.

Inside the house, there was no immediate sign of commerce, and not much evidence of the twentieth century. A few Victorian chairs and Persian rugs adorned the expanse of gleaming parquet in the hall, and a silver bowl on a tall mahogany stand held an arrangement of white roses and grey ferns.

A uniformed commissionaire escorted them up a magnificent staircase to an oak-panelled waiting-room on the first floor. There were oil paintings of horses on the walls, and current copies of *Tatler*, *Punch*, and the *Illustrated London*

News on the Sheraton table in the centre of the room.

The silence was uncanny. Somewhere in the house there had to be the usual noise and bustle associated with office activity; but here in this room it was quieter than a country churchyard.

Clays himself came out to greet them, doing his best to be amiable and ingratiating. It was not a role that sat easily on him. 'I have been in touch with the auctioneers about the two disputed paintings,' he said, 'and they are prepared, without prejudice, and without admitting any errors on their part, to refund the purchase price in full, and take the pictures back for re-appraisal.'

He ushered them into his office, accepting Tom's presence without question. Alison sat in a leather armchair, and waited until Clays had settled himself behind his desk, before asking bluntly, 'Why?'

'Why?' Clays looked startled. 'To protect their good name, of course. Ruisdel's has an international reputation in the art world; to admit that their own experts failed to detect two fakes, particularly in such an important auction, would seriously damage their image. Assuming that they are fakes, of course, which is not yet established for certain.'

'That's my point,' Alison said. 'Surely it would be more businesslike to check the pictures first? Suppose they're genuine?'

'I can only report their offer,' Clays said stiffly. 'I am merely guessing at their motives. In any case, I understand that your present objective is to sell the paintings and apply the proceeds to charitable purposes. This would seem to be a satisfactory start to such proceedings.'

'In good time. Right now, I want to show the provenances of those pictures—and any other related documents—to Mr Goring.'

'For what purpose?' The false geniality disappeared like summer mist.

'Because Mr Goring has expressed a wish to see them. It is good of him to be so interested.'

'Indeed? This is not the wisest course, Alison. These

papers are valuable. Let me have them photocopied for you.'

'Photocopy them by all means. I'll take the originals,' Alison said calmly.

Clays sighed his disapproval, and summoned his secretary. He gave the necessary instructions in graveyard tones. Then he turned to other business, handing over documents for Alison's signature, explaining each one as he did so with economical precision. When he had finished, his secretary returned with several folders and a bunch of keys. 'These are now your property. Here are the keys of Mrs Yelverton's house, and the documents relating to her art collection. These other files contain deeds, certificates, instruments of transfer, *et cetera*. If you wish to instruct us as your solicitors, we shall be happy to store them for you. Mrs Yelverton's deed-box is, of course, available.'

'Thank you.' Alison said. 'That will be very satisfactory.'

The interview seemed to be over. But Jeremy, as if turning over a page in his head, raised another subject: 'I have been thinking about that letter of your aunt's, and the reference to the boy—Clark, was it?'

Alison looked stubborn. 'I still think we should make an effort to find him.'

'Perhaps you are right, but that wasn't what was exercising my mind. When your aunt raised the matter at the time, I'm afraid I didn't attach much importance to it. It seemed —and still seems—such an obvious hoax, that I advised her simply to ignore it. I hadn't realized until I had sight of your aunt's letter how much the incident had preyed on her spirit. It explained a lot of things.'

'Such as?'

'Mrs Yelverton's conduct, in the last weeks of her life, was somewhat eccentric. Since I did not know her well, I had assumed that that was her normal behaviour. It now occurs to me that she may have been acting under considerable stress. It is possible that I was not sufficiently sensitive to her needs.'

It seemed to be a kind of apology, but Alison was more interested in other things. 'Eccentric? What do you mean?'

Clays hedged his position. 'Perhaps the word was too strong. In any case, I ought not to intrude my uninvited opinions into a client's affairs. I confess, though, that I was shocked at the distress evident in your aunt's letter, and I feel somewhat guilty that I was blind to it at the time.'

'I'm sure you did what you believed to be right,' Alison said. 'You mustn't blame yourself.'

'No. None of us can retrieve the past.' Clays closed the subject as if putting it away in a box. 'Now—you won't forget the car, will you?'

'The car?'

'Mrs Yelverton's Mercedes. The police released it after the inquest, and it is now garaged at Balmoral Creek, in the charge of the local constable. The garage rental is paid up only until the end of this month. All the details are in the statement of account.' He ushered them out briskly, waving aside the commissionaire and opening the front door for them himself. As they shook hands, he attempted to inject some warmth into his smile, but his heart wasn't in it.

As soon as they were inside the car, Alison opened the folder. 'I'm dying with curiosity to see what a provenance actually looks like.' She pulled out the top document, a single sheet of paper with a few lines of typescript. 'Is that all?'

Tom glanced at it. 'In this case, it's all that's necessary. It's a very simple history. Painted 1914; exhibited in Melbourne in 1919, and again in 1923; owned by a Mrs Powell 1923–43; sold by the Sherborne Gallery to a Mr Smith, of Newcastle, 1944; sold by the Warwick Gallery last year, to Mr O. Pepperidge of Ipswich. Here at the bottom, it says that the facts have been authenticated by the Warwick Gallery, and by Ruisdel and Co.'

'These look more exciting,' Alison said. 'Some of these files are quite thick.'

'Receipts, bills of sale, probably. Many owners like to know what their pictures fetched at previous sales.' Tom looked over at the documents as Alison leafed through them.

'Boring,' she declared flatly. She dumped the whole lot on Tom's lap, and started the motor. 'I can't think why

Lewis should be interested in all this rubbish.'

Tom rearranged the papers, and began stowing the files back in the folder. 'He's a collector. They have strange passions.'

'Oh, well. I'll drop that bumf off at his place, and we'll go and look at the house. If you don't mind, that is?'

'Of course not.' Tom took out all the files again and checked each one before stowing it in the folder. Then he sat nursing the heavy package in his lap, and staring out of the window with a puzzled frown.

Alison drove, letting the silence stretch between them. Then she said, 'Aren't you going to tell me?'

Tom shifted uneasily. 'I'm sorry. It's the curse of having been a cop. Suspicion becomes a conditioned reflex. You develop an instinct, a nose for the ripe aroma of graft.'

He tapped the folder. 'There's a con here somewhere: I can smell it. But I'm damned if I can see it.'

CHAPTER 12

Tom refused to say any more about his suspicions until they had consulted Lewis. He had spoken hastily; now he half-regretted having spoken at all. The trip to Lewis's house took them ten miles out of their way; and when they arrived, Lewis wasn't there. Tom groaned. 'I forgot. He's filming all day. I saw the schedule.'

'Filming? Shouldn't you be there?'

'I only do the running for him. The acting he does for himself.'

They left the package of documents, along with a lengthy note from Tom, with Lewis's housemaid, and drove on to Clare Yelverton's house. This was in the far western suburbs, in an area of steep-sided hills, thickly wooded with tall eucalypts. Near the top of one of the hills, a rutted track ran through uncleared bush to the house itself, a large half-timbered bungalow which extended around three sides of a paved courtyard. A timber-and-thatch carport was discreetly situated a few yards away, behind a thorn hedge.

They explored the house together, Alison drawing back curtains and opening windows on the way, uttering little cries of pleasure and surprise as she recognized this piece of furniture or that. 'So much of this was in their Melbourne house: I grew up with it. Everything looks so familiar, and yet so strange.'

The main living-room was huge and handsomely proportioned, with french windows and screen doors that opened on to a long, wooded verandah. Below the verandah, wide, unkempt lawns sloped down to flowerbeds, fringed with citrus and wild cherry. The far hills glowed a dark, opalescent blue, their outlines wavering in the heat-haze.

Alison stood next to him, silently looking out at the view. She seemed unnaturally still, unnaturally quiet: Tom wondered if she was on the point of tears. But when she spoke, her voice was steady. 'You know what I was thinking about?'

'Your childhood?'

She continued to look at the distant hills. 'No. I was thinking about your wife.'

'Ex-wife,' Tom said automatically.

'She is very beautiful, isn't she? And very talented?'

'Yes.'

'Am I being impertinent?'

'Not at all.'

'Would you rather not talk about her?'

'That depends. Why do you want to?'

'Because—' She hesitated, and seemed to lose track of what she wanted to say. She seemed fascinated by the outlook from the window. 'I suppose the real reason was, that I wanted to talk about my boyfriend.'

It was a jolt, to be warned off so brutally. Tom rode the punch as best he could. 'Why? Is he beautiful and talented too?'

'Yes, he is, rather. He's a doctor, with the WHO. I met him in India.' Although she had deliberately introduced the subject, she seemed disinclined to pursue it. She fell silent again, still refusing to turn her face from the window.

Eventually, realizing that Tom was not going to help her over this hurdle, she said, 'I'm sorry. That was crude. Seeing Clare's furniture and things made me very emotional, and a bit lonely. I'm afraid I panicked.'

'What were you afraid of?'

She did look at him then, and smiled wryly, without answering. She wandered away from him, towards the door, and it seemed that the moment had passed. Then she stopped. 'Are you still in love with her?'

It was a question he had avoided asking himself for years. But being faced with it suddenly, like this, the answer came readily enough. 'No.'

'I find that hard to believe.'

'Why? Because she's so special?'

'No. Because you are.' Absent-mindedly, she brushed the top of a table with her fingertips, making faint trails in the dust. 'You seem like the kind of man who would only love once.'

'Stubborn, you mean? Or just plain dull?'

'No, I don't mean that. I imagine that if you're in love you don't play safe: you don't hold anything back. You give everything. And you can only do that once.'

Tom wondered if the last remark was a statement or a question. He answered more brusquely than he intended: 'You're confusing love with innocence. Innocence, yes, you can only give once. But love isn't given: it's shared. And if the sharing stops, then the love drains away, like water out of a bathtub, as the poet says.'

'Very pretty. And did the poet say whether any scum got left behind?'

'Mercifully not. Why are we talking like this?'

'You know damn well why, Tom Grant!' The calmness of her manner belied the violence of her words. 'You're a damned attractive man. And, unless my feminine intuition has gone haywire, you fancy me like crazy. We're alone together in this empty house. So, I'm putting your wife, my boyfriend, and every other obstacle I can think of, between us before we go another step.'

'For your sake, or mine?'

81

'Mine, of course. I wouldn't presume to protect *you*. If there's anyone better equipped to look after himself than you, I've yet to meet him. If I didn't like you so much, I'd be scared stiff of you.'

He held up his hands in surrender. 'Let's just leave it there, shall we? We're both in danger of saying too much, too soon. This isn't the time, or the place. If it'll ease your mind, I promise to keep my hands to myself.'

'Mm.' She opened another window, using more force than was strictly necessary. 'That's the promise I was fishing for. I ought to feel pleased.'

Tom laughed. 'What's your boyfriend's name?'

'David.'

'Lucky man.'

'Lucky me,' Alison said, ambiguously. 'Come on, let's explore.'

There was a new intimacy between them, a dangerous feeling that made them more careful with words, and yet cancelled out the need for words. Tom felt recklessly happy, like a gambler on a winning streak; Alison was slightly ashamed to admit to herself that she felt insufferably smug.

At the end of the south-west wing of the house, they found Clare's studio. It was the only really untidy room in the house. Half-finished paintings stood against the wall, and a battered deal table was covered with the usual artist's paraphernalia: pots, jars, tubes, brushes, rags. There was a paint-splattered easel, and a handsome, leather-topped desk, covered in books and papers. 'So she really was interested in painting?' Tom said, wondering, even as he said it, why he was so surprised.

'She loved it. I knew *that*,' Alison said. 'What I didn't know, was that she was so keen on collecting other people's paintings.'

Tom looked through some of the canvases. He was no expert, but the paintings appeared very ordinary: a lot of flat-looking still-life, and landscapes with dodgy perspective. There was more art, Tom thought, in the way she had arranged her drawing-room furniture.

Alison peered at the papers strewn on the desk. 'There's

a letter here from Jeremy,' she said. 'Listen to this: *Dear Mrs Yelverton, I have today received your instructions re the Ruisdel art auction, to be held on August 23rd. While your instructions are perfectly clear, I should be failing in my duty as your adviser if I did not recommend caution in this matter. I am unfamiliar with values in the art world, but the upper limits you have set on your bids seem to me unreasonably high. Mr Smith, of the Walker-Smith Gallery, has agreed to bid on your behalf, but I have not yet communicated any details to him. Before I do so, I should like to be assured that you are determined, if necessary, to invest up to the limits you have indicated. If you are so determined, may I caution you not to divulge your intentions to anyone at all, prior to the auction? Yours faithfully, Jeremy Clays.'*

Tom glanced over her shoulder. The letter was dated August 9th. 'Ruisdel's—I wonder if that was the auction where those two fakes were bought. It looks as if Jeremy had serious doubts about your aunt's involvement—as if he was trying to warn her off it.'

But Alison was not listening. She was pursuing some thought of her own, shaking her head in disbelief. 'I never realized—so much happened in only seven weeks.'

'What do you mean?'

'Clare wrote to me on July 9th, remember? She was very distressed about the letter from Clark. Four weeks later, she's giving instructions to Jeremy to buy pictures at an auction. Three weeks after that, she dies in a bizarre accident five hundred miles north of here. Tom, if *you* wanted to buy pictures at an auction, would you ask somebody else to bid for you, and go away on holiday? It seems that's what Clare did.'

'People do strange things.'

'Not Clare. Not this strange. Then, two of those pictures were fakes. Tom, this whole thing is giving me a very creepy feeling.'

'You could be letting your imagination run away with you. We don't have enough facts. There could be a logical, non-sinister explanation for everything.'

'All right, then—' Alison began going through the drawers of the desk, plucking out papers and scattering

83

them on the leather top—'explain this: why did Clare go to Balmoral Creek instead of going to that auction?'

'I don't know.'

'Neither do I, but I can guess. She'd had another letter from Clark. She wanted to meet him "face to face", remember? I bet she went up north to do precisely that.'

Tom watched her ransack the desk thoroughly, if not very methodically. 'You're hoping to find Clark's letter?'

'Yes.' Her jaw set stubbornly.

'Clare might have taken it with her.'

'It wasn't mentioned at the inquest. And it wasn't in the list of her effects. It's got to be here somewhere.'

The desk, however, yielded nothing but receipts and cuttings from old magazines. Alison led the way to the small, booklined room that had been Clare's study. There was a modern desk in here, and a filing cabinet; and it soon became apparent that the task of finding Clark's letter was going to be harder than they imagined. Clare, it seemed, had been a compulsive hoarder of correspondence. There were hundreds of letters, crammed into every drawer of the desk, filling every spare corner of the filing cabinet, stacked untidily along a shelf behind her chair. Alison recognized a bulky package of her own letters, tied up with garden twine. 'She kept every single thing I wrote to her—even birthday and Christmas cards!'

'It looks as if she squirrelled away every letter she ever received,' Tom said. 'Which means—'

'Of course!' Alison began pulling out drawers and dumping their contents on top of the desk. 'Clark's letter must be here!'

After half an hour, Tom persuaded Alison that they needed to apply some method to their search. 'Clark's letter must have arrived on or about July 8th. If we work through this lot, discarding everything posted before, say, the middle of June, we should have a more manageable job on our hands.'

It speeded up the task, but it yielded no results. When they had sieved through the whole mass, they had twenty-seven letters, none of them from Clark. But it wasn't until they had gone through the whole house, opened every drawer and examined every cupboard, that Alison admitted defeat. 'It's not here. She must have taken it with her.'

'Or she decided it was a hoax, and destroyed it.'

'Yes.' After her flurry of activity, she seemed listless, undecided what to do next. 'You know, while we were going through those letters, I found myself getting more and more angry with Clare for dying. Isn't that silly? But her death has made me see myself in a new light. I'm finding things in myself I didn't know were there. And they're not very pleasant.'

'What sort of things?'

'Greed, for one. All that stuff I was talking about selling those paintings, and buying medical supplies. Even when I was saying it, images in my head were saying other things. Images of expensive clothes, famous hotels, world cruises. Images of big shareholdings, Rolls-Royces, power, self-importance. I've never had money, Tom, not this sort of money. When I talked about giving it away, I was still thinking of it as Clare's, do you see? It's easy to give away somebody else's money. Now, my mind keeps saying that money isn't Clare's, it's mine, *mine*, and I don't feel generous or charitable about it at all. In fact, I feel downright mean and miserly. And worse, I feel guilty and ashamed.' They were back in the study now, tidying up the stacks of letters.

Tom couldn't think of anything helpful to say. 'Are you telling me you're worried about your own opinion of yourself?'

'I don't know, Tom. I'm very confused.'

They worked in silence for a while. Then Tom said, remembering: 'You told me your aunt used to write her letters to you piecemeal, at odd times?'

'Yes, why?'

'I was just trying to visualize her doing it. Do you suppose she came back here, when she had a spare moment, and sat at this desk?'

'No, she told me she only wrote business letters in here. When she wrote to friends, she would carry her notepad into the garden, or the kitchen, or—' Her eyes widened. 'What are you getting at?'

'Nothing, really, I noticed some writing-paper in the kitchen, and I—'

'But we searched the kitchen!'

'We looked on the shelves and in the drawers, yes. There was an apron on the back of the door . . .' She was running down the corridor before he had finished speaking.

It was a carpenter's apron, big and practical, with huge pockets. In one of the pockets was a thick, brown envelope. Alison carried it to the kitchen table. 'Here, Tom. My hands are shaking too much.'

In the envelope was a wad of Press cuttings and a sheet of paper covered in spidery writing.

'Is it Clark?' Alison looked at the notepaper as if afraid to touch it.

Tom looked at the signature. 'No, it's from someone called Victoria Trowell.'

'Trowell? Clare mentioned a Mr and Mrs Trowell in her letter. Wasn't he one of Frank's employees? What does it say?'

The writing had a careful, laborious look. '"*Dear Mrs Yelverton, Vicki phoned us last night—*" Tom paused, distracted —'"*to say how kind you had been, and so understanding, she said. She specially asked us to send you these old Reviews that she has kept in her bureow ever since she got back from America. She told me which ones, but I couldn't make it out, so I've sent the Lot! She's 'Showing Off' I expect, you'll have to forgive her, still she was a lovely Dancer, tho' I suppose that's what you would expect a 'Doting Mum' to say! Well, I must end now, with many thanks for your kindness to Vicki, and every good wish for your Happiness from Dick and myself, yours sincerely, Victoria Trowell.*"'

'Of course!' Alison said. 'Don't you remember? The daughter was the one who said "I'm a hooker," when Clare asked her what she did for a living. She was giving it up, she said.'

'Yes, I remember. Vicki Foxe.'

'What?'

'That's what she called herself. Vicki Foxe.'

'You know her?'

'I know her boyfriend.' He would have to tell her what he knew about Vicki sometime, but he was reluctant to go into it now.

Alison was still disappointed that the letter wasn't from Clark. 'This was posted in June. She must have put it in her apron pocket and forgotten all about it.'

'Maybe she was still expecting Vicki to call, and wanted to keep the cuttings handy for her.'

'Yes, that's very like Clare. I suppose I ought to contact Vicki, and give the cuttings back myself.'

It was a cue to blurt out the truth: that Vicki was dead. But Alison was carrying enough of an emotional burden already; Tom didn't want to add to it. 'I'm going to see her boyfriend soon. I'll pass them on to him, if you like.'

It wasn't much of a lie. Anyway, what difference could it make?

CHAPTER 13

That evening, before he joined Alison for dinner, Tom tried to phone Ned Caton, without success. He found the address of the flat in Surfers' Paradise, and wrote a quick note, to enclose with the Vicki Foxe press cuttings. *'You probably have copies of all these, Ned; you may want to return them to her parents.'* He added an account of how he happened to have them, keeping it very brief: he was in a hurry. At the last moment, he reopened the letter and added a postscript: *'I've been meaning to ask—is that really Bas Underhill, in one of Vicki's scrapbook photos? Near the end of the book—lots of people sitting round a table. One of the other diners looks like "Slow Joe" Largo! If so, it must have been one of the last pictures ever taken of them. Legendary stuff!'* He gave the envelope to the Reception clerk to post, and forgot all about it.

His relationship with Alison had changed over the last twenty-four hours, and he wasn't yet sure that it was for the better. She seemed to think that the discussion that morning had cleared the air, since she had told Tom about her boyfriend, warned him off any romantic involvement. Yet curiously, a new intimacy had sprung up between them from that moment. She had, for instance, simply assumed that they would have dinner together that night; and unconsciously, in many ways, her conversation revealed that she was taking his companionship for granted. It was as if they had been friends for years, instead of only a few days. This was a mixed blessing, Tom decided: pleasant in one way, damned frustrating in another.

They tried hard to keep off the topic of Clare Yelverton, but eventually Alison, after a number of false starts, had to bring it up: 'I wish you were coming with me tomorrow, Tom.'

'Coming with you? Where?'

'Oh, I know it's impossible. You're filming soon, aren't you? I'm going to Balmoral Creek, to collect Clare's car. It would be nice to have you with me.'

'Nice for me, too. But that's a hell of a drive. You ought not to tackle it on your own.'

'I'll be all right. It's got to be done, anyway. And I have this morbid curiosity to see the place where Clare died.' She looked calm but her hands betrayed her: she kept crumpling her napkin into a ball, and then nervously smoothing it out again.

'Can't it wait? My job will probably be finished in another couple of weeks,' Tom said.

'No, I've got to get it over. I'm dreading it, that's why.' She put the napkin resolutely in her lap, and placed her hands on the table. 'I've hired a plane,' she added.

'Tomorrow?'

'Crack of dawn. I shall be gone at least a couple of days.'

'Shall I see you again?'

She looked shocked. 'Of course. Whatever do you mean?'

'I wondered if—or when—you were planning to move into your house?'

'I haven't faced up to that decision yet. To be honest, Tom, I'm scared.'

'Of the house?'

She nodded. 'Of living there on my own. There are too many ghosts there, too much sadness. Yes, you'll see me again. Do you mind?'

'Don't tease.'

'I'm sorry. You bring out the worst in me, Tom.' As if to prove her point, she added, even more teasingly: 'I shall have to break the journey back, of course. There's a very romantic beach-side hotel, near Miriamvale. I shall think of you, tomorrow night, while I'm sitting under the tropical palms, gazing at the moonlit sea.' She giggled at his expression.

One of the Second Assistant Directors had been watching them from the dining-room doorway. As soon as they stood up, he hurried over to their table. 'Didn't want to interrupt your meal, Mr Grant—' the boy looks nervous, Tom thought: it's bad news—'Mr Grigoros said I must speak to you tonight. Apparently there's some trouble with Mr Miller. He wants the tennis scene rewritten.'

'So?'

'Well—' the boy ducked his head nervously—'Mr Goring won't agree, and Mr Miller won't start work until he's got his way, and in the end Mr Grigoros—'

'Who doesn't like the scene anyway—'

'Yes, sir. He's cut the scene out altogether.'

'I see. So the schedule is completely up the spout. When will you need me again?'

'Well, sir, the fact is—Mr Grigoros doesn't think you *will* be needed again, on this movie.'

'You mean, I'm free?'

'I'm afraid so, Mr Grant.' The boy backed away slowly, his face clouded with anxiety. 'Far be it from me to advise, sir, but—I think you should ring your agent.'

Tom kept his face straight until the Second Assistant Director was out of sight. 'He was paying me a compliment. He would be shattered if he knew I don't have an agent.'

Alison looked mystified. 'What's going on here? That sounded to me as if you just got fired.'

'I did, sort of.'

'Just like that?'

'It's not as drastic as it sounds. I'm under contract, so I'll get paid for the work anyway. Only now, I don't have to do the work.'

'So you *can* come with me to Balmoral Creek!' Alison crowed. 'Who says a virtuous life is never rewarded?'

Tom slept badly that night: nameless, shapeless spectres drifted through his dreams. But he woke thinking of golden palm-fringed beaches.

The pilot of the little Cessna was very helpful. 'Nearest I can get you to Balmoral Creek's about 80 kilometres,' he said. 'There's a private airstrip on a property belonging to a friend of mine. I've fixed it so's you can hire one of his jackaroos to drive you over there.' It was the kind of casual efficiency that appealed to Tom as typically Australian: the miracle was that it seemed to work most of the time.

The 'jackaroo' turned out to be a grinning, nineteen-year-old youth who was too shy to speak except in monosyllables. He bullied the ancient car as if he had a personal grudge against it, which was probably true. It was a tough, two-hour journey, most of it over winding dirt road, in an old Holden saloon with terminally-sick suspension. They were rattled around like dice in a box, but as Alison remarked, it took one's mind off the petrol fumes.

Balmoral Creek wasn't much of a place, but they were glad to get out and stretch their aching limbs. A long, single-storey building combined the functions of pub, restaurant, post-office and general store. The only other building of note was an official-looking greystone hall, with large notice-boards on either side of the front door. A few notices, too small to be legible from the road, were pinned to the boards. Behind the hall was a cluster of wooden sheds and garages, and further along the road were two timber-walled bungalows, raised on stilts and shaded by mangoes and fig trees.

The local police sergeant lived in one of the bungalows. He was tall and wire-thin; dressed in khaki shorts and a shirt, long fawn socks and shiny brown boots. There was a countryman's slowness about him, particularly in his speech, which came in a measured, thoughtful rhythm, as if each word was being retrieved from a great distance. His name was Sergeant Darfield, but: 'Call me Eric,' he said, the leathery creases round his eyes increasing in number as he smiled. He shook hands solemnly, and explained: 'It's my first name.'

In spite of his manner, he wasted no time. He dealt efficiently with the paperwork, while his wife dispensed glasses of homemade lemonade; and then he led them to one of the lock-up garages behind the greystone hall. 'There she is. An't she a beauty?'

The white Mercedes was in showroom condition, sparkling like a jeweller's window display. 'I started her up once a week,' Eric said. 'Drove her a mile up the road and back. Cars is like dogs: need work to keep 'em healthy.'

'That was very good of you,' Alison said.

'It was good *for* me, ma'am.' Eric handed over the keys with a small bow. 'A pleasure.'

Alison hesitated. 'I have a favour to ask . . . Eric?'

'Yes, ma'am?'

'Could you show me the place . . . where my aunt was found?'

'I *could*,' he said doubtfully. 'It's a long way, mind. Are you sure—?'

'Please. I'd like to see it.' She had an inspiration. 'Perhaps you could drive us there? In the Merc?'

It was a master stroke. Eric didn't even have to search for words. 'Beaut!' he said.

He drove well, handling the car carefully, and with obvious pleasure, demonstrating its virtues for their benefit. He was not over-eager to talk about Clare Yelverton's death, and Alison didn't press him, since there was another question she wanted to ask. 'Is there a twenty-year-old boy named Clark living around here?'

'You mean . . . a resident? No, ma'am. No one permanent of that name. I don't know the names of all the holiday visitors, of course.'

'Clark is the boy's first name,' Tom pointed out. 'At least, we think it is.'

'Don't make no difference. An't more'n a score of twenty-year-olds hereabouts, and I know 'em all. Thousands of young folk down in the beach resorts, of course.'

As Eric had said, it was a long drive, but the big car smoothed out the road for them. After their earlier drive, it was the height of luxury. They climbed into a range of flat-topped hills, and turned off the main road on to an uneven, grass-grown track. A little way along, Eric stopped the car in front of a black-painted iron gate. There was a notice on the gate: WO PROPERTY—KEEP OUT. Under this, in red, there was a crudely-painted skull and cross-bones, and the warning: DANGER—UNEXPLODED SHELLS.

''Bout a kilometre walk from here,' Eric said. 'Don't worry about the sign—the track's safe enough. If there are any shells, they're forty years old by now.'

The path was not easy walking: sharply-ridged rock, littered with loose stones and shards of flint. Insects chirred and clicked in the scrub, and birds fluted pleasantly from the taller trees. There was a strange twanging sound in the distance, like a wire vibrating in the wind; and a hoarse mechanical whirring, as if someone was vainly attempting to start a car. 'Lyre birds,' Eric explained. 'Wonderful mimics. Love to imitate machinery.'

As he spoke, they were startled by a shrill, clear whistle, very close at hand. It was prolonged, and gradually increased in volume, ending with a ringing crack, like a revolver shot. 'I know that one,' Alison said, excited. 'That's a stock-whip bird. I haven't heard that since I was a kid.'

'Common enough round here, ma'am,' Eric said. He led them off the main track on to a much narrower path that veered steeply downhill, hugging the contours of the slope. Where it levelled off, the road divided: one branch plunging at right-angles down to a small clearing in the bush.

'Down there,' Eric said. 'That's where we found the car.'

'What are those big mounds?' Tom asked, knowing the answer before he had finished the question. 'Anthills?'

'Yep. Come on, I'll show you.' Eric led them into the clearing, sketching out the scene for them with his hands.

'The car was just here. Seems she'd run out of petrol. Anyways, Mrs Yelverton was good and lost . . . She got out of the car—we guess she was pretty confused: she had swallowed a handful of tranquillizers 'bout an hour earlier —probably when she first realized she was lost. She took a suitcase out of the car, and started to walk. Not a good idea, but like I said, she was probably confused and afraid. She got about fifty metres up the track, and then changed her mind. She dumped the case, and went back to the car. Beyond that, we don't know for sure what happened. Her body was just here, and the car keys over there.'

'The newspapers tried to suggest that she was killed by wild dogs,' Alison said. 'What do you think, Eric?'

Eric pulled himself up to his full height and turned slowly on his heel, surveying the surrounding bush. 'Mrs Yelverton *was* mauled by dogs,' he said slowly. 'The forensic boys said so, and I've got to believe them. But as for *killing* her, well, you want my opinion, that's a lot of baloney, if you'll pardon the expression.'

'Then what did kill her?'

'I don't think we'll ever know. Fear, would be my guess. The forensic boys were definite about what *hadn't* killed her —knives, guns, poison. Still, you can't blame them for being cautious. You see—' He paused, waving the flies away from his face. 'You don't want to hear all this?'

Alison looked pale but stubborn. 'Yes, I do.'

'Well . . . The bush is full of hungry creatures, ma'am. Scavengers. Insects, birds, rodents. A lot of them found your aunt before we did. Made the exact cause of death difficult to determine.'

Tom was squatting on his heels, looking at the ground. 'The car was here, you say?'

'Yes. As you can see, the track peters out here. We think she ran out of petrol at the top of the hill, and coasted down this slope. She had to swing the car hard to the right, to miss that big anthill. Actually, if it hadn't been for the car, we might never have found her at all. She was already three-quarters buried, when the car was spotted.'

'Buried?' Tom and Alison asked the question in unison.

Eric nodded. 'Ants. When they find a big source of food, they build a mound of earth and clay over it, to preserve it and hide it from other predators. They work incredibly fast.'

Alison shuddered. 'How horrible!'

Tom was still looking at the ground. 'I guess it's not important, but she must have run out of petrol right on this spot. She surely didn't coast down that slope.'

'Sure she did.'

Tom shook his head. 'There just isn't room to manœuvre a free-wheeling car of that size. If Clare had pulled left here, just beyond this flowering bush, she couldn't have hauled that car round to the right, to finish up on the near side of this anthill. There just isn't the space.'

Eric said patiently, 'If she had braked hard and pulled right, the car would have skidded into that position.' He squatted down to examine what Tom was looking at. 'Ah. I see what you mean.'

'Those three little saplings couldn't have survived the impact of a skidding car. And a skidding car couldn't have missed them. So—'

'So, the car must have reversed into that position. It couldn't have rolled backwards, because the slope is the wrong way. And if it could reverse, it couldn't be out of petrol. Neat. You want my job?'

His tone was mild, but Tom was quick to placate him, in case he had taken offence. 'It's nothing. Just a detail that interested me, that's all. Exactly where she ran out of petrol isn't important.'

'No,' Eric was wooden-faced. 'Have you seen all you want to see, ma'am?'

Alison scanned the clearing sadly. 'Yes. Thank you for bringing me here.'

They walked back to the car without speaking. The stock-whip bird was very active, whistling and cracking over their heads; and the distant twanging of the lyre birds rang like unearthly music. Tom felt oppressed by the loneliness of the place: he was glad to get away from it.

The detail of the abandoned car nagged at his mind. Its position, at the bottom of the slope, was too neat. A heavy

94

car, handled by a panicky woman who was drugged to the gills, would surely have inflicted some damage on the landscape? Or on itself? He shrugged. It hadn't, and that was all there was to it. He tried to stop thinking about it. 'Where did your aunt live, while she was up here?' he asked Alison.

It was Eric who answered. 'She took a place about five miles out of Balmoral Creek. We can go by there, if you like.' He manœuvred the car back on to the highway. 'Funny thing is, she was hardly ever seen there, after the first few days. Seems she travelled round a lot—only used it as a base, like.'

Alison caught Tom's eye. They were both wondering the same thing—had Clare found her stepson? Was she meeting him in some remote place, like that little clearing in the bush?

Very soon, Eric left the hardtop and took to the dirt roads, some of them no better than farm tracks. The land seemed totally uninhabited for miles on end, and Tom commented on it.

Eric grunted. 'All this used to be rain-forest: jungle, folks called it. They cut it all down, to get at the exotic woods. Theory was, because the trees were so big, the soil under 'em had to be rich and fertile, great for agriculture. By the time they found out different, it was too late to save the trees. So the developers put up a batch of retirement homes, Paradise for the old folk. Lots of old people want to emigrate here for their declinin' years, because of the death-duty situation. Only, they didn't tell the old folk about the humidity, the creepy-crawlies and the four-month wet season. Result: lots of empty retirement homes goin' very cheap. They're scattered along this road, facing the bit of forest that got rescued from the developers.'

They jolted past a few tumbledown shacks, cramped incongruously close together in a vast expanse of desert, and then drove through a more ambitiously-planned development of bungalows and cabins spaced at generous intervals along the narrow road. All the houses seemed deserted: the only sign of life was a slowly-collapsing plume of white dust drifting along the trail ahead of them. 'Probably an owner checking on his property.' Eric commented. 'A lot of these places were bought up by a Brisbane company, for tourist accommodation.'

'They don't seem to be having a lot of success,' Tom said.

Eric smiled thinly. 'You could say that.' He pulled up outside a small bungalow, indistinguishable from the others they had passed. 'Here we are.'

It was an anticlimax. The bungalow, empty and neglected, looked drably ordinary. Alison got out of the car and paced slowly along the overgrown path. A lizard, basking on the warm stone, darted out of the way, making her jump. The rational part of her mind knew that there would be no answers here, no dramatic new evidence; yet she was surprised at the sharpness of her disappointment when it proved true. She pushed through the unkempt shrubbery near the house, and a tendril of lawyer-vine hooked in her skirt. She tugged impatiently at it, and was rewarded by an untidy line of pulled threads across the material.

'Seen enough?' Eric asked.

She shrugged. 'I guess so.'

Tom stood with his back to them, looking at the view. Two hundred yards away, across a stony, weed-strewn wasteland, the jungle began: a high wall of dark, luxurious green. Above the trees, the blunt, bare hilltops poked through, angular and uncompromising. Tom thought one of the ridges looked familiar.

Eric followed his gaze. 'See the scar on that hill? Bloke was climbing there a couple of weeks back, and the cliff-edge gave way. He tobogganed on his backside all the way down, and landed on top of a seven-year-old skeleton. It's a tough country.'

CHAPTER 14

Eric clearly felt a sense of responsibility for Alison's disappointment. After some thought, he offered a crumb of consolation: 'The bloke who owns the pub, Cyril Keys, is the local agent for that Brisbane holiday company. He met your aunt, and remembers her well, he says. Maybe you should have a word with him.'

Alison stared apathetically out of the window. 'I feel I'm just wasting people's time.'

'Well—' Eric considered his response at length—'you'll need a meal before you go back. The pub does tolerably good tucker.'

Cyril Keys took it for granted that the principal reason for their visit was to talk about Clare Yelverton. He was a large, fleshy man with lascivious eyes and a creepy familiarity that set their teeth on edge. He sat at their table while they ate, and confided all he knew, which was not very much. He had in fact, only met Clare twice, but she had made a big impression on him; an impression that he reinforced by rolling his eyes upwards when he talked about her. It was meant to be humorous, but it somehow emerged as obscene 'What a tragedy! Such a lovely lady, so friendly.'

He put his hand consolingly on Alison's arm, and leaned closer.

Alison smiled, not very convincingly. 'Did she tell you why she chose to come up here?'

'Funny, I wondered just the same thing.' Keys absent-mindedly massaged her wrist with his fingertips. 'I mean, she didn't seem the type to go roughing it in the outback. Smart clothes—and that French perfume!' He rolled his eyes again, to illustrate the effect of the French perfume. 'I mean, your average bush-whacker isn't exactly the feminine type: you couldn't help but notice the difference.' He winked and nodded to emphasize the point, and squeezed her hand.

'But did she actually say anything?' Alison persisted.

'No. She was very friendly at first, but then she sort of withdrew into herself. She seemed very tired.'

Alison avoided Tom's eye. It was not difficult to imagine Clare backtracking from the pub-keeper's hot-breathed gallantry.

'Do you remember the date she arrived?' Tom made a vain attempt to distract Cyril from pawing Alison.

Cyril did remember, and seized the opportunity to show off his efficiency. 'It's all in the ledger here, look. She arrived on August 4th, and—'

'No, that can't be right,' Alison said sharply. 'She was at home in Brisbane on the 9th.'

'No.' Tom's detective instinct surfaced in spite of himself. 'We can't assume that. All we know is that she read Jeremy's letter sometime *after* the 9th.'

Alison was incredulous. 'Are you trying to tell me that she went back home sometime between the 9th and the 28th? And then came back up here?'

'It looks like it.'

Cyril waited impatiently for them to finish. 'Anyway, she arrived here on the 4th, and I drove her round to the bungalow and gave her the keys. See, she paid the deposit in Brisbane, and gave me the balance in cash when she got here. I saw her again the next—'

'Wait a minute,' Tom interrupted, 'did you say you drove her round to the bungalow? Didn't she have her car?'

'No, not then. It was being serviced, she said.'

'Where?'

'I dunno. Couldn't be local: nobody round here could handle it. Anyway, she obviously got it back, didn't she? As I was saying, I saw her again the next day. I called round at the bungalow to make sure she was okay.'

'And was she?'

'I suppose so. She had her radio on very loud, very jazzy. I thought maybe the loneliness of the place had spooked her —it does that, to some people—but she said it was okay.'

'Was her car there by then?'

'No. I asked her if she needed any supplies, but she said

no. I assumed she had been lying down—she had a robe on, and kept herself half-way hidden behind the door. She didn't ask me in.' Cyril's tone was tainted with resentment, at the memory.

That seemed to be all he could tell them. Alison had run out of questions, and sat glumly toying with her food. Tom asked, mainly to break the uncomfortable silence: 'Is there a big tourist demand for those holiday cabins?'

Cyril snorted. 'Not so's you'd notice. That smart-Alick Sydney firm must be losing a packet.'

'Sydney? I thought it was in Brisbane? Mrs Yelverton paid a deposit in Brisbane, you said.'

'Ah yes, there's an agent in Brisbane. Well, in Ipswich, to be precise.' Cyril slapped himself theatrically on the forehead. 'I forgot—I've still got a couple of receipts belonging to her. I meant to take them round, but what with one thing and another—' He went into the kitchen and came back with two grubby pieces of paper. 'I don't know whether you want to take them?'

Tom looked at them. 'Yes,' he said, 'we do.' He met Alison's look of surprise blandly. 'For the records.'

They hurried through the rest of the meal and went back to the car. When they were on the road, Alison said, 'God, I could do with a shower. Just having that creep look at me made me feel dirty all over.'

'Seems as if he made your aunt feel that way, too.'

'Yes. I wish we hadn't come here, now. I thought I knew Clare as well as I could ever know anybody. But the person that Eric and that slimy sod described was a perfect stranger to me. French perfume, jazzy music, tranquillizers by the handful . . . no wonder Jeremy Clays said she was eccentric.'

She concentrated on her driving, getting used to the controls, trying to blanket out her feelings of loss and confusion by racing too fast along the narrow roads. Gradually the tension eased, and she slowed to a more reasonable speed, looking shamefaced. 'Sorry. Would you like to drive?'

'No. You're doing fine.'

She glanced sideways at his face. 'What's the matter? Did I say something wrong?'

'No.'

'You look so grim.'

'I hate coincidences. They make me nervous.'

'What do you mean? What coincidences?'

'This, in particular.' Tom pulled the crumpled receipts from his pocket. 'Cyril just told us that the company that owns those holiday cabins has an agent in Ipswich. The agent's signature is on one of those receipts: Oscar Pepperidge.'

'So?'

'Don't you remember? One of the paintings your aunt bought at Ruisdel's auction belonged to a Mr. O. Pepperidge of Ipswich.'

CHAPTER 15

Alison swerved off the road, and skidded to a halt on the dirt shoulder. 'Let me see that!' She snatched the paper from Tom's hand. 'You said there was something phoney about that art auction. This proves it!'

'It proves nothing,' Tom said. 'At the moment, it's a coincidence, that's all. We can't link it with any crime; in fact we don't know for sure that crime's been committed.'

'This whole business stinks of something rotten, and you know it. What about those fake pictures?'

'That could be a genuine mistake,' he countered. 'And since the auctioneers admitted liability and paid up, we can't prove that anybody acted in bad faith. Look—' Tom could see that Alison's temper and frustration were building up to explosion point, and he tried to defuse the situation. 'I don't know all the facts, and I never knew Clare. But all the odd circumstances that we've found *could* be explained very simply, in terms of your aunt's temperament.'

'So now you're saying she was doolally, is that it?'

'No, all I'm saying, is that all these coincidences and odd happenings don't yet add up to anything tangible. I agree with you: my instincts tell me that those art sales were not completely kosher. But I can't tell you why. And instincts aren't evidence.'

Alison was clearly not impressed with Tom's caution, but made no attempt to challenge it immediately. She swung the car back on the road, and drove for several miles without speaking. Then, as if picking up a conversational cue, she said, argumentatively, 'Money is the root of all evil, right?'

'It's a commonly held point of view.'

'Right. So, lacking any other obvious motive, this crime must begin with the money.'

'What money?'

'The money that was paid for those pictures, of course. Jeremy Clays warned Clare that she was bidding too much. Why was she bidding too much?'

'I don't know. And neither do you.'

'No, but I bet Oscar Pepperidge of Ipswich could tell us. Somebody conned her into bidding too high, and then conned her into traipsing five hundred miles up-country while the auction was being held.'

'That's a powerful piece of persuasion. How do you suppose it was done?'

Alison warmed to her argument. 'The second part's easy. Somebody invented Clark, the phantom stepson, and lured Clare into the backwoods while her money was being squandered down in Brisbane.'

'That's pretty fanciful. She must have given permission for her money to be squandered, as you put it. The pictures aren't rubbish, or Lewis would have told us so. They must have some value.'

'Yes, but that's the beauty of it, don't you see? They *are* valuable. But suppose you've bought them for, say, a million dollars. If you can pass them on, at a public auction, for *two* million, you have a neat and virtually undetectable fraud.'

Tom was unconvinced. 'You're talking about a lot of organization here. Someone had to investigate Clare's personal life, buy the pictures, rig the auction, persuade Clare to go on a wild-goose chase up-country for several weeks—'

'She wasn't up here for the whole of that time,' Alison

interrupted. 'We know she was home sometime after August 9th, because of Jeremy's letter.'

'Yes, I'd forgotten that. But my point is that as a con trick, it was enormously risky. I mean, if Clare had had her accident only a week earlier, the crooks would have had a million dollars' worth of paintings on their hands, and no certainty of profit.'

Alison gave up. 'I guess the whole idea's too bizarre. But I'm certainly going to find Mr Oscar Pepperidge. And if Clark exists, I'll eat my hat.'

After nightfall, Alison turned off the main highway towards the coast, following the signs to Agnes Waters and 1770. 'The Tourist Bureau recommends the motel there,' she explained briefly. It was the first time she had spoken in over an hour.

'Down here?' Tom stared doubtfully at the road ahead: a narrow, lumpy dirt track.

'They've only just started to develop this area,' Alison explained. There's a new motel near 1770—'

'1770? Is that a place?'

'It used to be called Round Hill. Captain Cook landed there.'

'In 1770, of course. Silly me.'

Alison sounded smug. 'The motel's on the beach, at one end of a secluded bay, with magnificent views and great surfing.'

'Surfing? That's not likely. The Barrier Reef's in the way.'

'That's all you know, smarty. There's a gap in the reef. This is probably the most northerly surf beach on this coast.'

'You got that out of the guide book,' Tom accused.

'So? People who don't read guide books have to ask silly questions.'

Well, at least they were talking again, Tom thought. Many miles back, he had offered to take over the driving for a while, and her curt refusal had provoked an awkward silence between them. He could think of no reason for the tension that was infecting the atmosphere, other than their difference of opinion over her aunt's pictures, which hardly

102

seemed a sufficient cause. His attempts at casual conversation were so clumsy that she had no difficulty in ignoring them, and he quickly gave up the attempt. Last night, she had teased him with her reference to 'romantic' hotels and tropical palms, but now, she seemed as cold and distant as a suspicious stranger. Probably, she hadn't been teasing at all: he had simply read a sexual invitation into her words because that was what he was hoping for. Tom felt a momentary spasm of irritation. He was doing this girl a favour, and she was making him feel about as welcome as a two-day migraine.

The beach-side motel did indeed have palm trees in the courtyard, their leaves clattering in the brisk southerly breeze. Alison parked the car, and they walked together to the foyer of the main building, still without speaking. Then, just before they reached the reception desk, Alison touched his arm. 'I've just got to go to the loo,' she murmured. 'You don't mind booking us in, do you?' She disappeared before he had fully realized the extent of her treachery.

When she reappeared, he was fuming. She, however, had recovered her good humour. 'Everything all right? What did you get us?'

'There was a choice,' Tom said evenly. 'We were offered studio units, with sundecks, single beds, and showers en suite; or, a beach cabin with a king-size bed and a tropical bathroom equipped with a vast sunken bath.'

'Oh.' Alison tried to look nonchalant, but spoiled the effect by giggling nervously. 'Which did we choose?'

'We chose the bloody studio units,' Tom snarled bitterly. 'David would be proud of us.'

Later, they dined in the motel restaurant, sitting at a table by the window, overlooking the floodlit beach. The wind flattened the dune grasses, and raised little puffs of white sand here and there. Beyond the expanse of light, the surf gleamed thinly, like a steel blade.

Alison said, 'Are you still mad at me?'

'I'm not really mad, just confused. Was that some sort of test? And if so, did I pass?'

'Oh, you passed all right. You did for me what I couldn't do for myself.' Alison straightened the table-mat, and arranged the cutlery in front of her with scrupulous neatness, unwilling to meet his eye. 'I wrote to David last night. I had to do something: I couldn't sleep.' She paused nervously, as if expecting some comment, then went on: 'I wanted to tell him that I missed him, that I loved him, but I simply couldn't write the words. In the end, I just wrote that I was thinking about him, which was true enough. I've always prided myself on my honesty, Tom Grant.'

'Look,' Tom said irritably, 'there's no need to labour the point. I like you just fine. But you don't *have* to warn me off every five minutes. Crazed with lust I may be, but I'm not yet going completely berserk.'

Alison went very pink. 'You great thick Scottish oaf, you still don't understand, do you? I'm the one who's going crazy. I want you so badly, I could scream with frustration. When I look at you, I get longings and desires no respectable girl would ever admit to. And stop gaping like a fool,' she added unfairly.

Tom took some time to gather his wits. 'Why the hell couldn't you have said this a couple of hours ago? Don't you realize there's a king-size bed going begging under this very roof?'

'I'm not going to bed with you, Tom.'

'But—'

'You're right, I owe you an explanation.' She didn't, however, seem in a hurry to give it. 'I wish I were drunk: this kind of truth needs a little help. I'm not doing my chastity bit out of loyalty. I'm not in love with David, and I never have been. I went to bed with him for a number of reasons, none of them to do with love. No, my problem is sillier and more serious than that. I'm jealous of your wife.'

'I've told you, I'm not married.

Alison ignored the interruption. 'She's beautiful, she's famous, and she's immensely talented; and if that wasn't bad enough, you love her.'

'*Loved.* Past tense. It's over.'

'So you say. Did you get engaged to Maria before you got married?'

'Her name was Mary, when I knew her. Yes, we were engaged.'

'For how long?'

'Nearly a year. It took us that time to find somewhere to live.'

'And how long had you known her before you got engaged?'

'About three years.'

'Exactly!' Alison thumped the table with her fist, making the cutlery rattle. 'That's what I'm jealous of. You courted Mary for three whole years. I'm damned if I'll give you full conjugal rights after only three days!'

CHAPTER 16

Tom slept better than he expected to, on his narrow bed, but woke early, just after dawn. He put on swimming trunks, went down to the beach, and jogged along the flat, wet sand. He needed to work some of the stiffness out of his body, and the frustrations out of his mind. His relationship with Alison had turned awkward. They were not lovers, and yet the physical attraction between them made simple friendship virtually impossible. Was he in love with her? It would be very easy to believe so; and yet how could he be sure of his feelings, in so short a time? On the other hand, he had courted Mary for three careful years; and see how that had turned out. He ran faster, to try to distract his mind from these problems. Thinking was no use: time would sort it out. At least last night was over, thank God: today was a whole new adventure.

The thin, dark-blue clouds on the eastern horizon scattered like minnows as the sun poked up out of the sea. The warmth caressed Tom's skin, produced a momentary feeling of exhilaration. The world was full of good things: the dazzle on the sea, the squeaking of the sand under his feet, the steady beat of his heart. The wind dropped, as suddenly as if someone had closed a door, and he began to sweat. He turned aside, and waded into the sea.

The surf was too boisterous to swim in: he allowed himself to be knocked over and rolled about in the high, breaking waves, frolicking like a child. The surging water pummelled his chest, knocking the breath out of him; it dragged his feet away, dumping him on moving sand. He was a cork, a piece of driftwood. He found he was laughing out loud, whooping and jeering and talking to himself. He discovered something else, too: as the white water broke over his head, and the giant waves picked him up and tossed him about, he realized that he was a pompous, over-cautious idiot. Alison Easterbrook was beautiful, desirable and totally adorable. He loved her. His love for her was the best thing that had ever happened to him.

It was perfectly in keeping with this miraculous moment to find that Alison was there in the water with him, gasping and grinning, her blonde hair plastered tight against her skull. She reached out and clung to him just as another roller dumped them under tons of water, and tumbled them about like drifting weed. They bobbed up, coughing, spluttering, and laughing. Alison held on to him tightly, as if in fear, hiding her head against his shoulder. Then, abandoning all pretence, she kissed him passionately on the mouth, and wrapped her arms and legs around him as the next wave surged under them, and dropped them smoothly down the other side. 'I love you!' Tom yelled: it was good to shout, to compete with the boom and thunder of the surf. Her weight bore them both under again, and the fierce pull of the ebbing wave forced them to break apart and kick for the surface.

Eventually, exhausted, they managed to crawl out of the sea, and collapsed panting on soft, dry sand. 'There was no need to say that,' Alison gasped. 'That wasn't fair.'

'That wasn't a game, Allie. I meant it.'

'We'll see.' She rolled over and raised herself on one elbow, smiling wickedly. Sand caked her hair, and glinted like frosting on her shoulders. 'You'll have lots of opportunity to prove it, believe me. Did you sleep?'

'Not much.'

'Nor me. But I thought of something, in the night.'

'So did I.'

'Not that, you idiot. Well, not just that. I remembered Clare's luggage. It's still in the boot of the car. I got up in the middle of the night to have a look at it. It suddenly occurred to me that Clark's letter ought to be there somewhere.'

'Surely the police had searched the luggage?' Tom tried to be interested, but Alison's legs, even heavily coated with sand, were a powerful distraction.

'Yes, I thought of that, too. Eventually.' Alison shivered, as the water from her hair dripped on to her bare skin.

'So, no letter,' Tom said. 'What did you find?'

'Nothing. In the end, I couldn't face it. Just the sight of her suitcase spooked me badly.' The tone of her voice warned Tom that she was not being completely candid. After a short silence, she admitted it: 'I did find something.'

'What?'

'On the top of her things, in the case, was a sponge-bag. In the sponge-bag was the filthiest pair of panties I've ever seen in my life. They are revolting: I can't imagine anyone touching them, let alone wearing them. I dropped them back in the case, and locked it quickly. Tom, if I could make myself believe that Clare actually wore those—*things*—in that state—then I'm more than half way to believing the obvious explanation for all this mystery. I'd be forced to think that Clare was mad, after all.'

When they got under way again, Alison was content to let Tom drive, and leaned back at ease in the passenger seat, commenting favourably on the universe. Everything pleased her that morning: the distant hills, the cloudless sky, the brightly-plumed birds grazing at the roadside. Tom half-listened to her chatter, making appropriate conversational noises whenever it seemed necessary. He too felt astonishingly cheerful. It was interesting, the way happiness changes the landscape: images become sharper, colours brighter.

Best of all, life becomes simpler; for the first time in years, he was where he wanted to be.

Afterwards, neither of them could say exactly why they chose to stop at that particular petrol station. It was not the obvious place to stop; in fact, from the road, it was not visible at all. Perhaps it was the sign that did it. Hand-painted on a square board, hanging from a branch of ti-tree, it announced laconically:

PETROL
REPIARS
HAMBERGERS

An arrow pointed the way down a dirt-track to where a cluster of shacks sheltered behind a group of stunted trees. As they drove up to the pumps, a grey-bearded man in blue dungarees and a straw hat trotted out from the repair-shop to serve them. 'G'day! Fill 'er up?' He had to repeat the question.

'Thanks.' Tom answered for both of them, since Alison had succumbed to an attack of the giggles, inadequately disguised as a coughing fit. Ahead of them, the farthest wooden shack had been painted in vertical stripes of red, white and blue. In the front, a canvas awning was supported on iron posts embellished with plastic vine-leaves; and over the awning, a painted sign decorated with wrought-iron curlicues, read CAFE MOMUS. There were two white tables under the awning, and leaning against the nearest table was a blackboard with a carefully-chalked legend:

PROLLY
THE BEST HAMBERGERS
IN THE WORLD
(WITH ALL THE TRIMINGSES)

'Tom,' Alison murmured weakly, 'I am suddenly famished with hunger.'

'Would you like—' Tom chose his words with care—'the best hamberger in the world, ma'am?'

'Only if I may have all the trimingses, Mr G.'

They left the car on the shady side of the repair-shop, and

sat at a white table under the canvas awning. They drank ice-cold beer, and ate the Café Momus de luxe Jumbo Special with homemade bread rolls and garden-fresh salad. 'By God,' Tom said, 'it *is* the best hamburger in the world!'

'Too right.' The grey-bearded man ambled across the dusty yard. 'Ma is not given to hyperbole, are you, Ma?' He sat down at the other table, took off his hat, and mopped his bald head with a grey rag. The top of his head, protected by the hat, was white as fine porcelain, but below the hat line, his face was burnt mahogany-brown by the sun. The quiet, shy woman who had served their meal emerged from the kitchen, set a glass of beer in front of him. 'There y'are, Ben.' She disappeared again.

'She hasn't given you any trouble, then?' Ben asked.

Tom and Alison looked at each other. 'The meal was wonderful,' Alison said. 'Your sign ought to say "Definitely", not "Probably".'

'I don't mean Ma.' The old man mopped his head some more. 'I know the tucker's all right. I was talking about the car.'

'Why should the car give us trouble?' Tom asked.

'No reason, I suppose. I noticed you hadn't changed the unit, so I guess she's waterproof all right.'

It was Tom who caught on first. 'You've seen the car before, then? Repaired it?'

'I surely have. Prolly no one else within a hundred miles could'a done it that quick. You can wait up to three weeks for them parts.'

'What part was that?'

'Rear-light unit, off-side. All smashed up it was. Nothing working: indicators, brake-lights, nothing. Couldn't go no further like that: the traffic cops are very keen on roadworthiness along this stretch of highway. Thousand to one chance brought her in here. Got her back on the road in a couple of hours.'

'You mean, you just happened to have that part in stock?'

'Not exactly.' The old man chuckled. 'But I just happened to have the identical model Merc in the garage there. Storing it for the owner, who's over in Europe for three months. So

I borrowed the unit from that car, and replaced it later, when I got the part from the supplier. Pretty neat, eh?'

'When was this?' Alison asked excitedly.

'Couple of months ago.'

'And you're sure it's the same car?'

'Certain. See, I wasn't sure the fit was waterproof, so I squeezed a bit of sealant into the crack. You can't see it unless you bend down and look real close. That's my work all right. I checked when I was filling 'er up.'

Alison impulsively held on to Tom's hand. She was trembling and close to tears. 'Imagine us coming to the same place,' she whispered. 'Perhaps she sat at this very table, and ate a Café Momus Special. I can just see her doing it.'

'Who?' Ben cocked his head, his eye bright as a sparrow's.

Alison smiled wanly. 'My aunt. She was the driver: the car belonged to her.'

Ben guffawed and slapped the table. 'Damn funniest aunt I've ever seen. Driver of that Merc was a feller. Thin, nervy-looking bloke. Wore a red hat with a long peak, like them American ball-players.'

CHAPTER 17

'I didn't know you could draw,' Alison said. 'How many other talents are you hiding?'

Tom made some alterations to his latest sketch, then put it aside and started another. 'I've never done this before,' he said, 'but I've watched police artists at work. The end result is only as good as the witness's powers of observation.' After a few minutes, he showed his latest effort to Ben, who had been patiently cooperating for the last hour.

'That's pretty good,' Ben said. 'The jaw and the mouth are about right. But the ears are too big, and the freckles go right over his nose.'

Tom made a couple of alterations, and Ben nodded. 'Yep. That's as close as I can get.'

Alison studied the drawing over Ben's shoulder. 'Who is

110

he, do you think? Does Clark exist, after all?'

'I think we should talk to him, whoever he is,' Tom said. 'Let's go find him.'

They managed to get back to Brisbane early enough to catch Jeremy Clays at his office. He was unimpressed with Alison's suspicions, and made no bones about saying so. 'What you seem to be suggesting is a conspiracy to defraud your aunt. If so, it was a conspiracy in which your aunt was a willing participant. She made her own decisions on what to bid for each lot, without—indeed, in spite of—any outside advice.'

'But,' Alison insisted, 'weren't you at all bothered by the fact that Clare wasn't even present when her money was being spent?'

Clays frowned his astonishment. 'What on earth are you talking about? Of course Mrs Yelverton was present at the auction. Who told you she wasn't?'

'But—I thought she was at Balmoral Creek at the time. She died up there only three days later.

'I think,' Clays said heavily, 'that you are letting your imagination run away with you. I can see no reason why Clare Yelverton should not be in Brisbane on August 23rd, and in Balmoral Creek three days later. Can you?'

'I suppose not.' Alison was unwilling to let go of her suspicions. 'But on that very day, August 23rd, Clare's car was being repaired at a garage nearly two hundred miles from here!'

Clays looked shocked, as if she had just slapped his face. 'Are you telling me that someone claims to have seen Mrs Yelverton—'

'No. Someone else was driving her car.'

His brow cleared. 'Ah. Then it seems obvious to me that she asked someone else to drive her car up north, to save her the effort.'

'Who?'

'I have no idea, and I refuse to speculate. As for your other suspicions, I advise you to beware of making any accusations, however oblique, against anybody, without much weightier evidence. I sympathize with, and understand, your grief over your aunt's death; but I beg you to take care that your grief does not warp your judgement.' Under his pompously courteous manner, he seemed to be seething with anger. He summoned the commissionaire and dismissed them with barely perceptible politeness.

As they went back to the car, Alison said, 'I don't think I've ever before seen Jeremy so het up.'

'He thinks you're accusing him of professional carelessness. Lawyers don't like that.'

'I didn't realize that Clare was at that auction. That alters things, doesn't it?'

'Yes. But it doesn't make them any less confusing.' They sat in the Mercedes, disinclined to get involved in the peak-hour traffic. 'One thing that really puzzles me,' Tom said, 'is that your aunt seems to have disappeared for most of the last month of her life. She was at Balmoral Creek on August 4th and 5th; and at the art auction in Brisbane on the 23rd; but where was she the rest of the time? What was she doing? And who was the man in the red hat?'

'I thought you had an idea about that. "Let's go find him," you said.'

'Spoken in haste. Finding him may not be easy. But it might be a notion to stir things up a bit.'

'How?'

'It'll be expensive, and there's no guarantee it'll work.'

'Hang the expense. Tell me about it.'

Tom outlined his idea. It didn't seem as clever in words as in his head, but Alison was enthusiastic. 'I'll fix it up tonight. Afterwards we'll have supper, and then—'

'And then?'

Her eyes sparkled. 'Your place, or mine?'

There was a whole sheaf of messages waiting for Tom at the hotel reception desk. Sam, Nikos, Lewis and Julian all wanted him to call as soon as he got in; and it seemed that Ned Caton had been phoning every couple of hours. Ned's messages were all the same: 'Phone. Most urgent. Ned.'

Tom phoned as soon as he reached his room. His call was answered on the first ring. 'Tom? Where the hell have you been? I've been going crazy here.' Ned sounded breathless, from excitement or drink. Possibly both.

'Take it easy, Ned. What's the problem?'

'Those Press cuttings you sent me—did you look at them?'

'Only a few. They looked like duplicates of the ones you have.'

'Not quite. Come and look at them now.'

'Now? Ned, I have things to do. I know how you feel about the girl—'

'*Please*, Tom! This is important. I've never been anywhere near anything this big, before. I need help, son, and I need it right now!'

'Ned, make some sense. What's so special about those cuttings? Why can't you bring them over here?'

'I can't. Look, I don't want to talk about it over the phone. Tom, I'm scared to go out! Come over here now—please!'

'Okay.' Tom yielded reluctantly. 'But I'll have to see if I can borrow a car. Listen, if I have a problem, I'll get back to you; if not, I'll turn up there as soon as I can.' He rang off and started calling the other people who had left messages. The only person who was in his office was the Second Assistant Director, who was delighted to hear from him. Did Tom know they were having second thoughts about the tennis scene? So they might need him after all. Yes, of course he could borrow a car—the white Renault was out in the parking-lot, and the keys would be at Reception. Tom tried to let Alison know where he was going, but couldn't contact her. He left a message for her at the desk, and drove to Surfers' Paradise.

The traffic was still dense and slow-moving; it was after dark when he arrived at the white apartment house. Tom rang the bell, and stooped to speak into the entry-phone. There was no reply, and he jammed his thumb impatiently on the button. At last the box squawked, the buzzer sounded, and Tom pushed his way inside.

On the third floor, Ned's door was open, and a deep buzz-saw sound of snoring came from inside the room. Ned was obviously dead drunk. Trying to control his irritation,

Tom pushed the door wide, and felt for the light switch. The door swung back on him, striking his shoulder and pushing him sideways, off-balance. He heard a swish, and ducked instinctively. Something struck his left arm. The sharp pain was followed by instant numbness: he felt that his arm couldn't move at all. Suddenly, there was pandemonium in the darkness: a fist punched him in the ribs, and another crashed against the side of his head. Somebody cannoned into his back, and he stumbled forward, arms flailing. He hit someone in the face. Then a kick rattled his legs from under him, and he crashed down, knocking over chairs and tables in the darkness.

There were three of them, he was almost sure. They were still fumbling, getting in each other's way. One of them had some sort of weapon: a stick or a truncheon. The numbness began to leave Tom's arm, and the throbbing began: a deep, sickening ache. Any second now, they would switch on the light, and he would be at their mercy. He crawled forward, arm outstretched, found the wall. With the wall at his back, he crouched, waiting.

The scuffling stopped. The only noise in the room was the loud snoring, which came from somewhere to his left. Tom held his breath and crouched lower. The darkness was not absolute: light from the street filtered around the curtains. He could begin to make out shapes, black against deeper black.

A voice whined out of the darkness: 'Christ, Merv, did you have to hit him so hard?'

'Shut up, you stupid prick!' The other voice was deeper, but still sounded young. Tom saw movement: a re-arrangement of the shadows. That was good. Now he knew where one of them was. It wasn't much, but it was something. There was a sudden rush of movement, and he braced himself, straining to see. The door was wrenched open, and light spilled into the room. The three youths crammed into the doorway, obstructing each other, using their fists and feet in their struggle to escape. Tom got a fleeting impression of ragged tank-tops, blue jeans, long hair. One of the boys carried a baseball bat. The smallest of the three looked back

114

in panic, but with the light behind him, most of his face was invisible. Tom could see only the angular planes of his brow, and the high, sharp ridge of his cheekbones.

By the time Tom reached the door, they had gone from the corridor: he could hear them clattering down the stairs. He started to follow, but a harsh cry from inside the room stopped him. He turned back and switched on the light.

Ned Caton was no longer snoring. He was sprawled on the floor, holding his head and moaning. There was blood on his hands and on the back of his shirt. His eyes were wide open with pain, dark against the grey pallor of his cheeks. He seemed to recognize Tom, and tried to speak, but could only make strangled, guttural sounds, as if his tongue was paralysed. With an effort, he snatched something from the floor, and thrust it into Tom's hand.

It was the letter Tom had posted in Brisbane two days before. Ned struggled to speak, his eyes pleading, but could only manage those strained animal noises. He choked on the sound, and began to cough. Blood ran from his nose. He collapsed and began to snore again, raggedly. An obstruction in his throat sounded like a rag fluttering in the breeze.

Ned's phone was wrecked. Tom tried to raise help from the other flats in the block, but could get no answer to his knocking. Finally, he had to go down to the street to find a phone-box. He called the emergency ambulance service and the police, and then had to wait on the street because he had locked himself out of the apartment block.

The ambulance arrived first, and the two attendants were breaking the front door open when the police turned up. Tom led the whole party upstairs.

Ned was still alive, but he looked bad. One of the ambulance men briefly examined the back of his head, then nodded to his companion. 'Fast as we can make it, Danny.' They strapped Ned to a stretcher, and left at a trot, handling their burden with incredible speed and gentleness.

Then Tom began his explanation to the police. At first, he hoped to keep it simple, and mentioned only that he had come over in answer to Ned's phone-call, and surprised the

115

intruders in the flat; but it was soon apparent that this account left too many questions unanswered. In the end, he told the whole story, from their meeting in the hotel bar.

The two officers looked at him in silence, as if in some doubt as to what to say next. They were young, tough, streetwise; scepticism glinted frostily behind their eyes. It was clear to them that Tom wasn't telling the whole story.

'You say the injured man gave you a letter?' one of them asked.

'Yes. This one.' Tom handed over the bloodstained envelope.

'There's nothing in here.' The man's tone was neutral, but his eyes were suspicious. 'Why should he give you an empty envelope?'

'I don't know. That was the envelope I sent to him. It contained press cuttings about his girlfriend, who was an actress.'

'Yes, you told us that. We found these newspaper clippings scattered on the floor. Would they be the ones you sent?'

'As far as I know. I didn't examine them closely. I sent a letter with them.'

'We haven't found that.' The young officer had a knack of making a simple statement sound like an accusation. 'You said that Mr Caton asked you to come over and look at these newspaper clippings? And he was very insistent about it?'

'That's right.'

'And you have no idea why?'

'None.'

'Would you cast your eye over them again, Mr Grant, and see if anything at all comes to mind?'

Tom looked carefully through the papers. 'Nothing. They all refer to Vicki Foxe, Caton's girlfriend. He was besotted about her.'

'Why was Caton so insistent that you come over and look at these cuttings? What's so special about them?'

'I have no idea.'

'Was he drunk?'

116

Tom hesitated. 'He may have been. He certainly drank heavily when he came to my hotel room.'

The other policeman took up the questioning: 'You say there were three assailants? And one of them was called Merv?'

'That's what one of the others called him, yes.'

'Could you identify any of them?'

'Not so's it would stand up in court. The light was dim, and behind them. They were slim, young-looking: that's all I can say.'

The officer went back through his notes. 'At your first meeting with Caton, he told you he was being harassed by punks. Did he say why?'

'No. He was fairly drunk when he said that, and to be honest, I put it down to alcoholic paranoia.' Tom frowned in an effort to remember. 'As a matter of fact it seemed that the kids turned the tables on him. They reported him to the police for threatening behaviour. Caton was ticked off by a couple of your men.'

'That's interesting. We'll check that out. Now, sir, can I ask you to come round to the station with us? There's so much in your statement, that I think we'd better get it down formally, to make sure we've got it right.'

It was a polite way of telling Tom that he was still under suspicion, and Tom accepted it with a good grace. In their shoes, he would probably feel the same way. At the station they tape-recorded his statement, asking him to elucidate points as he went along; then they typed it up and he signed three copies.

It was getting late: he phoned the hotel; but Alison was not back yet. He left a message to say that he had been delayed, and went to the hospital.

But at the hospital, he wasn't allowed to see Ned; he was still in the operating theatre, they said. No, they didn't know what his chances of survival were, but they were doing their best. No, there was no point in waiting; there wouldn't be any real information until tomorrow morning at the earliest.

A pretty young nurse was standing by the desk while Tom was making his inquiries, listening unashamedly to their

117

conversation. 'Excuse me,' she said, 'but are you Tom?'

'Yes.'

'A friend of Mr Caton's?'

'Yes.'

'Well, I suppose you must be the right one. Mr Caton came to briefly, when we were preparing him for the op. He was very agitated. He said, "Give Tom this, give Tom this," and then he passed out again. So perhaps I'd better give it to you.'

It was a key-ring, with three keys.

CHAPTER 18

'Tonight?' Alison said, in some confusion. 'I didn't think it would be so soon. I mean, I'm hardly dressed for the occasion—'

'It's up to you. We've got the time, if you've got the money. We'll stay in close-up all the time, except when we cut away to the captions, so it doesn't matter what you're wearing. Touch of make-up, a comb through the hair, and you're away.'

Alison made up her mind. 'I'll do it,' she said recklessly. 'But this is the only photograph I've got, I'm afraid. It's very small.'

'Graphics can cope with that.' The director grinned. 'They can work miracles. Now, if you've made up your mind. I'll take you to Accounts. They take all major credit cards. And remember—rehearse your piece. Three minutes is all you get.'

After that, everything seemed to happen at top speed. Alison phoned the hotel, and left a hurried message for Tom: 'I'm on the *Say It!* show tonight! Love, Allie.' Tom would be pleased: it was his idea.

She paid for her 'slot', as the Accounts clerk called it, and then sat in a corner of the foyer to write and memorize her lines. Surprisingly, she didn't feel nervous at all.

There was a disappointing lack of showbiz atmosphere at

this TV studio. People came and went, carrying papers or bits of equipment; but mainly, they went. During the evening people drifted away, shouting goodbyes, getting into their cars and driving off. The canteen closed. A security guard checked offices and dressing-rooms, switching off lights. It felt a little like a night-shift at a factory.

There was what the director called a 'rehearsal' for Alison and the other participants in the show, but it consisted mainly of showing them where to sit while they were waiting, and where to stand when they were on camera. The studio 'set' looked distinctly shabby and down-at-heel: a few badly-painted canvas screens, a coffee-table, two chairs, and a plain wooden lectern provided all the décor for the show. It was no wonder the director concentrated on close-ups.

Suddenly, things began to liven up. The studio lights came up, and the set looked a whole lot better. Nancy Grafter, the show's presenter, swept in, accompanied by her dresser, her make-up girl, the producer, and a nervous youth carrying a clipboard. Nancy listened, nodding to the producer while the two women fussed around, dabbing her brow with powder, arranging pleats and creases in her dress. She took the clipboard from the nervous boy, and surveyed the set with no noticeable enthusiasm. 'Flowers,' she commanded tersely. 'And a bloody bookcase. This looks as if I'm working in a bloody tent.'

The flowers and bookcase were forthcoming with such speed, it was clear that the demand had been anticipated. A bespectacled floormanager, complete with headphones and walkie-talkie, wished the participants luck, without noticeable enthusiasm. 'I'll look after you,' he said. 'Don't worry about a thing.'

Then the screen monitors flickered into life, and Nancy smiled out at her public. 'Good evening, and welcome to another edition of *Say It!*—the programme where ordinary people get it off their chest, let it all hang out, and tell the world! Do *you* have a message for the world? Do you have a bee in your bonnet? Or fairies at the bottom of your garden? Do you want to jump for joy? Cry for help? We believe that everyone has something to say, and *we* say—as long as it isn't illegal or obscene—*Say It!*'

The title-music came in on cue, and the opening credits rolled. The make-up girl darted in to dab at Nancy's nose, and a stage-hand changed the cue-cards. Nancy smiled and spoke again. 'Remember, none of our speakers is sponsored by any charity, organization or professional body. They are spending their own money to speak directly to *you*, because they *care*. If you want to answer back, the number to ring is on the screen now. We will broadcast a selection of the phone-calls we receive, at the end of the programme. What can our first speaker, the lovely heiress Alison Easterbrook, want to talk about? Find out, after the break.'

After the commercials, Alison stood at the lectern, and addressed the camera directly: 'Someone out there can help me solve a mystery.' She nodded a cue to the director, who flashed up the photograph of Clare Yelverton. 'This is my Aunt Clare, who died some weeks ago in an accident on the Wooroora Tank Range. You may have read about her death in the papers. Shortly before her unfortunate accident, Mrs Yelverton, a widow, confided to me that she had a stepson, whom she had never seen. This boy, Clark, had been born before Clare even met her husband; in fact, she didn't know of his existence, until he wrote to her, last July.

'So, it seems that I have a cousin: but where is he? I haven't been able to contact him, because I haven't got an address; all I know of him is his name, Clark.' Alison paused for dramatic effect; she was surprised to find that she was enjoying herself. 'But there's another mystery: who is this man?' Tom's drawing of the man in the long-peaked cap filled the screen. 'This is an artist's impression of a man who was seen driving my aunt's car on August 23rd—three days before she died. Is he Clark? If not, who is he, and why was he driving Clare Yelverton's car? Someone, somewhere, must know the answers to these questions; if it's you, won't you please help me? Contact this programme as soon as you can.'

Tom had said that he was sure that there would be a response to the programme, but she didn't expect it to be so immediate, or so big. Before the end of the show, more than a hundred phone calls had come in for her. Some were facetious, some were silly; many more were simply crude. But one was a shock. Alison recognized the voice of Cyril Keys, puzzled yet belligerent: 'There's some mistake. That wasn't a picture of Mrs Yelverton. She was nothing like that at all.'

CHAPTER 19

'Where the hell have you been?' The connection was weak, and there was a sound like frying bacon on the line, but she could hear the anger in his voice.

'Half the damn phone-boxes are out of order,' the woman said sullenly. 'I've driven around for miles.'

'Okay. Make my day. Tell me the whole thing isn't falling apart, up there.'

'I'm worried about the man. This thing on the TV tonight has really spooked him.' The woman hurried to explain: 'The Easterbrook girl went on the *Say It!* show tonight. She had a picture of Red—a drawing, by some artist, she said. But it was a good likeness all right.'

'That stupid bastard! I said that cockamanny scam was crazy, right from the start. Greedy and dangerous. If they get to me through your goddam greed—'

'They won't. Nothing leads back to you. Nobody can prove a damn thing. The Easterbrook girl thinks Red is her cousin. There's nothing to worry about.'

'Except the man.'

'He's the nervous type.' The woman didn't try to hide her contempt.

'Too nervous.'

'He's been useful. But—' She let the word hang in the air for a long moment. 'When this thing cools down, you could do me a big favour.'

'Like that, is it? You want to borrow my right hand? It comes expensive, even to me.' Some of the tension had gone out of the man's voice: he sounded almost amused. 'Now tell me about the cop.'

'He's in hospital.'

The static on the line made the man's silence even more ominous. When he spoke, she had to strain to hear him: 'That's not what I wanted to hear. You're telling me he's *alive?*'

'He's not expected to live.' The woman prayed for it to be true. 'It was down to Brumby and Red, but Brumby won't leave the farm while the dog is sick. He told some punks to rough him up, and they knocked him cold.'

'Why didn't they finish the job?'

'They don't have the balls for it. Anyway, they were interrupted: a guy walked in on them.'

'You mean, they were *seen*, for Chrissake? This gets worse. This other guy—he's in hospital, too?'

'No.' She was dreading the next question, but it never came. The man said abruptly, 'I'm coming up there. Tomorrow.'

'Do you want me to—'

'No! You don't know me, understand? Don't meet me, don't talk to me, don't even look at me. And don't tell anyone I'm coming.'

'I understand. Will you be alone?'

This time the man really did laugh. 'Don't be silly. Would I leave my right hand behind?'

CHAPTER 20

One of the keys fitted the street door, and one was presumably for the door of the apartment itself, but what was the third, and smallest, key for? Tom decided to check it out before he went back to Brisbane. He climbed the stairs yet again.

The two young detectives, Allen and Paisley, were in the apartment, along with a photographer and two older men.

'The lab boys have taken over,' Allen said. 'Forgotten something, Mr Grant?'

'Ned Caton asked a nurse to give me his keys.' Tom held them up. 'I didn't know whether it was significant, or—'

'Or if his mind was wandering,' Paisley finished for him. 'He also gave you an empty envelope, according to your statement. If he was trying to tell you something, he sure was cryptic.'

Tom watched the technicians at work. 'You're being very thorough.'

'If Caton croaks, it's a murder case,' Allen said bluntly. 'We wouldn't want to be accused of negligence.'

Something in his tone warned Tom that their attitude had changed, over the last hour. He guessed at the reason. 'You've been checking on Caton's background?'

'Too right, we have. When the Press get on to this, they'll have a beanfeast. A Pommie cop, sent out here to investigate the local force, inheriting a flat that belonged to a prostitute who committed suicide—Christ, there'll be purple prose a mile thick.'

'Hang on a sec.' Paisley had been thinking. 'What do you suppose that titchy little key is for?'

'I was hoping to find out,' Tom said.

'Think. He gave you an envelope. He gave you a little key. What does that suggest?'

Allen cheered. 'Gad, Holmes, you're a genius!'

'A mailbox?' Tom asked.

'Downstairs in the lobby. If you'd arrived five minutes earlier, you'd have saved us the trouble of picking the lock. Mind you, as a clue, that mailbox rates pretty low on any scale of values. Here's what we found: Two leaflets from a Chinese takeaway, an offer from an insurance company, a reminder from a TV rental firm, and an electricity bill.' He thrust the envelopes and papers into Tom's hand. Under the bantering tone, Tom sensed a challenge: he wondered if they had done some checking-up on him, too. He glanced down at the bundle of papers in his hand, and his temper rose. If they had been under his command, he'd have bawled them out till their toes curled.

He thrust the papers in his pocket and turned to go. Allen called after him, seemingly off-hand: 'We came up with a suspect on this mugging, but we had to let him go.'

'One? There were three of them.'

'You only gave us one name,' Allen explained patiently. 'We found one Mervyn Rowell, a young larrikin who seemed to fit the bill, but he had an alibi.'

'An alibi? Did it check out?'

'Unfortunately. Some senior citizens—regulars of an establishment called Annie's Palace—vouch for the fact that young Merv was playing pool in that hostelry this evening.' There was a mocking undertone to his words that needled Tom, as he was sure it was meant to. The man was a fool, as well as being a sloppy detective. Tom kept his temper with some difficulty, and left.

If he had not been so angry, he might have driven straight back to Brisbane. As it was, he found a phone directory, and looked up the address of Annie's Palace.

Even armed with the address, he had difficulty finding the place. It was on the northern edge of town, near the highway, in an area where two buildings out of three had been demolished for redevelopment. Annie's Palace was in the basement of a squat, small-windowed building that looked as if it had once been a warehouse, or an industrial workshop. There was a weatherbeaten sign, painted in large Gothic lettering, and below it two neon arrows blinked alternately, pointing the way down a flight of stone steps.

The décor of the place was intended to represent an English country pub, but the original design had been savaged over the years. Now, glittering poker-machines outshone the horse-brasses, and pool tables occupied the oak-panelled alcoves. Near the bar, loudspeakers blared out pop music at a volume that made Tom wince; he ordered a beer in sign language, and took it down to the end of the room where the pool tables were. The noise down there was below the pain threshold, but it was still horrendous. Tom sipped his beer, and watched the players.

The place was not crowded, but there were plenty of people there, most of them young, and most of them male.

A few girls congregated in groups of three or four at tables near the wall. At the bar, a line of middle-aged men looked with sad and longing eyes at two slim boys dancing together.

A beefy youth appeared from behind one of the pool tables, stood directly in front of Tom, and stared unblinkingly into his eyes. He had a soft, round face with a double chin which concealed some of the gold chains around his neck. There were so many rings on his fingers, it seemed as though his hands must be incapable of movement. Tom shook his head, smiling so as not to cause offence, and moved away.

The smile was a mistake. The young man followed him, sidled up close. 'You with anyone?' He had to shout.

Tom shook his head, still looking round. He hadn't really expected to find the three youths here, or even to be able to recognize them if they *were* here. It had been an impulse, born of irritation. He would finish his beer, and go. Back to Alison.

The plump boy touched his hand. 'Looking for someone?' His eyes were beseeching, pathetic.

Tom felt pity and distaste in about equal measure. He ought to have snubbed the youth unmistakably right at the start. In the middle of his embarrassment, he had an idea. He faced the boy, and nodded vigorously. 'Merv,' he shouted.

The young man was taken aback, disappointed. 'Merv?'

'Mervyn Rowell.'

Tom spoke louder than was strictly necessary. The players at the pool tables looked up, startled. One of them continued to look, after the others went back to the game. He had a narrow face, pointed, like a fox; and there was a purple bruise high on his right cheekbone.

The plump boy shrugged, and wandered away. Tom and the foxy-faced youth went on staring at each other. Tom addressed him directly: 'Merv?'

The youth made no response, but his lips parted a little, and his face seemed paler and thinner than before. He seemed unable to tear his eyes away from Tom's face, until someone nudged him and pointed at the table. He walked

125

round to take the next shot, but he found it difficult to concentrate. Tom moved round the table to face him. There was a familiar feeling in the pit of his stomach: that instinct that told him when a suspect was about to lose his bottle.

Foxy-face was nervous, under Tom's stare. His hands trembled, and he muffed the shot, to the jeers of the few onlookers. Tom backed away, found a chair, and sat down to watch.

Foxy-face lost the game, and stood, undecided what to do next. He no longer wanted to play, but he was reluctant to leave the security of the table. Tom looked on patiently. He had unnerved tougher customers than this. The kid was falling apart under his very eyes.

The boy came to a decision. With a desperate attempt to appear casual, he crossed the room, and keeping his back to Tom, began feeding coins into one of the poker machines. He spoke to the youth working the next machine, a child so small it was a wonder that he was allowed in the place at all. The smaller youth glanced round in obvious surprise, met Tom's eye. The overhead light caught the high cheek-bones, the vertical ridge of the brow. That's two, Tom thought: where's the third? He walked over and stood behind them, watching them lose money. He thought of Ned Caton, lying on the operating table with his head smashed in. He moved closer. The youths pretended not to notice.

The sound system developed a fault. The tape slowed and the music deepened to a low growling, punctuated by a barking noise, like a hungry seal. Somebody switched it off, amid whistles and catcalls. The relief from the din settled on the room like a blessing.

The silence only served to unsettle Foxy-face even more. He fed coins into the slot, and pressed buttons as if his life depended on it. Tom said conversationally: 'If he dies, that makes it murder. That's twenty years inside, even with a soft-hearted judge.'

'What are you on about?' Foxy-face snarled over his shoulder. 'Don't you harass me, you pervert, or I'll have the law on you.'

'Where's Merv?' Tom could smell the sweat on the youth;

and, more pungent than the sweat, the smell of fear. 'Where's your friend Mervyn Rowell?'

'Never heard of him. Leave me alone, or I'll call the police.'

'Good idea. Let's tell them how you helped your friend Merv beat in a man's head with a baseball bat.' There was a gasp from the smaller boy. He had abandoned all pretence of playing the machine, and was tense, listening, afraid to turn round. Tom pressed on: 'You're in trouble, sonny. We know all about you. Merv's been called in once. How long d'you think it'll take to break his alibi?'

'It was a mistake!' Tom had heard that high, shrill voice before, in Caton's flat. The younger boy was almost crying with panic. 'We didn't mean to—'

'For Chrissake, Derry! Can't you see what he's doing?' Foxy-face rasped.

'Derry's a sensible lad. He doesn't want to spend twenty years in pokey for somebody else's mistake, do you, son?'

Derry's nerve broke. He dodged round Tom and started to make a run for it, but stopped after only a few paces. Barring his way was a tall, slim man with lank, shoulder-length hair. He was older than the other two by several years; but he wore the adolescent beach-bum uniform: tank-top, cut-off Levis, scuffed trainers. He motioned with his head for Derry to stand aside, and faced Tom square on, feet braced apart, thumbs tucked in his belt: a pint-sized John Wayne. 'Are you looking for me, Daddy-oh?'

'Mervyn Rowell?'

'Yeah.'

'I wanted to know why you smashed Ned Caton's head in with a baseball bat.'

It rocked him, but he recovered fast. 'That's libel, Daddy. I've been here all night. Got witnesses to prove it.'

'Who?'

'Respectable citizens. You wanna meet them?' Merv turned on his heel, and marched to a table near the door. 'Walter, tell this guy where I've been all this evening.'

Walter looked up blearily. He was old, bald and wrinkled, and he needed a shave. When he spoke, his purple-stained teeth clicked as if they were on a ratchet. 'Me an' Mo been here all night,' he said. Mo ignored them. He was staring at his hands, which were twitching on the table like insects preparing to do battle. He was old and wrinkled, too. His nose was a dark maroon colour, and spread monstrously in bulbous growths over his face.

'That wasn't what I asked, you dozy old fart,' Merv said. 'I asked you where *I* was.'

'Oh. You been here.'

'All the time?'

'Oh yes. All the time.'

'And what does Mo say?'

Walter fidgeted, clicked his teeth. 'Mo says the same as me.'

'You see, Daddy?' Merv grinned into Tom's face.

'What I see is a couple of winos who would perjure themselves to hell and back for another drink.'

'Now there you are wrong, my friend.' Another old man rose from the next table and shambled over to join them. He was unshaven, like the others, and had a leonine mane of white hair. He wore a jacket, but no shirt; and his baggy canvas trousers were held up by a striped necktie. 'You must not leap to conclusions, nor judge by appearances.'

Merv guffawed over-loudly. 'You tell him, Perfessor.'

'The fact is,' the white-haired man continued, 'that should you question the veracity of these two venerable pillars of society, others will appear, willing to swear on their mothers' graves, to the unblemished purity of this young man's reputation.'

'Why?'

'Why indeed? If my throat were not so dry, I might elucidate.' The old man stepped in front of the boys, who seized the opportunity to run for the door. Tom made to follow them, but the old man gripped his arm with surprising strength. 'Let them go,' he said firmly. 'You owe me a drink.'

'Do I?'

'Indeed. I hate to lapse into melodrama, but I may have just saved your life. If you had actually assaulted those children, you would have roused the whole establishment here to their defence. You are *not* among friends. Now, you will be so good as to buy me a large whisky. The cheapest brand, please: my palate has absolutely no appreciation of quality.'

The barman had a word of advice, when Tom bought the drinks: 'You don't wanna get stuck with the Perfessor. He's a right nutter.'

But nutter or not, he was quite an impressive old boy, with his white hair and stately demeanour. Tom handed him his drink and sat opposite him at the table. 'Why do they call you the Professor?'

'Ignorant exaggeration, dear boy. I was a lecturer in one of the sterner disciplines at a University of small repute, until my weakness for whisky and nubile undergraduettes became too blatant to ignore. You have the appearance of a police officer, but not, I fancy, a local one?'

'No.'

'Otherwise, you would hardly have been so misguided as to come in here unaccompanied. Now, you wanted to know why those two geriatric alcoholics should be willing to perjure themselves on that mindless hooligan's behalf? Fear, my dear fellow; sheer craven funk. Intelligence test: what is the oddest thing about those two old fellows?'

Tom thought about it for the first time. 'Well—they're the only old people here. Except—'

'With the exception of myself, exactly. They were, as you might say, imported for the purpose of providing an alibi.'

'Imported from where?'

'There's a doss-house nearby that takes in about forty of these unfortunates, in return for most of their Government relief money. On top of their rent, all of them pay five dollars a week protection money to a gang which includes those charming children who were engaging your attention. The membership of the gang varies, but it is, I assure you, too numerous to take on alone.'

'Thank you for the warning. Is Merv the leader of this gang?'

'He is. A thoroughly obnoxious young man. I take care

129

to insinuate myself into his favour as often as possible.'

'Aren't you taking a risk, talking to me like this?'

'As long as you keep buying me drinks, people will assume you're just a mug.'

Tom took the hint, and ordered another drink. 'What's the old fool on about?' the barman asked.

'Philosophy.'

The barman looked shocked. 'He's a blagger. You don't want to let him take you for a mug.'

'Are you telling me,' Tom asked the Professor, 'that whenever these punks need an alibi, they trot out a couple of old soaks from the geriatrics hostel?'

'Precisely. The old folk live in mortal terror of these hooligans.'

'So those kids do more or less what they please?'

'By no means. They themselves live in mortal terror of even bigger hooligans. Ah, I see I have caught your interest. If you could see your way to providing yet another draught of hemlock, I shall tell you something that may save your life.'

'An offer I can hardly refuse.'

'As you say.' The Professor leaned back in his chair, and scratched his bare chest, as relaxed and urbane as if he were taking a tutorial. 'First principles: what, would you say, is the largest industry, hereabouts?'

'Tourism?'

'Very good. People come here in large numbers to enjoy themselves. Many of these people wish to enjoy themselves in ways which are not—officially—socially acceptable. They take drugs, for instance; they consort with prostitutes, both male and female. These services do not, of course, feature in the official guide-books; but they are tourist attractions, none the less. I need not explain to you that a situation where the public cooperates with the criminal against the police is a very profitable situation for the criminal. Along this stretch of coast, the profits from prostitution and the sale of illegal substances run into many millions of dollars a year. Tax free, of course.'

'Very interesting. But I believe I read all this in a magazine, months ago. How will this information save my life?'

'Wait.' The Professor finished his whisky and held out the glass. 'Prime the pump, dear boy.' When the glass was safely back in his hand, he began again: 'The unspeakable Merv is accused of breaking into a flat, and assaulting a man called Caton.'

'How did you know that?'

'My dear fellow, Merv had only just got his alibi in place when the law officers arrived. I listened in, of course: I eavesdrop whenever I can, as a matter of policy. The officers departed empty-handed and unconvinced. But my point is this: Mervyn's trade is petty extortion: he's a street shark, a mugger of old women. He would not attempt a job like this, except under orders.'

'Whose orders?'

'One of the bigger sharks. In this case, one of the local agents of the Sydney gangster who runs the illegal operations along this strip of coast.'

'And who is this Sydney gangster?'

'Now there, I cannot help you. His identity is, as they say, shrouded in mystery. What is certain is that he took over this territory about four years ago, with a ruthlessness that has assumed the force of a legend, locally. It is rumoured that nine people perished in the power-struggle—disappeared, that is to say, without trace. The legend has it that they were eliminated by a merciless professional killer, so adept and secretive that he is nicknamed "Old Funnelweb" by the criminal fraternity.'

Ned Caton had talked about 'Old Funnelweb' too; but Tom hadn't been paying much attention. Had Ned merely been quoting local gossip?

'Your mind is wandering,' the Professor said severely. 'And you are not following the logic of my story. If Mervyn was under orders, he will have asked for further orders, namely what to do about you. It is not difficult to guess what those orders will be. Mervyn, and as many hooligans as he can muster, will even now be out there, waiting to do you a mischief.'

131

CHAPTER 21

After the TV show, Alison drove back to the hotel, well satisfied with her night's work. The studio had logged nineteen calls from viewers claiming to have seen Clark, all within a radius of a hundred miles from Brisbane. That was something to follow up—an achievement of sorts. And that extraordinary message from Cyril Keys—she was impatient to tell Tom about that.

At the hotel, she had barely stopped the car, when a young man hurried across the parking-lot to greet her. She recognized him as one of the Assistant Directors on the film. He looked gaunt with anxiety. 'Have you seen Tom?—Mr Grant?'

'Not since this afternoon.' Her stomach turned over. 'Is he all right?'

'Oh yes, as far as I know. *I'm* the one who's up the creek. Have you any idea where he is?'

'No, but he may have left a message for me at the desk. Let's go and see. What's the panic?'

'It's the tennis scene. It's been on–off, on–off, ever since the picture started. Now it's on again. Even worse, it's scheduled for tomorrow.' In his impatience, he was walking backwards, urging her to hurry.

'Tomorrow? But I understood that he'd been sacked.'

'Well, yes—I was the one who told him, remember? But the producer says that since nothing was written down, and as Mr Grant is still being paid, he's still under contract. The movie industry's a bit weird, miss.'

At the reception desk, Alison picked up her room key and the two messages from Tom. 'He had an urgent call for help from a friend in Surfers'. He's gone over there. This note says he expects to be back by dinner-time, but this one just says he's been delayed. There's a phone number here. Do you want me to try it?'

'Please.'

After a minute she returned, shaking her head. 'The phone seems to have been disconnected.'

'Oh well, thanks for trying. He's bound to come back tonight.' The boy was feeding himself crumbs of comfort. 'God, I hope he makes it soon. He's needed on the set in under twelve hours.' Alison left him in the lobby, biting his fingernails, the picture of misery.

It was a disappointment not to see Tom tonight; it was a disappointment to be going to her room alone, if she were to admit the truth. It wasn't what she'd had in mind at all. Perhaps if he turned up in the next few minutes . . .

The suitcase was a shock. She thought she had left it in the boot of the Mercedes, but the porter must have brought it up with her overnight case. She had intended to leave it in the car, and deal with it later. She was being ostrich-like about it: hoping it would go away if she didn't look at it. She really must have the courage to face up to things. She opened the case, and lifted the contents out on to the bed.

The sound of the telephone made her jump. It was Lewis, sounding very bright and chipper. 'Saw you on the telly tonight, looking devastating. Is Tom there? No? I hope he knows he's on call tomorrow. If you see him, tell him I'll bring his coat up to the Club.'

'Yes.' Alison absently sorted the clothes out into separate heaps. 'But it's getting late. I don't really expect to see him tonight.' Especially since he has an early call, she thought wryly.

'It doesn't matter. It's you I wanted to talk to. About your pictures.'

'Have you found any more fakes?'

'No, as far as I can discover, they're genuine enough. Actually, I've had a great time, playing detective, ringing up people, going through art books, auction catalogues. It's my opinion you've been swindled, young lady.'

'Tom thought so too,' Alison said eagerly, 'but he couldn't figure out how it was worked.'

'It could be difficult to prove. What I've found out so far is that all the paintings sold to Mrs Yelverton at that auction had been bought from various art dealers within the previous

133

three months. *At* the auction, every picture more than doubled its price. A hundred per cent mark-up at these values represents a million-dollar profit for somebody.'

'I'd worked that out for myself. So the auction was rigged. But how?'

'This is the sneaky part. The bidding was done for Clare Yelverton by an art dealer called Praga—an expert, a man with an international reputation for honesty and fair dealing. I talked to him this afternoon. Apparently, Mrs Yelverton gave him strict instructions which pictures to bid for, and in each case, her ceiling price. In spite of his skill and experience, he was mortified to have to go to the maximum for every item on his list.'

'Wasn't he suspicious?'

'His client was present at the sale. She had only to signal to stop him bidding.'

'So you . . .' Alison lost track of what she was going to say. She stared appalled at the heaps of clothing she had taken from the case. 'Oh my God!'

'What is it? What's the matter?'

'Oh my God, oh my God!' Alison was frozen in shock. Slowly, she stretched out her hand, and picked up a lacy bra from the pile of underwear on the bed.

'Alison! What is it? Are you all right?' Lewis was shouting in his anxiety. Alison swallowed, tasted bile. 'These are mine,' she whispered.

'Yours? What are yours? What are you talking about?'

'Underwear. In Clare's case. It's mine. Don't take man-made fibres to the tropics, they said: only cotton. So I bought cotton; left these behind.'

'Honey, you're not making sense. I'm trying to tell you about Praga, and you're talking about bras.'

'It's just—don't you see?' Alison was too muddled to explain. 'I'm sorry.'

'Listen, honey, this is the really juicy bit. Praga saw you on TV tonight. Then he rang me. Very upset. The Clare Yelverton in your picture . . . he's almost sure . . . was not the Clare Yelverton at the auction.'

'No.'

'Alison, don't you see what that means? Who told you that she *was* there?'

'Jeremy Clays.'

'Right. And he was also the person who passed on the instructions to Praga. Honey, Clays cheated your aunt of over a million dollars!'

'He did more than that,' Alison said bitterly. 'He murdered her.'

CHAPTER 22

The Professor's head began to shake under the impact of the whisky. One eyelid drooped, and his speech became slower and more studiously articulated. 'Do not underestimate the peril in which you stand,' he said solemnly. 'The attack on Caton puts a dangerous new perspective on this situation. If Mervyn believes he has killed once, he has nothing to lose by killing again.' He stood up and bowed courteously, then walked with careful dignity past the long bar to the men's lavatory. Tom finished his beer, waited exactly three minutes by his watch, and left by the front door. He ran quickly up the steps to the street level and looked round. There was a sudden blare of sound from across the street as a door opened and pop music pounded out from a car radio. Merv ducked out on to the far pavement, and beckoned to the car behind. More doors opened, then slammed shut. Merv had called up plenty of reinforcements: eight youths faced Tom across the narrow street. They fanned out to right and left, moving with exaggerated menace, enjoying themselves. They were rôle-playing, Tom realized: they had watched this scene a dozen times on TV. Tom backed towards the steps, looking worried, playing for time.

The little MG roadster came round the corner like a greyhound at full stretch, and roared along the block, its exhaust growling and popping in protest. The Professor crouched behind the wheel, his white mane streaming in the wind, his mouth stretched wide in a mad war-whoop. He changed gears with a clatter like a rifle-volley and Tom began to run. As the little car drew abreast, he dived head-first into the passenger seat, and drew in his legs quickly as the Professor accelerated away.

It was a struggle to get upright again in that confined space, and the Professor was swinging the car round corners like the madman of Le Mans, but Tom finally managed it. 'Now what?' he shouted, struggling to make himself heard above the noise of the wind and the engine.

'That depends on them. Once we know their response, we must plan our strategy. At the moment, they are following us, and I fear we have little chance of escaping them. Lucy is past her best.'

'Lucy?'

'The motor. I call her that because virtually every part is loose.' The Professor hoho-ed like a demented Santa Claus, and fumbled in an inside pocket. With an effort, he pulled out a pair of wire-framed spectacles. 'That's better. Now I can see the road.' It didn't make any perceptible difference: the car continued to wobble like a puppy wagging its tail.

They were travelling along a busy main highway, but Tom had no idea which way they were headed. The Professor reluctantly abandoned a suicidal attempt at overtaking, and pushed the rear-view mirror back into place. 'Yes, they are definitely following us. What shall we do now?'

Tom manfully resisted the temptation to close his eyes. 'What are the options?'

'Excellent question. We have neither the speed nor the fuel to outrun them. Therefore we must outwit them in some way. What do you suggest?'

'We could drive to a police station.'

The Professor snorted. 'Point one out to me.'

'I can't.'

'Neither can I. Tell me: why did you seek out Mervyn in the first place?'

'To find out why he attacked Ned Caton.'

'And have you found out why?'

'No.'

136

'Precisely!' The Professor crowed in triumph. 'State the objective and the strategy becomes clear. Ah! Here we are.'

He swerved violently across the path of the oncoming traffic, acknowledging the hooting and catcalls with a cheery wave. 'That may delay them for a moment.'

They had turned on to a side road that curved and meandered like an English country lane. The road narrowed dramatically, and they thundered over an insubstantial-looking plank bridge. After a mile or two they crossed another, this one made more alarming by the lack of rails on either side. 'Drainage canals,' the Professor explained briefly. Then after a moment: 'Ah, here they come.'

Behind them, two sets of headlights carved through the darkness. The Professor urged the MG on, rocking his body forwards and backwards, and mumbling what sounded like a Latin invocation. Curiously, the car responded with an unexpected surge of power. 'Equipment!' the Professor shouted. 'Torch in the glove-compartment; jack-handle under the seat; coil of rope in the back. You take them. When I stop, get out and run.'

'Run where?'

'Don't be a jackass. Do as you're told!'

The next bridge was coming up, even narrower than the others. The cars behind were no more than two hundred yards away, and closing fast. The Professor drove a few yards on to the bridge, and stopped the car. 'That's it! Run!'

They hopped out and scuttled to the far side, while the cars behind slowed to a halt. The Professor made good time, but the effort clearly exhausted him. At the end of the bridge he staggered a few yards along the canal bank, out of the range of the headlights. He was in pain and gasping for breath. 'Give me the torch. Now, you must not worry about me. Go and deal with them.' He waved a hand to silence Tom's protest. 'You wanted to interrogate Mervyn. This is the best opportunity you will get.'

There was no time to argue: Tom doubled back across the road, through the headlights' beams. There was a shout from the other bank: he had been seen. Two of the youths began to run across the bridge after him, but slowed uneasily to a halt when they realized that the others were not following. Tom's eyes were not yet accustomed to the dark; he stumbled and slid down a muddy bank, ending up in a patch of reeds at the water's edge. The bridge was only a dozen yards to his right: if he stood up, his head would only be a foot lower than the planking deck. He had no plan. The Professor had rescued him from the ambush outside Annie's Palace, but dumping him out here in the middle of a swamp didn't seem to have done him any favours.

There was a lot of activity on the far side. The boys were pushing the MG backwards off the bridge. Suddenly, Tom had a clear picture of what the Professor was up to. The old madman had talked about strategy, hadn't he? Now, he felt sure he knew what it was. Cunning old sod, he thought.

The bridge was no more than forty feet long, constructed from concrete posts anchored by metal cross-ties supporting a deck made from old railway sleepers. Crouching low, and treading cautiously on the slippery ground, Tom crept to the bridge and ducked underneath it.

The darkness seemed absolute at first, but after a few seconds Tom could make out the shape of the cross-ties, silhouetted against the sky. With these offering him firm hand- and footholds, crossing the canal was as easy as climbing a ladder.

The youths were talking a lot; the excitement of the chase had loosened their tongues. With a lot of shouting and laughter, they pulled down a flimsy wooden fence, and pushed the MG down the bank and into the canal. The front wheels sank into the mud and the bonnet nosed the water, like an animal stooping to drink. Tom crouched in the shadows only a few yards away as the youths capered and hollered.

Merv's voice sounded immediately above Tom's head. 'That's cut off their retreat. We'll take my car over to the other side. Lenny, you and Mick stay in your car here, and watch the bridge. The rest of you come with me. The old guy can't move fast. We'll pick him off first, and then track down the other bastard.'

'You gonna top 'em, Merv?' another voice asked.

'I got my orders,' Merv said.

'From Brumby, is it?' A childish voice, this: quivering with excitement. 'How much is he paying?'

'Enough.'

'What about us?' several youths wanted to know.

'You'll get your share. Now, get moving!'

A few seconds later, the car trundled overhead. Tom moved under cover of the noise, and scrambled crabwise along the sloping bank of the canal. The ground was wet and slippery, and ribbed with dead roots the thickness of a man's wrist. He moved fast, on all fours, hoping to reach some vantage point before the kids got themselves organized. The slope levelled off a little, and the canal became a shallow, ever-widening ditch, and finally lost shape altogether. Behind him the headlights went out, and Tom was momentarily disorientated. He inched forward. The ground was soggy: water seeped into his shoes. Suddenly, he sank up to his knees in quaking mud. He threw himself backward and scrambled on to firmer ground. As he lay on his back, his heart racing like an overworked engine, the moon emerged, dazzlingly bright, from behind a ragged edge of cloud. Tom could now see that behind a tangle of rushes and marsh weed were tall sand dunes, pimpled with tufts of grass. But between him and the dunes was the quaking mud. Further off, to his right, was a dark mass that looked like a thicket of trees.

Tom circled back to the bridge. There was some cover here: clumps of ti-trees and fern; and he soon realized that these plants had established themselves on the only firm ground available. Everywhere else was soggy marshland, intersected by treacherously deep trenches and channels. Frogs chorused hoarsely, and mosquitoes whined in delirious welcome. He reached the slope beneath the wrecked wooden fence and climbed diagonally to his left, where a few stunted bushes offered some cover. When he reached the road level, he was no more than five yards away from the driver's door. Cupping his hands around his mouth, he said in a hoarse stage whisper: 'Lenny! Lenny!'

The car window came down. 'What? Who is that?'

'The Perfessor's sneaking back this way!' Tom whispered. 'Down by the river, near his car. You and Mick wanna come?'

'Yeah.' The two youths got quietly out of the car and crept to the edge of the road, peering down the bank. 'Where is he?' one whispered.

Tom flattened himself against the slope. His eyes were used to the dark now, and he could see the boys quite clearly. His silence and the blackness beneath their feet unnerved them. Lenny dropped to his hands and knees. 'Are you there?'

They froze, listening hard. Then, Mick lowered himself to the ground and swung his legs over the edge. 'Bastard din' wait for us.' He began to slide cautiously down the bank, and after a second's hesitation, Lenny followed.

Tom daren't risk slipping on the damp, uneven ground. He scrambled up to the road, moving swiftly behind the youths. Then, coil of rope in one hand and jack-handle in the other, he went down the slope after them. He felled Lenny with a blow to the side of the head, and as the other boy turned, jabbed him brutally under the ribs with the jack-handle. It was over in seconds; the swiftness and savagery of the attack knocked the fight out of them. Tom trussed them up, threw their shoes into the swamp, and stuffed their socks into their mouths. In Lenny's pockets, he found the car keys and a cut-throat razor; Mick's yielded a flick knife with a needle-sharp point. Taking their belts with him, he climbed into the car and drove across the bridge.

Merv had left two of his men to guard the other car: Tom's headlights showed him their faces, pale and goggle-eyed, behind the windscreen. There wasn't much room to manœuvre, but he pulled round in a tight arc and rammed the other car in the side. The youth behind the driving-wheel screamed and fell sideways. Tom abandoned his car, and ran round to where the other boy was struggling to open the passenger door. As he ducked to get out, Tom kicked the door shut. The boy's head cracked through the window, and his face began to stream with blood. Tom wrenched open the door again and dragged him out. He didn't look as if he would give much trouble, but to be sure, Tom picked him up bodily and threw him into the canal. The driver had dragged himself clear of the wrecked car, and was hopping on one foot, wailing in agony. 'Man, I think you've broken that leg,' Tom said. He kicked away the sound leg, to be sure. 'Aye, I was right.'

He thought the noise must have raised the alarm with the rest of the pack, but they were too far away and making too much of a din themselves to notice. The noise came from the direction of the sand dunes, and there was the glitter of flashlights. Tom set off at a run, keeping to the high part of the canal bank, where the ground was firmest. The channel petered out and the ground levelled off. Tom slowed to a walk, testing each step, wary of quicksands. Water squelched underfoot and the mud sucked at his shoes. There were some tussocky mounds to his left: he sidestepped towards them, and came on firmer ground. There were footprints here, too: several tracks of them, deeply imprinted in the mud. He followed the footprints, moving fast again.

The dunes were high and featureless; but for the footprints and the moon, Tom could easily have lost his sense of direction. Then he breasted the last rise, and plunged down the other side, through the soft dry sand to the beach.

The four youths were a hundred yards ahead of him, at the sea's edge, jeering and yelping with laughter. In the centre was Merv with his baseball-bat, prodding the Professor backwards into the water. The beach shelved sharply here, and the sea had a sleek, oily flatness to it that threatened swift currents and a treacherous undertow. The Professor stood a few yards from the edge, waist deep in the water, bracing himself feebly against its force. Merv gave up trying to reach him with the bat, and began throwing pieces of driftwood. The Professor ducked, and the current pulled him off-balance. He tumbled forward, arms flailing, thrashing about in the water like a hooked salmon.

Merv leaned over, one foot down the slope, trying to prod the old man with the bat. 'You're going to die, you crazy old soak,' he shouted. 'You're going to die because you forgot who your friends are.' He lunged again, lost his

141

footing on the wet sand, and slid on his knees into the water. The other boys shrieked and whistled. Merv, maddened, scrambled to his feet and began to beat the Professor savagely on the arms and shoulders.

Tom took out Denny first, because he was the nearest. He body-charged him, shoulder down, putting all his weight into it. Denny went flying, fell face down in the sand. Next was a fat, moon-faced youth in a gorilla sweat-shirt. Tom straightened up, and stiff-knuckled him in the throat. The blow took the youth up on to his toes; Tom stepped in close and punched him with all his strength under the heart. The fat boy doubled up in slow motion, gagging horribly, unable to cry out. That left just Merv and Foxy-face. Foxy-face had been joining in the fun with a length of steel piping. He saw the danger before Merv became aware of it, and ran back, lashing out at Tom's head. Tom turned and leaned away, taking the blow on his right shoulder. They circled round each other warily, the sand squeaking under their feet. Foxy-face scythed to and fro with the steel bar, intent only on keeping Tom at bay. Merv, at last alerted to the danger, began to wade back to the beach.

Tom stepped backwards and stumbled over a piece of driftwood, lurching perilously off-balance. Foxy-face saw his chance and charged, arm upraised. A second later he yelped in dismay, knowing he'd been suckered. Tom had his arm gripped at wrist and elbow, and was applying unsubtle pressure. He pushed the youth's elbow upwards and outwards, and forced his hand in towards his own armpit. Faced with the prospect of jabbing himself up his own nose, Foxy-face dropped the steel bar and concentrated on screaming with pain. Tom could now turn his attention to Merv, who was coming at a run, bat swinging. Tom shuffled forward, made a quarter-turn, and transferred the grip on Foxy-face's wrist to his left hand. Now, when he applied pressure, the youth would either move where Tom wanted, or have his arm dislocated.

Tom wanted to get this fight over quickly. He was worried about the Professor, who was still flopping about feebly in the water. He used Foxy-face as a shield between him and

Merv, looking for an opening. It was not a clever move. Tom had assumed that Merv would back off, reluctant to see his friend hurt. In fact, Merv simply clubbed him out of the way, and struck viciously at Tom over the falling body.

It nearly worked. Tom was slow to let go of the boy's wrist, and the bat caught his left forearm. The blow really hurt, and Tom grunted with pain and anger. He snatched at the bat with his free hand, and held on grimly. Merv tried desperately to pull it away, using both hands. Tom pushed forward, forcing the lighter man back. The bat was trapped between their bodies, no use to either of them. Keeping up the momentum, Tom pressed harder, hooked Merv's feet away, and fell on top of him. His temper was beginning to fray. This thug thought he was tough: but he wouldn't last ten minutes in a Glasgow street brawl. It was time to finish him off. Tom rolled away and stood up, swaying out of range of an aimless swipe from the baseball bat. He rapidly assessed the situation. One youth was laid out, the fat boy was being sick, and Derry was nervously backing away, ready for flight. The Professor still lay motionless on the wet sand. Merv, however, was full of pep. He had watched a thousand fights on the telly, and identified himself with the winner every single time. He knew he was invincible; and the experience of beating-up helpless old men had taught him the headiness of power. He came on at a crouch, swinging the bat threateningly. Tom flung the handful of sand he had picked up into his eyes, stepped in close, and head-butted him on the nose. 'That was for Ned Caton, Noddy,' Tom growled. 'Now, this is for me.' He took Merv's left hand, and used a simple finger-lock with rather more force than absolutely necessary. Merv screamed and his knees buckled, but he kept swinging the bat. Tom twisted away, not in time: the bat thudded against his ribs. In a fit of cold rage, Tom broke Merv's fingers. He took his wrist in both hands, and swung it upwards in a wide arc. Merv keeled over backwards, and the bat skidded away over the sand. His nose was bleeding, and he was sobbing with pain and wounded pride.

143

'How very satisfactory,' the Professor said. He was dripping wet and not very steady on his legs, but he struggled gamely up the beach, wheezing like an antique steam engine. 'I see you're interrogating him already. Has he told you anything yet?'

'He will,' Tom said grimly. 'Are you all right?'

'Well—' the Professor flopped down and wheezed some more. 'I could do with a drink.'

CHAPTER 23

'I'm sorry about your car,' Tom said.

'Don't worry about it, dear boy. It's insured for more than it's worth.'

They were sitting in the living-room of the Professor's bungalow. It was nearly two o'clock in the morning, and the Professor had his drink. They had driven back to Surfers' Paradise in Lenny's car, which was the only one working, leaving the punks to their own salvation. Tom was poised to leave, as he had been for the past half-hour; but somehow the old man kept him talking. His name, it turned out, was Philip; and his insatiable curiosity was matched only by his craving for adventure. 'What will you do now?' he asked.

'Tell the police about this Brumby, I suppose. It was a lot of effort for very little information.'

'Oh, I don't think you can go to the police, can you? I mean, won't they ask how you came by this information? You broke a few bones tonight: the authorities tend to frown on that sort of interrogation. Officially, that is. Now, what do you know about the man Brumby, who, it appears, gave Mervyn his orders?'

'Nothing.'

'Then I can enlighten you. To begin with, his real name is Kilkee. Sergeant Kilkee.'

'Sergeant?'

'They still call him that, around here, although he resigned from the police force some years ago. He and his partner Erwin are reputed to run half the brothels in this area.'

'But I thought you said that prostitution here was controlled by a Sydney gangster?'

'Exactly. Kilkee and Erwin are his lieutenants.'

'How do you know all this?'

The Professor shrugged, 'Being the neighbourhood drunk has its compensations. People talk to me, and in front of me, as if I were a block of wood. But we digress. Ned Caton, you say, was a Scotland Yard officer brought in by the State Government to investigate allegations of police corruption. Kilkee and Erwin are patently corrupt now, and probably were then. Perhaps they were forced to resign, as a result of the investigation? That might provide a motive for the assault on Caton.'

'It might.' Tom was only partly convinced. 'But that wouldn't explain why Ned was so excited about those Press cuttings. He said, "This is too big for me to handle," or something like that. It certainly sounded more important than a cops' vendetta.'

'Press cuttings?' The Professor's tone was sharp and his eye was bright. 'You have said nothing about Press cuttings before. Explain.'

Tom yawned. He was weary and his bruises had begun to throb. He wanted to go home to his bed. Still, this man had probably saved his life. He owed him something. As concisely as possible, he recounted the unspectacular history of Vicki Foxe, born Victoria Trowell: failed actress, successful suicide.

The Professor listened attentively, as if judging some student's literary composition. 'And you have no idea why Caton was so excited over these Press cuttings?'

'None.'

'Baffling. Two things strike me, however: you say Vicki came here from Sydney?'

'Yes.'

'And she admitted to being a prostitute?'

Tom remembered Clare Yelverton's letter. 'Yes.'

'Well, it's tenuous, but one could postulate a link between

her and the Sydney gangster. Had you thought of that?'

'No.' Tom gave it some thought. 'You're suggesting that she posed some sort of threat to the boss man?'

'I'm offering it as a theory.'

'But—if it's true, why didn't she tell Ned? She was living with him.'

'Not when she committed suicide. You said he was back in England.'

'Mm.' Tom was feeling quite groggy with tiredness: he had to leave soon. But the Professor was still worrying at the problem. 'Tell me again why you went to Annie's Palace tonight?'

'The police said they picked up Merv there. They didn't seem impressed with his alibi. I thought I'd check for myself.'

'No, that isn't what I meant. You said something made you angry.'

'What?' It took Tom a few moments to recollect. 'Oh yes, I got exasperated because I thought the two detectives were sloppy in their work. It wasn't important.'

'Wasn't it? In what way were they sloppy?'

'They made an assumption without checking it out.' Tom took some papers from his pocket. 'This stuff was in Ned Caton's mailbox. Junk mail, they said, and so it is. But they assumed that this was an electricity bill, because it looks like one. They didn't bother to check. If I'd been their boss, I'd have to put them through the mincer.'

The Professor took the windowed envelope. 'I would have made the same assumption, I suppose. But if I suspected that Caton was trying to communicate with me—' He ripped the envelope open with his thumb. 'Ah! What do you make of this?'

Folded inside the official form, was a page of newsprint. And a note: 'Tom—you were right!'

CHAPTER 24

It was an eventful morning.

Jeremy Clays breakfasted alone. Francesca had left early, to watch the filming at the Club, she said; but it was possible that she was simply avoiding him. She had been doing that a lot, lately. When they *were* together, she seemed tense and nervous: almost suspicious, as if she had some inkling of what he had been up to. But that wasn't likely: he had been very careful, and he was very clever.

He rang the bell, and the maid brought him more coffee. There was plenty of time: the bank didn't open for another hour. He was glad, now, that he had planned it all beforehand, prepared for the impossible, foreseen the unpredictable. 'Money, and an escape hatch,' he said, not realizing he was speaking aloud. That was the secret formula: lots of money, and a foolproof way of disappearing. If he could manage it for others, he could surely manage it for himself. He had seen the necessity for it, all of seven years ago; and he had perfected and refined his plan over the years. The others might go under, but he would survive. He smiled over his coffee cup.

Part of the plan was to behave normally, give no cause for alarm or question. There were things he would have liked to take with him, but it would be better, less suspicious, if he left them behind. His preparations for today were outwardly the same as for a normal day at the office. The maid gave him his briefcase at the front door, and commanded him, as was her nerve-grating custom, to have a good day. Thank God he would never have to hear her say that again.

He would have liked to have driven the Rolls one last time, but he always used the Porsche on ordinary working days. He could always buy another Rolls. He flipped the electronic switch that controlled the garage door, and reached for his seat-belt. In the rear-view mirror, he saw a middle-aged man walking up the drive, carrying a small case. The man stooped slightly under the weight of the case, and he walked as if his feet hurt. His suit was about five years out of fashion: he had the anxious, defeated air of the unsuccessful door-to-door salesman. Jeremy started the car. The salesman broke into a shambling run, waving and pointing at the offside rear tyre. Jeremy lowered the window, poked his head out. 'What is it?'

The man was puffed out: obviously out of condition. He doubled up, clutching his side, then leaned near the back of the car, head down, unable to speak.

'What is it, man?' Jeremy repeated irritably. 'Is there something—' The middle-aged man straightened up, suddenly much closer. Jeremy recognized him, too late. He reached for the key, but never made it. The salesman took a revolver from his pocket and shot him in the side of the head.

The man they called Funnelweb leaned through the open window and felt Jeremy's neck for a pulse. Satisfied, he addressed the corpse amicably. 'Move over,' he said. 'I'll drive.'

Tom Grant felt like hell. He had not had more than three hours' sleep, and he was not sure that he understood what was happening. It seemed that he was still under contract to the movie, and they were going to shoot the tennis scene that morning. The whole idea was ludicrous: he told them so several times, but they simply bundled him into a car, drove him out to the location, and dumped him in the Make-up caravan. Make-up had seen more flaked-out actors at six o'clock in the morning than she could shake a stick at. She settled Tom in the chair, turned off the radio, and propped his head back under the lights. At least this time she wouldn't have to fake the shadows under his eyes. She dabbed away gently, and watched him go to sleep.

Alison felt like a fool. She realized now that she ought to have phoned, and made an appointment. She should have thought out what she wanted to say, and organized it into a coherent, consecutive order. She ought to have taken a lawyer along with her, to warn her what she could say and what she couldn't. Now, after hours of talking, explaining, arguing, she knew that she had achieved nothing. Worse than that, this kindly, avuncular detective-inspector was treating her with an elephantine tact that made her want to batter him into a pulp. He read through his notes, humming tunelessly under his breath. When he reached the end, he said, 'Would you just run through the underwear bit again, miss?'

This made the fifth time this morning, and with each telling Alison felt less confident. 'The point is that it is *my* underwear, in *her* suitcase, don't you see?'

'Yes, I've got that point. What I don't quite see is its sinister significance.' There was a musical, Irish lilt in his voice that hinted at a gentle tolerance, a lifetime of dealing with loonies and cranks. Alison tried not to let her own voice get out of control.

'Aunt Clare was kidnapped,' she said. 'The kidnapper packed a suitcase with what he thought were her things, but in fact they were mine.' ·

'So your theory that she was kidnapped rests on the fact that your underwear was in her case. How do you know she didn't simply make a mistake?'

'Inspector, a woman just doesn't make that kind of mistake.'

The Inspector coughed. 'No offence, miss, but that is just an opinion. A lawyer would make mincemeat of it in court. Now, let me see if I have understood the rest of it. You say there has been a conspiracy to defraud your aunt's estate of about a million dollars. The conspiracy must have involved at least three people: the lawyer, Jeremy Clays; a woman to impersonate your aunt at the auction; and a kidnapper— possibly, you say, the man in the red hat. Is that a fair summary of your statement?'

'So far as it goes. But you've missed out—'

'I have missed out a mass of circumstantial evidence which can be interpreted in different ways. So far, your case depends on two things only: a retouched photograph, shown on television; and a few items of underclothing. Some people might consider that flimsy.' He smiled, to show that the pun was intentional.

'So you intend to do nothing?'

'Oh, we shall do *something*. Conspiracies involving fraud, kidnapping and murder are not everyday humdrum experiences for us; you may be sure your story will evoke the keenest interest. However, I should caution you that our inquiries could take considerable time. To be frank, Miss Easterbrook, this is not the kind of information that sends squad cars squealing through the city streets.'

Still feeling foolish, Alison left. She needed to talk the whole thing over with Tom, but he wasn't in his room. He seemed to have been out all night.

Lewis Goring started the day by being sick. 'Those goddam pills!' he growled. 'They may keep me alive, but they make damn sure life isn't worth living.'

In spite of Brian's protests, he insisted that he was going to watch the location filming that day. 'I wanna see Tom's face, when he sees my new coat,' he said.

There was another reason too, which he confided to Brian a little later: 'In all the years I've known him, I've never seen Tom lose his temper. But then, he's never come up against a sumbitch asshole like Zee Miller.'

The dog died in the night. Brumby had been expecting it for days, knew in his heart of hearts that it had to happen; knew by rights he should have put the creature out of her misery. He just hadn't been able to do it. Now she was dead, and he wept over her. He carried the carcase out of the house, grieving at how thin and wasted it was, and buried it in a shallow grave.

The thin, pale-eyed man watched him. The other man's tears excited him, made his flesh tingle. He still felt naked without his cap, but the woman had made him get rid of it. 'Burn it,' she had said, jumpy because of that TV thing. The cow. One day he would mark her card all right. But right now, the important thing was to get out of this fix.

That lush down in Surfers' had turned out to be a real pain: that whole mess had to be cleaned up double-quick. If only Brumby would get his ass in gear . . .

Brumby still squatted by the grave, but he was no longer weeping. 'Waddyer think poisoned her, Brumby?' the thin man asked.

Brumby spat. 'I think she et a toad.'

'One o' them big buggers down by the gully? Thousands of 'em down there, big as jack rabbits. Some o' them buggers stands a foot high.'

'I'll kill them. I'll kill the lot of them.'

It was strange, the thin man thought, how matter-of-fact Brumby sounded, when he was really mad. Strange and thrilling. He was like a bomb, with the fuse already burning. 'Talking of killing,' he said lightly, 'we oughta go. The Cow wants us over at the Club.'

'The punks first,' Brumby said.

The middle-aged man no longer stooped, and he no longer looked like a third-rate salesman. His sports shirt and slacks were Italian and expensive; his soft leather mocassins and heavy gold wristwatch proclaimed that he was wealthy and proud of it. Now, he looked like a tourist with money to burn.

He had to show his membership card at the gate. That was good: security ought to be efficient. He hated inefficiency almost as much as a late payment.

The cab-driver lifted the man's golf-bag out of the boot and carried it on to the clubhouse verandah. The middle-aged man thanked him politely—after all this time, he still had to remind himself not to offer a tip—and strolled into the bar. This was the part of the job he hated most: the smell of tobacco smoke and stale beer nauseated him. However, he liked to think of himself as a soldier; and this was the smell of the trenches. The conceit pleased him, made him smile. He bought an orange juice at the bar, and walked over to the window, which overlooked the eighteenth green. After one sip of the drink, he put it down: as usual, the muck was poisoned with additives.

'Great view.' The speaker was a cheerful, roly-poly man with a bald head like a speckled brown egg poking up from a nest of black curls. The middle-aged man regarded him with some reserve. His stiffness of manner indicated a certain distaste for casual encounters of this kind. However, he nodded politely enough, but ventured no other comment.

'New member?' the plump man persisted. 'Don't think I've seen you around.'

The middle-aged man hesitated, as if it was in his mind to snub the fellow, but in the end, politeness won. 'A temporary member only. A guest of Jeremy Clays.'

The bar steward came across the room at a trot. 'I'm sorry, Mr Venn, I didn't see you come in. What can I get you?'

'Oh, just a bourbon, Jack.'

'Duggie, sir. Jack's the other one.'

'Just a bourbon, Duggie. And a refill for my friend.'

The middle-aged man shook his head firmly. 'I have a drink here, thank you.' He was being drawn into the conversation in spite of himself.

'Friend of Jeremy Clays, huh?' Venn chirped familiarly. 'Is he here, today?'

'No.'

'Smart feller. His wife's here, though.'

The bar steward raced back, with the drink on a tray. Venn acknowledged it with a nod, and went on: 'Saw her in that crowd over by the tennis courts. They're makin' a movie over there, you know.'

'Really?' The tone was as bored as he could make it, but the bald man was not to be put off. 'Fine-looking woman ain't she, that Francesca Clays?' He grinned.

'I—I haven't seen her for many years. My business has been with her husband.'

'I'll point her out to you,' Venn said. 'Could be embarrassin', not knowing your host's wife. My name's Venn, by the way. Mike Venn.'

'Ah. Have you been a member here long?'

The bald man guffawed. 'You could say that. I own the place. What did you say your name was?'

The question nearly caught the other man off guard. What the hell was his name today? He remembered in time. 'Pepperidge,' he said, offering a perfunctory handshake. 'Oscar Pepperidge.'

Zee Miller moved the dial up a notch, and pedalled even harder. First thing he was gonna do when he got back Stateside, he was gonna fire that crummy agent. Correction: first thing he was gonna do was to bust his fat ass. *Then* he'd fire him. The right to see the rushes ought to be in his contract: *then* he'd know what was going on. He was being treated like crap on this picture: like Zee Miller was a nobody. He was getting a bum deal from every direction: the script, the camera angles, even the accommodation. He'd paced it out last night: Lewis Goring's caravan was a full metre longer than the one they had allotted him. He wasn't born yesterday: he knew when every man's hand was against him.

And now this latest insult: making him play the tennis scene with a crummy stand-in, for God's sake! And on top of that, he had to *lose*. All his fans knew he had been junior tennis champion at Crowside High: what were they gonna think?

He had been too easy-going: let himself be pushed around. Not this morning, though. From now on things were gonna be different.

CHAPTER 25

'Where we goin', Brumby?' Merv asked for the third time. 'My hand hurts real bad. I ought to get somebody to look at it.'

Brumby lounged in the stern of the boat, smoking one of his thin cigars. The dog lay at his feet. Red was at the wheel, and the three youths, Merv, Derry and Dave, the foxy-faced boy, sat in a row on a port-side locker.

'Thought we might do a little fishing,' Brumby said.

153

'Heard there were sharks breeding in that old wreck off Stradbroke Island.' The boat rolled in the light swell, and Derry grabbed nervously at the gunwale. Brumby's tone hardened. 'But mainly, I thought this talk ought to be private. After last night, I didn't want to be seen around with you scumbags.'

'We did what you tole us, Brumby,' Dave whined. 'We went after that Caton feller, like you said. We didn't expect no other guy to turn up.'

'And we fixed Caton good,' Merv said eagerly. 'He's still in a coma. He's a dead man, as good as.' He leaned forward, chopping at the air with his good hand, to emphasize the point. The dog growled a warning.

'Careful,' Brumby said mildly. 'Don't let him think you're not my friend. He'd tear your throat out if he thought that.'

'Yeah, Brumby, I know.' Fear, and the motion of the boat had tinged the youth's cheeks with a ghastly shade of green.

'All right,' Brumby said. 'Tell me again about the other guy.'

'Hell, Brumby, he just come up out of nowhere. I don't even know who he was.'

'I know who he is. Just tell me how he managed to get away from eight of you heroes.'

'He had help, man. The Perfesser helped him. Who would of thought that that crazy old wino—'

'Where's the Professor now?'

'We—we don't know. We think he took a coach out, first thing. He wasn't gonna hang around, not after what he done. He's running scared: he won't come back here, not ever.'

Brumby arranged cushions at his back, put his feet up on a locker. He looked back over his shoulder. The thin line that marked the beach had disappeared; all that could be seen of the land were the blue hills, misty and insubstantial-looking as clouds. To the east, the sea looked featureless and empty as a desert. 'One little thing I don't understand,' Brumby said. 'The Professor left by coach, huh? Why didn't he use his car?'

The boys looked at each other. Derry hastened to explain: 'We wrecked his car. We ran it into the creek.' He sniggered at the memory.

'So you caught up with them? You wrecked their car, and yet they still got away. How come?'

The three boys started to talk at once. Merv shouted the others down: 'The Perfesser suckered us into this swamp. He knew the area: we didn't.'

'So you lost them? And they had to walk home?'

Merv didn't meet his eye. 'Yeah.'

Brumby stood up and stretched lazily. He turned round a full circle, scanning the empty horizon. Then in a sudden violent flurry of movement, he plucked Derry up by his shirt and pushed him backward over the rail. Within seconds, Derry was yards astern, screaming and thrashing about in the water. The dog barked excitedly. Red throttled back, spun the wheel, and began slowly circling the struggling figure. 'Christ, Brumby!' Dave shouted. 'He can't swim!'

Brumby made himself comfortable again. 'Wouldn't you know? Seventy miles of beach on his doorstep, and the lazy bastard can't swim.'

'Pick him up, Brumby, please! He's drowning!'

'I do believe you're right. Well now, perhaps you'll start telling me the truth.'

'The truth?' Dave couldn't tear his eyes away from the drowning boy. 'We wouldn't lie to you, Brumby.'

'That's good. That's very good. You see what happens to punks who lie to me. Now, how did you get that nasty bruise on your face? And what happened to Merv's hand?'

'He's gone under!' Dave shrieked, pointing. 'He's drowning, Brumby, don't you understand? You can't just leave him!'

'What happened last night?'

Dave was frantic, shaking with emotion. 'If I tell you, will you go back and pick him up?'

'Just talk, sonny. Then we'll see.'

'Okay, yes, we cornered the guy and we had a fight. He won. He took our car, and we had to walk home. That's all there was to it. Now go back, for God's sake!'

155

'That's all?' Brumby's eyes glittered. 'What did you tell him?'

'Nothing. Nothing.'

'You're telling me he didn't ask you any questions? He wasn't curious about why you beat up his friend? *What did you tell him?*'

'*I* didn't tell him anything. I swear it.'

'*You* didn't tell him anything? Merv did, is that what you mean?'

Merv lurched to his feet. 'No! We've told you, we didn't tell him anything. Who do you—'

The dog leapt and sank its teeth in his arm, its weight throwing him off balance, and pushing him almost to the far end of the deck. Merv yelled and beat at the brute's head with his injured hand, but the jaws clamped even tighter. The black snout moved patiently, pitilessly to and fro. Merv's back arched, and he flopped about on the deck like a landed fish. Red throttled the engine right back, and turned to watch, one hand on the wheel, the other to his mouth. Merv fainted, but the dog went on worrying at his arm, dragging the inert body along the deck. Brumby snapped an order, and the dog backed away reluctantly, grinning and ducking its head.

'Look at that!' Brumby said. 'Bleeding all over my nice clean deck.' He hauled Merv upright, and toppled him overboard. 'I sure hope there aren't any sharks about. They go crazy if they smell blood.' He lit a cigar from the stub of the last one, and threw the butt over the side. 'Looks like you're the only one I can trust. What happened last night?'

Dave made himself small, his knees drawn up and his arms hugging his body, as if he had a stomach ache. 'It's like you said. The guy beat us up—broke Merv's finger. Then he asked questions—who sent us? Why? Well, Merv didn't know why, and he wasn't gonna say who. But the guy just picked him up like he was a rag doll or something, and threw him into this mud swamp. Merv was just sinking down and down, sliding under . . . The guy just watched him. When the mud got up to his chest, Merv talked.'

'He told him my name?'

'Yes.'

'Anything else?'

'He didn't know anything else.'

'Where was the Professor, all this time?'

'He was away, down by the beach. He wasn't feeling too good. We'd roughed him up a bit. Now, can we get the fellers out of the water, Brumby? Please? Merv would have told you the truth, but he was afraid to.'

'Well, Dave—' Brumby drew on his cigar—'them two aren't making much commotion out there. They could be dead.' He unclipped a boat-hook from the side of the cockpit while Red manœuvred the boat alongside the drifting bodies. Leaning over the gunwale, he drove the metal spike into Merv's neck just under the ear. Then, hooking the body closer, he speared the other boy in the same way. 'Yep. They're dead, all right.'

Brumby and Red looked at Dave. 'Your turn now, sonny,' Red murmured. His eyes were so pale, they looked like white pebbles under his eyelids.

Dave began to stammer. His lips shook, unable to form any words. His eyes pleaded, without hope.

'You know too much, son,' Brumby explained reasonably. 'Over you go. Swim for it.'

Dave shook his head. He could never make it that far. He couldn't even see the shore.

'Please yourself,' Brumby said. 'Maybe the dog can persuade you. He's a devil when he's roused. You're between the devil and the deep blue sea, how d'you like that?' He drew luxuriantly on his cigar. 'Sonny, this just ain't your lucky day.'

CHAPTER 26

At the Venn Country Club, the film encampment had grown to the size of a small village. They had found a space for the invading hordes of cars, coaches, trailers, caravans, trucks, and pantechnicons on a strip of waste land between the golf-course and the perimeter fence; and a makeshift path, bordered by parallel lines of plastic tape, marked out the way to the tennis courts. The path ran through a small copse of ornamental trees that skirted the seventh and ninth greens.

Activity had been building up since before dawn. Platforms were erected and tracks laid for the cameras; lights rigged—even in the brightest sunshine, the cameramen would ask for some extra light somewhere—and around the boundary of the action, mounds of equipment were strewn like the abandoned impedimenta of a defeated army.

Tom felt a little better for his sleep in the make-up chair. If he could take a nap in his dressing-room before the day's work began he might be ready to rejoin the human race. His dresser, as usual, looked apprehensive: this hour of the morning brought out the worst in actors. He had laid out Tom's gear for the day: tennis whites, and a couple of sweaters. And a coat. A familiar coat. A splendid, eyeball-searing coat. 'That's my blazer!' Tom said.

'Yes, sir.'

'Brian brought it in, I suppose. It's good to have it back.'

'Yes, sir. We're wearing it in the scene, sir.'

'What!'

'Yes, sir. It seems Mr Goring liked it so much, he wants to wear it in the picture.'

'But it's my blazer, dammit?'

'Mr Goring's had it copied, sir. In Hong Kong. He's like a puppy with two tails, Mr Brian says.'

Tom didn't know whether to be flattered or offended. It was so typical of Lewis, of his bizarre enthusiasms and quirkish sense of humour. 'All I'm doing in this scene is play tennis. I don't need a coat.'

'No, sir, but you're seen wearing it, I understand. I was just told to lay it out for you.' Alfie pressed his temples with the tips of his fingers, as if to squeeze out an incipient headache. Some days, the pressure just made him want to scream.

'Okay.' Tom stretched out on the sofa. 'Pop out and see

158

if my call's imminent, will you? If there's time, I'd like to crash out for half an hour.'

But before the dresser could leave, there was a knock at the door and Alvin Hurley bustled in, looking harassed. 'I've been watching this guy Miller,' he said, without preamble. 'He's practising with the Club pro right now, in front of a crowd of people. Tom, he's very good.'

'So I've been told. Alvin, it's all down to the director. All I have to do is to look half-way competent. And you've seen to that, bless your heart.'

'Well, I dunno,' Alvin said awkwardly. 'Maybe you ought to do a little warm-up. Going in cold is bad for the muscles. I mean, you could look awful silly, out there.'

Tom's tiredness made him slow to comprehend. 'You mean, *you* might look awful silly if he humiliates me in front of all the posh people.'

'Well . . . People know that I've been coaching you . . . I just thought . . .'

'All right.' Tom succumbed with what grace he could muster. 'I'll do battle for your reputation. I'll see you down there in five minutes.'

He changed rapidly, putting on the blazer as a concession to Alfie, who looked as if he would burst into tears if Tom refused, and tried to summon some enthusiasm for the day's work ahead.

'Mr Grant?' The tall, dark-haired woman was lounging as usual, in the shade of a tree; and as usual, she had a glass in her hand. 'How that wig changes you! I would never have recognized you. But I would know that blazer anywhere.'

The name flashed into Tom's head just in time. 'Mrs Clays, isn't it? Nice to see you again.' Even if you *are* plastered, he thought.

'Call me Francesca, please. I feel that we're old friends. You really do look like Lewis Goring, don't you? It's astonishing. Is he here today?'

'I don't think so. He's not needed for today's schedule, so he'll probably stay home and rest.'

She nodded owlishly, as if he had said something very profound. Tom was quite certain that she hadn't heard a word. 'Actually—' She swayed dangerously, and a middle-aged passer-by gave her a wide berth, eyeing her with disapproval. 'Actually, I was hoping to have a little chat with you.'

'Well, I'm afraid I haven't time just now—'

'Of course not. You're much too busy. Later, perhaps. I'm sure you'll find it interesting. And rewarding.'

'You're very mysterious.'

'Later, if you wish, I shall reveal all. Metaphorically speaking, that is.'

'Of course.'

'There's no "of course" about it, you gorgeous beast!' Her throaty laugh followed him along the path down to the courts.

Alvin was more wound-up and nervous than Tom had ever seen him. He was too tense, he said, to do court practice, but he put Tom through some flexibility and stamina exercises. 'You don't want to go up against this guy with your muscles all cold.'

Strangely enough, although Tom would have preferred to rest, the exercises did make him feel better. Last night's events seemed distant and dreamlike: a whole world away from this bright, bustling activity.

Some details of the previous night were rather blurred: the Professor had decided that he had to go to the police in Sydney, and Tom had agreed; but he couldn't remember now why it seemed such a good idea. Also, he had said that he would go by coach, which meant that he wouldn't be there for hours yet. Tom wondered what the police would make of his story when he got there. It had seemed so satisfying, so watertight, when they had pieced it together last night; but now, in the clear, rational light of day, it seemed as fragile as a house of cards.

Tom longed, momentarily, for the comfort of the police Establishment: the back-up, the collaboration, the teamwork. In the old days, with the leads he had, he would have cracked this thing wide open in a couple of days. But now he was an outsider; now, the Establishment would probably treat his story as the ramblings of an over-imaginative crackpot. He thrust it to the back of his mind: he had a job to do.

He was aware of an unusual degree of tension as soon as he arrived on the set. There was the normal appearance of chaos, as the extras were shunted into place by harassed stage managers; and people scurried about adjusting bits of equipment, or checking endless lists; but over it all was an atmosphere that was strangely depressing, and strangely familiar. Tom had never experienced it before, but he had heard actors speak of it and he recognized it instinctively: it was the stink of failure. Everyone was behaving as if the picture was already a flop.

Nikos pretended to make light of it. 'It's nothing. We're a bit behind schedule, is all. We had to settle for a couple of shots yesterday that were a little below standard, technically. These guys are perfectionists: they take it hard.'

It was disastrous news. The ship was sinking, and the captain was whistling in the wind. Sloppy work on a movie endangered everybody's future in the business, from the director downwards. Everybody knew that today's shortcomings could haunt them for years. No wonder morale was poor.

Nikos talked fast, as if to avoid awkward questions: 'This is another long sequence. It's right at the top of the picture, Tom: before and under the credits. There'll be a lot of editing: cutting in close-ups, crowd shots, and so on. What we want today are full-court master-shots of you and Zee playing some dynamic tennis. I want three minutes—or more—of hard-hitting action—'

'I know,' Tom said resignedly. 'Real sweat, real pain.'

'Right. I'm just using two cameras, so the change-over for the different angles oughtn't to take long. And I've got video-jockeys rigged, so we'll know immediately what we've got. We're going to make this a good day, Tom!' He couldn't quite hide the anxiety in his voice; he was infected with the same sense of defeat that afflicted his whole crew. Tom wondered why, but not for long.

Zee Miller, it turned out, was the equivalent of a one-man bubonic plague. His evil temper and intimidating physical

161

presence dominated the entire location, and everyone on it. The only people who were spared the full force of his boorishness, were the extras, on whom he lavished a kind of contemptuous bonhomie. He referred to Tom as 'that stand-in jerk', and refused to speak to him directly, sending messages through a harassed and sweating gopher.

Nikos had clearly lost control of the situation. He discussed the shot with Miller, and then trotted over to give Tom his instructions, only to be called back because Miller had changed his mind about some detail. The minutes ticked by. Among the crew, tension gave way to boredom, and then to irritability. Nothing seemed to happen for an age; and then at last they began to rehearse.

It was agreed that Miller should serve to Tom's forehand, and that they should keep up a hard-hitting rally as long as possible. As Nikos said, it didn't matter who won the point in this first shot: the action was the thing. After all, they weren't planning to film a whole match. Good photography, clever editing, dramatic music, could compress the drama of a three-hour match into three minutes. The trick was to film those three minutes.

The rehearsal was fine. Miller put his serve where he said he would, Tom returned it, and after some fiercely-struck ground strokes, Miller finished off the point with a fine overhead smash that brought spontaneous applause from the crowd.

The camera operators made some minor adjustments, and pronounced themselves ready; the sound technicians bickered over the placing of the effects microphones; but on the whole things were going well. Nikos allowed himself a faint smile, and the atmosphere began to feel almost cheerful. The unit began the elaborate ritual that preceded a take, and at last, the relief evident in his voice, Nikos called 'Action!'

Zee Miller began the scene exactly as he had rehearsed it, glaring at his opponent, walking menacingly to the serving line. He stooped, bounced the ball twice, then straightened up and tossed it high over his head.

The serve came to Tom's forehand, but it was a foot

deeper and nearly twice as fast as they had rehearsed. Tom missed it completely, his stroke only half-completed as the ball thudded into the fence behind him. 'Somebody tell that fairy to wake up!' Miller jeered; and Nikos's cry of 'Cut!' was submerged in the crowd's laughter.

They rehearsed again. This time Tom was ready for the faster serve, and scrambled it back over the net, but the rally that followed was not impressive. After more rehearsal, they managed to recreate their first success, and Nikos decided to go for another take.

This one was no more successful than the first. Miller produced a vicious, in-swinging serve that caught Tom hopelessly out of position. He hit the return tamely into the net, and had to endure a temperamental outburst of abuse from his opponent for his incompetence.

The pattern was now clear: Miller served gentle, worka-day stuff in rehearsal, and savage thunderbolts when the cameras were turning. It was so obvious that Tom waited confidently for Nikos to call the actor to order. He waited in vain; and after yet another abortive attempt to shoot the scene, he realized with a jolt, that Nikos was afraid of the man. Zee Miller was totally in control.

The crew insisted on a break at eleven o'clock. They had worked for five hours, and had not achieved a foot of usable film. Tom was beginning to understand the aura of defeat that hovered over the whole company. When they got this far behind with the day's work, the temptation to cut corners was very strong.

As if to aggravate his mood further, some clown was wearing his blazer. He looked again. It was Lewis. Of course: that clown had had his coat copied. Lewis was looking wryly amused. 'Having trouble, I see.'

'Nothing the director couldn't control, if he wanted to. The guy isn't doing on camera what he does in rehearsal.'

'No, but he appears to be. You're the one who's making the mistakes.'

Somebody brought Tom a cold drink. It was Alvin, look-ing angry and anguished at the same time. Lewis motioned for him to stay. 'Hang around, you may be able to help. I'd

163

better wise you up about what's going on here. Zee Miller's an asshole, but he's a cunning asshole. He's not just trying to humiliate you, Tom, although he's enjoying that, too: he's got a bigger fish to fry. He wants a bigger slice of this picture.'

'If he goes on like this, there won't be any picture to carve up,' Tom objected. 'What's the point?'

'The point is blackmail. Let me explain. Miller is employed on this film on a limited-time contract. If the company hasn't got his performance in the can in the time allowed, it has either to re-shoot, with another actor, which is murderously expensive; or they have to renegotiate his contract, beg him to finish the movie. At that stage he can virtually dictate his own terms.'

'But that's crazy! A contract like that practically begs him to be disruptive. How can he get away with it?'

'He's smart. He makes sure that any delay on-set can never be blamed directly on him. What he does is to create so much tension around the lot that other people get nervy, start to make mistakes. This scene with you is tailor-made for his particular talents.'

'But why does anyone ever employ him?'

Lewis sighed. 'I hate to say this, but in fact he's a very good screen actor. He may be a shit in life, but on celluloid, he's a star.'

'So what can we do?'

'I've been thinking about that,' Lewis said. 'Maybe we can cook up a little blackmail of our own.'

CHAPTER 27

It was too hot in the car, even with all the windows open. Brumby left the keys in the ignition in case they had to leave in a hurry, and stood a few yards away, in the inadequate shade of a young fig tree. It would have been more comfortable to wait inside the hospital, but neither he nor Red could guess how things would turn out. It was safer this way.

164

He was uneasy. He and Red were being forced into taking more risks than at any time in the last seven years. They were being used like garbage men, cleaning up other people's mess. That wasn't any part of the original deal. They had made a lot of money these last years, taking virtually no risks at all—as the lawyer had pointed out, that was the beauty of it. 'Murder for profit is a mug's game,' Clays had said, 'because the profit points at the murderer. But if the murder isn't a murder—officially—then the profit doesn't look like a profit. Then it's not a mug's game at all. It's a licence to print money.' It sounded crazy, but it worked. And there had been good sport, too. Until now. Now, they had to scuttle about like lackeys, doing other people's work. Somebody was sure as hell going to pay for this.

At last Red came out of the hospital doorway, and cut across a corner of the lawn towards the car. He walked easily, not hurrying, showing no sign of alarm. But to be on the safe side, Brumby had the engine running, and the car on the move, as soon as Red slid on to the passenger seat. 'What happened? I was beginning to think you'd booked yourself in for the night.'

Red scowled. 'I had to make sure, didn't I? I hung about in case I could catch him alone. No chance. He's wired up like a telephone exchange. There's people watching him the whole time.'

'So you didn't do anything?'

'What could I do? I couldn't get near him. I talked to the nurse.'

'And?'

'If he comes out of the coma, which they doubt, he'll be a cretin. His brain is damaged beyond repair. He's no danger to anybody.'

Brumby slowed down, as if he considered turning back. 'I hope the Cow will buy that. She wanted him dead.'

'Then she can hire somebody else. I'm not putting my head in a noose. I don't understand what's so special about the guy, anyway.' Red gnawed impatiently at a thumbnail, making clicking sounds with his teeth.

Brumby grinned his dog-grin. 'We're just being used as

165

lackeys, is what. And there's a distinct smell of panic in the air. Maybe we should take out some insurance.'

'What insurance?' Red chewed some more at his finger-nails, thinking about it. 'You mean, the lawyer?'

'Or that wife of his. Or both. It's just an idea. Let's see how things develop.'

They were on the main highway now, travelling fast. The air flowing in through the window cooled them, but it was tainted with dust and diesel fumes. Red thought of another problem. 'What are we going to do about this guy Grant?'

'I phoned in while you were in the hospital. He's being taken care of.'

'Who by?'

When Brumby told him, Red whooped and clapped his hands. 'Let's get up there quick. This, I gotta see.'

A few miles over the NSW border, the coach made one of its scheduled 'comfort' stops. The Professor hobbled down the steps and walked along the road a little way to ease the stiffness out of his legs. He was already half-regretting the journey. What had seemed so brilliantly obvious last night now seemed hopelessly implausible. Would anyone believe him? Would anyone even listen to him?

He had fallen asleep soon after the coach started, his head lolling sideways against the seat cushion. When he woke, he was dismayed to find he had dribbled down his chin and made a wet patch on the front of his shirt. It made him feel old and vulnerable and depressed. He needed a drink really badly.

The police interview had left Alison disillusioned and de-pressed. She ought to have talked it over with Tom first, instead of charging in like that, on her own. She wanted badly to see Tom, right now. But he was working, doing that tennis scene at last. Where on earth had he been all last night?

On impulse, she decided to go up to the Club and wait for him to finish work. She could take some exercise while she was there: work off this depression. She got out her sports bag, checked its contents, and carried it down to the car.

The man who called himself Oscar Pepperidge carried his golf bag through the clump of bushes at the side of the seventh fairway, and trampled a path through the nettles to the perimeter fence. The position was perfect: when he knelt down he was almost completely hidden from view. Once through, he would have about forty yards of uneven ground to cover, but that couldn't he helped. There was plenty of time to reconnoitre it, check out any serious pitfalls. He took a pair of long-armed wire-cutters from his bag and patiently clipped out a large square section of fence, tall enough to duck through easily. He would be coming through here in a hurry: he couldn't risk being snagged up on the wire.

Satisfied, he shouldered the golf bag, and plodded across the fairways to the car park, with the defeated air of a man overcome by the heat. He drove out of the Club by the main entrance and began to explore the side roads. It was stifling and uncomfortable work, but he did it methodically and with the thoroughness that had kept him alive through three decades of murder, made him a legend.

When he was sure he knew the layout, he parked the car off the road and scouted on foot. He was luckier than he expected to be. Less than a hundred yards from the gap he had cut in the perimeter fence, was an unfinished spur of concrete-paved road. The relic of some long-abandoned grandiose scheme, it cut a straight, white gash through four hundred yards of stony scrubland, and finally petered out in an unsavoury rubble of stones, broken concrete slabs, and dumped refuse. Best of all, the mounds of earth and rubble were big enough to conceal the car from the Club grounds. The surface of the road was cracked, littered with stones and overgrown with weeds, but it was still usable. As he made his way back to the car, he carefully moved the larger boulders and other debris off the track, concentrating on perfecting his plans, seemingly oblivious of the sweat dripping from his face and the ever-increasing cloud of flies that swarmed around his head.

He moved the car to its new hiding-place. His plans were almost complete: there was only one decision still to be made. He unzipped one of the pockets in the golf bag and took out an oilskin package. He unwrapped the package and took out the two pistols, weighing them thoughtfully and affectionately in his hands.

CHAPTER 28

Zee Miller threw a tantrum as soon as he saw Tom's new racquet. Within minutes, he had involved the director, the set designer, the property-master, and all the crew who happened to be nearby, in a shouting-match that made the windows rattle. It was all part of the same rotten conspiracy, he raged. *He* could recognize the new carbon-fibre-shafted, super-tension, hi-tech racquet when he saw one. It was typical that they should provide one for the stand-in, for Chrissakes, a goddam no-hoper who couldn't even hit the ball, while the star had to make do with a crummy piece of spaghetti strung like a fishing-net. If they thought he was going to put up with this insult, on top of the other insults, they were out of their tiny, nit-picking minds.

Acutely aware of the expensive minutes ticking by, Nikos lost heart in the face of this new dilemma. He had seen Lewis talking to Tom, during the break: it seemed probable that the new racquet was Lewis's idea. The prospect of being caught in the crossfire between two warring screen giants filled Nikos with terror.

He was saved by Alvin. The tennis-coach explained that it had been his idea to re-equip Tom, since his game seemed to need improvement; but he had another, identical racquet in his bag. Would Mr Miller care to borrow that?

The racquet was produced, and since it appeared to be brand-new, Miller sulkily conceded that it would do. The charade began again. Tom went over in his mind Alvin's hurried instructions: 'Watch his feet when he sets himself up for the serve. They give away his intentions. If they're like *this*, it's the pat-ball serve he uses in rehearsal; like *this*, the ball will swing to your right; like *this*, to your left.' Alvin demonstrated the positions several times in quick succession, making a little dance of it. 'If he does anything else, it'll be something new: I can't help you there. Luckily, he's not as good as he thinks he is: his game will disintegrate under pressure—especially with an audience.'

Simple, Tom thought: all you've got to do is outplay the guy. So much for Lewis's brilliant plan. To make matters worse, the heat and humidity were really building up, now. In these conditions, equipment and humans became increasingly cranky and temperamental. Make-up girls waited anxiously under parasols, their precious creams and lotions in refrigerated boxes. The extras, bored and uncomfortable, began to fidget and grumble; the stage-managers roamed around them like sheepdogs, keeping them in order.

Another half-hour passed fruitlessly. The rehearsal was fine, the take a disaster. Nikos looked sick, and snapped bad-temperedly at the production assistant. Wearily, the crew began to set up for another rehearsal.

Then, suddenly, Lewis was by Tom's side. 'This is it, General,' he whispered. 'Time to go for it.'

'What? What are you talking about?'

'Don't ask questions. Trust your uncle.' Turning away, he shouted up to the camera platform: 'Nikos, Tom wants to go for another take right away. He's rehearsed enough. He'll get it this time.'

'Are you sure?' Nikos appealed to Tom directly, a glimmer of hope showing through the despair.

'Of course he's sure!' Lewis took full responsibility for Tom's state of mind. Then, lowering his voice, he drawled out of the side of his mouth: 'Go take him, tiger: he's all yours!' It was a famous quote from Lewis's most famous film; only that famous voice could make it funny and inspiring at the same time.

Lewis climbed up to join Nikos, and put his arm round his shoulders. The pre-take formalities began. 'Rolling—Speed—Action!'

Zee Miller served a fault. The ball thumped into the net,

spun against the mesh with a sound like a hissing snake, and trickled back into the server's court. There was a moment of hushed surprise before Nikos remembered to call 'Cut!' and the set-up ritual began all over again.

'Don't print that!' Miller shouted. He looked as surprised as everyone else. He stared intently at the palm of his right hand, as if blaming it for the failure, and then rubbed it vigorously on the side of his shorts.

The set-up was achieved quickly, and Miller prepared to serve again. Tom tried to study the position of his feet, but it was more difficult than Alvin had made it out to be. The best he could manage was an educated guess that the ball would curve to his right. He made a slight adjustment to his balance, but without much confidence.

In fact, the service curved right, but was so short and slow, that Tom almost got there too soon. But he managed to control the return, and after a satisfactory base-line rally, he was able to come forward and volley a cross-court winner. There was a round of applause from the spectators, and Nikos let the camera dwell on Miller's furious face before he cut the shot.

Tom was baffled. All the fire and fury seemed to have gone out of Miller's game. Lewis had known that it was going to happen. But how?

Nikos was ecstatic. The camera operators were happy, the sound technicians said it wasn't perfect, but it would do, which was what they always said: and the video recordings looked stunning. At last he had some footage. The day was no longer a disaster. In fact, if he could get another master-shot as good as that, the day would be a triumph.

It had to be Miller's racquet, Tom decided. It must have been doctored, the strings softened in some way. Alvin approached, looking like an anxious nurse: a rôle that didn't suit him. 'I've brought you a salt tablet,' he said. 'You're going to need it.'

Tom took the tablet, and allowed himself to be pushed into a chair by the make-up girl, who wanted to check his wig. 'What's wrong with the racquet you foisted on Miller?' he asked Alvin.

Alvin tried to look sheepish, another feeble performance. 'You'll have to ask Lewis that. It's his recipe. Anyway, we didn't foist it on the guy: he practically tore my arm off to get it.' He seemed to be having difficulty keeping a straight face. 'Anyway, Lewis has been explaining to me about this scene: about how the important thing is the ball whizzing to and fro across the net. I mean, it's different from proper tennis.'

'Alvin, I know all that. I've been trying to explain it to you for weeks.'

'Yes, well, that just happens to be your strength, doesn't it? Biff-baffing the ball to and fro. I mean, you practically drove me crazy doing it. Just think what it might do to this guy.' That, it seemed, was to be the sum total of his encouragement. He went away, cackling like a deranged witch.

The new camera set-up took so long, that it was finished only twenty minutes before the scheduled lunch-break. There was time to rehearse, but not to film. But Lewis had a suggestion: 'I'm sure Zee can handle Tom's serve. Why not just risk a take? If you get something usable, it's a bonus: if you don't, all you've wasted is film.'

But Miller was not happy with that suggestion. 'There's something wrong with this goddam racquet,' he complained. 'My hand's swelling up. And it hurts like hell.'

Alvin crossed the court at a gallop, carrying a first-aid box, almost as if he had anticipated such an emergency. 'Sweat rash,' he announced tersely, after examining Zee's hand. 'Lots of amateurs suffer from it,' he added tactlessly.

'Never had it before,' Miller said.

'Ever been in Australia before?'

'No.'

'There you go then,' Alvin said ambiguously. 'Here, I'll spray it with this pain-killer. Not too much, or you won't know whether you're gripping the racquet or not. You want some talcum powder to soak up the sweat?'

'I guess so.'

'Here you are. Better put some on the racquet handle as well.'

Time was slipping past, but everyone agreed that it was worth going for one more take before lunch. When Nikos called 'Action!' Tom took his time, steadied himself, and served. It wasn't a bad serve: Miller could do no more than return it short to Tom's backhand. Tom played it hard and deep, forcing Miller back. Miller had to scramble to return: his shot was short and without authority, an easy kill. Tom played it deep to Miller's forehand, and took possession of the centre of the court. He played steadily, rhythmically, from one side to the other, using the full width of the court, but never punching the ball through for an outright winner. His opponent had the choice of either running or surrendering.

Miller ran. He retrieved from either wing, sometimes performing miracles of agility to keep the ball in play. He ran, and jumped, and struck, and ran some more. Tom played him like a salmon on a line, patient, implacable; and in the end Miller broke. He began to swear, breathlessly but doggedly: a high-pitched, staccato stream of abuse, punctuated by grunts of effort. Finally, he put up a feeble lob, and advanced down the centre of the court, screaming, as Alvin had done, 'Kill it! Kill it!'

Tom obliged. He smashed the ball hard over the net, a clear winner. Then stared in dismay, as his opponent keeled over in agony.

Carrying her sports bag, Alison walked over to the courts where the filming was taking place. There was a huge, football-crowd roar from the spectators as she approached: something very dramatic was happening. Before she reached the scene of the action, a figure stumbled towards her, evidently in pain. It fell to its knees and bent over like a giant grasshopper. It took a moment for Alison to recognize the figure, in these unfamiliar surroundings. 'Alvin! Are you all right?'

Alvin was not all right. He rolled over on to his side, holding his stomach. Tears blurred his eyes, and laughter hacked into his speech. 'I trained him!' he gasped. 'But it wasn't any use, because he lacked the killer instinct—that's

172

what I thought. Eee, how wrong I was!' He wiped his eyes, and began cackling all over again.

'Tom? What's he done?'

'He's just turned that bloody ape into a bloody soprano!'

'It was an accident!' Tom protested. 'Even if I'd wanted to hit him in the—like that—I don't have the skill.' He could tell that nobody believed him.

He and Alison were having a hurried lunch with Lewis in his trailer. Alvin was in attendance too, still sniggering like an adolescent schoolboy. Alison, who only knew the end of the story, was mystified by the atmosphere of barely-suppressed hysteria. She wanted to talk to Tom about her visit to the police station, but she realized that this was not going to be the time.

Lewis took pity on her bewilderment, and tried to explain: 'Zee Miller was trying to sabotage today's shoot by making Tom look foolish in the tennis scene.'

'It was easy for him,' Tom said, 'because he's a lot better than me.'

'So,' Lewis continued, 'we decided—Alvin and I—to even up the balance. We dummied Miller into using a doctored racquet—'

'Doctored with what?' Tom asked.

'Well, I got the idea from watching the pro tennis tournaments. You've seen how some guys carry powder in their pockets, and rub it on the racquet handle, to improve their grip? Well, I've often thought, what if some cunning bastard snuck some itching-powder in there, instead of talc?'

'Is that what you did? Put itching-powder on the handle of his racquet?'

'Sort of. I had to invent something, so I used three parts talcum powder to one part fibre-glass dust, and a generous flavouring of citric acid. It seemed to work just fine.'

Tom was appalled. 'You sneaky bastards! When he works it out, he'll think it was my doing, particularly after that—accident. He'll be after my blood for real.'

Lewis chuckled. 'Man, that "accident" has saved the picture. The whole scene is on video, remember, as well as film. If Zee Miller isn't the model of good behaviour until this picture is finished, there'll be ten copies of that video on board the next plane to New York.'

'That's why I could never be a real actor,' Tom explained to Alison in a glum aside. 'I don't have the stomach for it.' He pushed his plate away, and stood up. 'I'd better go and make my peace with that poor slob. We've a whole afternoon's work ahead of us.' Alison started to get up too, but Tom said. 'I'd better do it alone. Be back in a few minutes.'

He left an awkward silence behind him. 'Hell!' Lewis grumbled. 'Now, that son-of-a-bitch has made me feel guilty. I'd better go and eat humble pie, too.'

In the copse behind the seventh green, the man who called himself Oscar Pepperidge sat in the piebald shade, watching the players come and go. All his preparations were made, and the only thing he could do now was to wait. He didn't mind that. He had the still, cold patience of a snake. Or a spider: he knew his nickname, and it amused him, as much as anything did. The girl would be waiting, too; on edge, because she didn't know what was going on. Well, that was her bad luck.

He had decided to use the Wesson revolver. He was more accurate over a longer range with the Remington target pistol, but he couldn't see that this job needed that kind of fancy shooting. He had added his own refinements to the Wesson: a longer barrel, heavier trigger-pressure, soft-nosed Magnum cartridges, which spread on impact. Up to fifty yards, it was totally reliable. He knew he had a ninety per cent chance of stopping a man at twice that range, but ninety per cent wasn't good enough. He knew his business. One shot, then *move*, before anyone got over the shock. Don't even wait to see the man fall. He rarely loaded more than one round, anyway; the extra weight reduced accuracy. And if you couldn't do the job with one shot, you probably couldn't do it at all.

The man he was planning to kill came down the steps of a large caravan parked in the waste land with all the other

174

film vehicles. He hesitated a moment, and then walked the opposite way from where Pepperidge waited, towards a sort of mobile canteen, where a crowd of people laughed and chatted. Pepperidge relaxed. His chance would come: it always did. He was ready.

A few moments later he was alert again. His target, the man in the incredible jacket, had changed his mind and was walking along the path in his direction. Pepperidge stood up and moved to the spot he had chosen, on the side of the copse farthest from the golf-course. The concealment here was good: with luck, he might even get through the gap in the fence without being seen.

He moved without haste. The target would not be in range for a full minute; plenty of time to go through the routine. He took the gun from a small canvas hold-all, and checked the safety-catch. He began to breathe deeply and slowly, stretching his lungs. As always, he held the spare cartridge in the palm of his left hand: he had never yet needed to use it, but it was part of his routine, part of the carefulness that kept him successful, kept him alive.

He had paced out the distance, and left a scrap of rag under a stone as a marker. One step beyond that, and the hit was dead. He was still intrigued by the mystery of it, after all this time, all those deaths. Life could be humming like a motor inside a guy, then—click!—it was gone. Stillness. Blackness. Nothing. Like switching off a light.

Seventy-five yards. Another twenty seconds. Breathe deeply. Wait. Don't rush anything. Go through the routine in your head: raise—aim—steady—first pressure—squeeze. Then run. Don't think about running, yet. Don't think about the girl. She'll be there. Trust her. Damn, he's stopped. Sixty-five yards: too far. Wait.

Pepperidge waited. Then, in spite of himself, his pulse began to race. There was something very wrong. Suddenly there were two targets: two identical guys in tennis shorts and technicolor coats. There had been a foul-up: nobody had told him about this. Which was the target? Should he take them both? Was there time? They were on the move again, both advancing towards him. Nearly in range.

175

Which? Or both? He raised the gun, his mind in a turmoil of doubt.

The blow took him on the side of the head, and slammed him hard against the tree-trunk. The gun exploded at the same instant, and one of the blazered figures stumbled and fell. The big man battered Pepperidge to the ground in a storm of anger and disbelief. 'This bastard's got a gun!' Zee Miller yelled furiously. 'He's trying to kill somebody!' He whacked the gunman again with the twisted wreck of his carbon-fibre-shafted, hi-tech tennis racquet.

CHAPTER 29

Lewis was badly hurt. The bullet had torn a monstrous hole in his right thigh, and he was losing a lot of blood. Tom shed his jacket, tore off his shirt, and wadded it into a pad, which he pressed against the jagged exit wound. Lewis was in shock: the pain had not yet fully registered, and he was swearing in a low, disbelieving monotone.

People arrived at a run, among them someone who knew first aid. Between them they improvised a crude tourniquet, and little by little, made shift to stop the bleeding. Tom saw Alison briefly in the crowd. She seemed to grasp the situation quicker than anyone else, and set off at a run, presumably to phone for an ambulance.

Tom had registered the flash, and the brittle crack of the gunshot up ahead. He had heard Miller shouting, and the sounds of some sort of fight. His first thought was that Miller, humiliated on the film set, had gone completely berserk: but that seemed too far-fetched, even for that unstable character. He wanted to go and investigate, but he daren't leave Lewis until proper help arrived. The pain was reaching Lewis now: he hung on to Tom's arm, and his face looked squeezed and wrinkled, as if he had aged twenty years in the last minute.

The news spread; the crowd around them became bigger by the second. At last a doctor appeared. He gave Lewis an injection against the pain, and made a professional job of the bandages; but he confessed that there was nothing more he could do. Lewis needed a hospital, and fast.

The waiting seemed interminable. The crowd milled around aimlessly, unable to help, unwilling to go. Some of them had heard the shot, but there were conflicting accounts of where it had come from: and it seemed that the gunman had disappeared. The film crew was confused; Lewis wasn't called for today's action, and they didn't know whether the director would go through with the scheduled shooting or not. Nikos himself was undecided: until he knew how seriously Lewis was injured, he couldn't make up his mind whether the scenes were going to be usable or not. He hated to waste working time; but if Lewis died . . . He began to worry about insurance. He went off to phone Sam.

Zee Miller carried the unconscious gunman into the Administration block assisted by a small, plump man he'd never seen before, but who said he was the owner of the Club. They carried Oscar Pepperidge into an empty office and dumped him on the floor. 'Best keep him under lock and key until the police arrive,' Venn said. He found an extension lead under one of the desks, and used it to tie Pepperidge's hands behind his back. 'That ought to slow him down a bit. Can you guard him, while I find something to tie his feet with?' He was gone before Miller could answer.

Ten minutes later he was back, carrying Pepperidge's golf bag. 'Lots of goodies in here. It weighs a ton. Look.' He reached in and pulled out what looked like the skeleton of a rifle. The wooden stock and pistol grip had been replaced by aluminium frames, and the long, thin barrel had a naked look. A sniper's rifle, stripped of every ounce of unnecessary weight. There was a revolver in one of the side pockets, along with two boxes of ammunition, a kitchen knife in a leather sheath, a telescopic sight, a metal tripod and four lengths of thin rope.

'Looks like he was ready to start a war,' Venn commented. He tied the gunman's ankles together.

Pepperidge was conscious by now, but he made no

attempt to speak, or even move. He lay completely passive, not even trying to turn his head to look at them. There was no sign of fear or dismay, or even tension, about him. He simply lay on the floor, apparently as relaxed as a cat.

'Hell,' Miller said, 'I'd better get back to the set. This picture's goin' right down the tubes, and they're trying to blame it on me. Can you manage here?'

'Sure. But you'll have to answer questions when the police arrive, film or no film. Your publicity agent ought to be around, too. You're a goddam hero, son. You copped an assassin single-handed.'

'I know,' Miller said sourly. 'But they'll find a way to cheat me out of the credit. You can bet on it.'

As soon as he had gone, Venn locked the door behind him, and went back quickly to the desk. From separate drawers, he took a stub of candle, a metal spoon, and a first-aid box. 'The lawyer didn't give you any trouble, then?' he asked in a conversational tone.

Pepperidge sighed, but still didn't turn his head. 'No.'

'Where is he?'

'In his car.'

'And where's his car?'

Pepperidge breathed very deeply in, and then slowly out. 'My head hurts. I should like it if you would untie me now.'

'In a minute. Just want to be sure that punk doesn't come back.' There was the scrape of a match as Venn lit the candle.

Pepperidge did turn his head then. 'What are you doing?'

'Just cooking up a little scag. Want some?'

'You know I don't. Look, cut me loose. The only witness is that punk who laid me out. I can take care of him.'

'Of course you can.' Venn took a hypodermic syringe out of its sealed wrapper. 'There's no hurry. First, I'm gonna have a little shoot-up here.' He chuckled at his own wit, and concentrated on his preparations. 'What is it they call you, over here? Old Funnelweb? We've come a long way together, Joe.'

'My first mistake,' Pepperidge said bitterly. 'And it wasn't my fault. The girl only fingered one hit. She didn't say

178

anything about identical twins. The job was set up too fast.'

'Take it easy. Nobody's blaming you. We've just got to think what to do next.' Venn carefully filled the syringe, and walked around the desk holding it high, examining it as if it were a rare jewel.

'That stuff is going to help you think?' Pepperidge asked contemptuously.

'It already has,' Venn said. He kicked the gunman over on to his face, and knelt on his back. Pepperidge squirmed, but he was helpless under the pudgy man's weight. With his free hand, Venn pressed the other's head against the floor, and with almost surgical care, sought with the point of the hypodermic needle for a vein in Pepperidge's neck. Slowly, he injected the contents of the syringe, and stood up. 'We go back a long way, Joe,' he repeated softly. 'And that was the first time I ever lied to you. That wasn't scag. That was two hundred dollars' worth of pure horse. It really is a great way to go.'

The police arrived a few minutes before the ambulance. The two cars parked nose to tail, and four wary officers approached the scene. A shooting incident was always potentially unstable; until you knew the score, it was like walking through an uncharted minefield. And this particular incident looked more confusing than most: it was a sports club, so naturally there were golfers, tennis-players, even people in wet swimsuits: but who were the weirdly-dressed guys carrying sheaves of paper, and with stop-watches and other gismos round their necks, like medallions? Strangest of all, kneeling by the victim, was the guy's identical twin brother, who appeared to be wearing make-up, and an enormous man in skin-tight white strides, who was sobbing his heart out.

When the ambulance finally arrived, Brian insisted on accompanying Lewis to the hospital. Nobody gave him any argument. As the ambulance left, it passed a police van bringing the armed back-up: two sharp-shooters and a detective-superintendent. More reinforcements were on the way, the superintendent said. Now, what was this all about?

The facts were easily ascertained, once a few misunder-standings were cleared up. The victim had been shot by a gunman hiding in a clump of trees some fifty yards away. There seemed to be no motive that anyone could think of; although the super got the impression that one or two of the witnesses were not being completely frank. But that problem could wait: the important thing was, where was the gunman now?

With immaculate timing, Zee Miller opened the door of his trailer and took a commanding pose on the top step. 'I've got him for you, pal,' he announced over the top of the crowd. 'Trussed up like a Thanksgiving turkey.'

But in fact Pepperidge was not trussed up at all. He lay face down on the floor of the office in the Administration block, apparently still concussed. The bruises on his face and neck showed up darkly on his pale, damp skin. After some consultation, it was decided that he too should be taken to the hospital; the super rode with him in the back of one of the police cars. The man who called himself Oscar Pepperidge never regained consciousness. The diagnosis of heroin poisoning came too late to save him.

In the middle of the excitement, Alison was called to the phone. It was the detective who had taken her statement at the police station earlier that day. He wanted to interview her again, as soon as possible. 'There has been a develop-ment,' he said.

'What development? I got the impression that you didn't believe a word I said.'

The man was silent, as if debating something with himself. Finally he said, 'I'm sorry if you thought us uncooperative, miss. As I said, there's been a development. Mr Clays has been found dead—by his own hand, apparently.'

It soon became clear that he was not going to tell her any more over the phone. He repeated that he wanted to see her as soon as possible: would she be at the hotel that evening?

Alison arranged to meet him about eight o'clock. There was a question she wanted to ask: 'Have you told Mrs Clays yet?' But the man either didn't hear, or didn't want to answer. He rang off before she had finished speaking.

At last the questioning was over, and people were allowed to leave. The day's filming was abandoned, and shouts of 'It's a wrap,' were repeated with idiotic frequency, like words of some mystic invocation. Tom removed his wig and make-up and changed into his own clothes. His dresser insisted on keeping the blazer, in case it got lost. Tom was too weary and depressed to argue. Also, he couldn't rid himself of an oppressive feeling of guilt. Had the bullet that had felled Lewis really been intended for him? Was the ambush somehow connected with last night's happenings? Tom had the feeling that it was, and yet it was difficult to see exactly what the connection was. True, Tom and the Professor had worked out a sensational and potentially explosive theory, in the early hours of the morning; but it was hard to see how that could have provoked so swift a reaction. Unless ... with a gut-wrenching pang of alarm, Tom wondered where the Professor was.

With all the drama and excitement, the long day had passed quickly: the sun was already sliding below the western horizon when Tom stepped out of the dressing-room trailer. Francesca Clays was standing in almost the same place, by the trees, as she had stood this morning; but now she was coldly sober. 'Mr Grant? I was told you were down here, but I couldn't make out which of these vans you would be in. I have a message for you. Alison has been arrested.'

'Arrested?'

'At any rate she was taken away in a police van. She left her own car keys for you.' Francesca produced them from a capacious shoulder-bag.

'Arrested for what?' Tom asked.

'Perhaps I was being over-dramatic about that. The police whisked her away in a hurry, that's all I know.'

'Where have they taken her?'

'Well, the local nick is about five kilometres away. You could try there. I'll show you the way, if you like.'

'Please.'

The last piece of the jigsaw was falling into place, but Tom didn't recognize it at the time. If he had stopped to organize his thoughts, he would have seen then how the unholy pattern fitted together. The truth came to him suddenly, but it came too late. As he bent to unlock the door of Alison's car, he saw that it was not empty. On the back seat was a man he had never met before: a small, plump man, with a domed bald head speckled like a brown egg. On the floor at his feet, Alison lay bound and gagged. The plump man nursed a pistol on his knee: a Smith and Wesson M59. Behind Tom, Francesca said, 'I have a gun too, Mr Grant. Please don't force me to use it. Get behind the wheel.'

CHAPTER 30

'There are sixteen rounds in this piece, friend,' the plump man said. 'It's on automatic and the safety is off. One burst from this would split the girl's head open like a meat-cleaver. Unless you do exactly what I say, that's what's going to happen. Got the picture? Good. Let's go. Follow the Jag.'

Francesca got into a black car parked a few yards away, and drove smoothly out of the Club grounds. Tom followed.

He drove for more than two hours, on dirt roads that zigzagged bewilderingly through the hills. He lost all sense of direction. Sometimes the trees pressed close, turning the road into a long, claustrophobic tunnel: and in places, the ground seemed to fall away on all sides, and they could see nothing from the side windows but black, star-strewn sky.

They left the road for farm tracks, running across open fields. Once they rattled over a cattle grid, and once Francesca had to get out to open a rickety wooden gate. It grew even darker; black clouds swept up from the east, blotting out the stars. The headlights flicked across a ragged sprawl of buildings: the two cars halted in the middle of a big yard, pot-holed, rutted and in places overgrown with weeds. No lights showed from the buildings. The house directly in front, in the glare of the headlights, looked derelict: broken windows, peeling paintwork, splintered wood. When Tom cut the engine, the silence closed in, absolute, shocking.

'Now,' the plump man said, 'understand this. I'll kill you if I have to. The only reason I don't do it right now is that you just might be useful to me alive. But if I were you, I wouldn't gamble on that. Any heroics—any lack of co-operation—and I'll waste both of you. The girl first.'

Tom cleared his throat to speak, but the man leaned forward, jabbing with the barrel of the gun. 'No questions, Grant. You either know all the answers, or you don't. Either way, your life ain't worth spit, right now.'

Tom had to help Alison from the car, and then support her until some strength came back into her cramped limbs. Francesca took a small flashlight from her bag, and led the way across the yard into a low-ceilinged room in one of the outbuildings. The room smelt of leather and seed-oil, overlaid with a sickly smell of rotting wood. A long workbench stood to one side; there were rusting metal hooks at regular intervals along the ceiling beams, and matching them, massive staples bolted to the walls. At the far end, a filthy stove, with its gas bottle, stood next to a square stone sink with a single tap. There were a few pieces of shabby furniture: a couple of kitchen chairs, a sagging sofa, a broken card-table.

'Sit there,' the bald-headed man said, pointing at the chairs. He stationed himself behind Alison, resting the gun-barrel against the back of her head. 'And keep still.'

Francesca handed him the torch, and went out of the room. She came back a few minutes later, carrying a metal tool-box, staggering slightly under its weight. She took a pair of handcuffs out of the box, and clipped one on Tom's wrist and the other on to a staple on the wall. Then she cut the ropes around Alison's wrists and as swiftly handcuffed her to the opposite wall. 'What about the gag?' she asked the plump man.

'Take it off. We're safe enough here. Anyway, she knows that if she screams, I'll shoot her.'

Freed of the gag, Alison swallowed painfully, her breathing harsh and rasping. When she was able to speak, her voice was clogged and unnaturally husky. 'So now we know.'

'Know what?' Francesca sounded inexplicably apprehensive.

'Who murdered my aunt. And why.'

'You know nothing,' Francesca said bitterly. 'You understand nothing.'

'How many others?' Alison persisted. 'How many other helpless old people have you slaughtered, you and your disgusting husband? Clare couldn't have been the only one, and I can't be the only suspicious relative left behind. Other people have been asking questions, haven't they? The police are breathing down your neck. Is that why you killed him, too?'

'What are you talking about? Killed who?' The flashlight in Francesca's hand danced crazily, sending long shadows leaping round the room.

'The faked accident, the faked suicide: they're your speciality, aren't they?' Alison croaked. 'You—'

'Shut up!' The bald-headed man took command. He whipped the barrel of the gun across Tom's cheek, drawing blood. Then he crossed the room and shouted at Alison, leaning so close that the spray from his mouth spattered her face: 'Get this into your head: you two are responsible for each other. If you offend me, I shall hurt him. If he offends me, I shall hurt you. He understands that well. Do you?'

'Yes.' Alison fought against the panic that threatened to engulf her. She knew she ought to try to think coolly, rationally, not give way to this red tide of anger and fear. Tom's eyes sought hers, steadying her. 'Yes,' she said again, quieter now.

'Good.' The man turned to Francesca. 'Wait here. Watch them. I shall be gone half an hour, no more.' He looked at her more closely. 'You're shivering. Are you cold?'

'Is it true about Jeremy?' Her voice was almost childishly shrill.

'Of course not. She was trying to scare you. And it seems she succeeded. You have to trust me. Can I trust you?'

'Yes.' But her hands still shook.

The man closed the door behind him, and stood for a long time just the other side of it. He might have been making sure that the prisoners stayed quiet, or he might have been waiting for his eyes to adjust to the darkness. At last they heard him move away, his shoes scuffing the hard-packed mud of the yard.

Tom said quietly, 'Who is he?'

'Don't ask, don't talk!' Francesca pleaded in a whisper. 'He might hear you.' Then, ignoring her own warning, she asked urgently, 'Who was killed, who? Was it Jeremy?'

'You know it was,' Alison said.

'No. I *didn't* know. Can't you see I'm just as much a prisoner as you are?'

'What I don't see,' Tom said, 'is how old Baldy fits into all this.' The lie was worth trying. 'Who is he?'

'It's best you don't know. If he thought you knew, he'd kill you for sure. And if he thought I'd told you, he'd kill me.'

There was the sound in the distance of breaking glass, splintering wood. They were quiet, listening. They could hear only vague noises: creaks, bumps. It sounded as if the man was walking over a bare wooden floor, moving furniture.

'He probably plans to kill us in any case,' Tom said.

'No. Not yet, anyway. If he was going to, he would have done it by now. I think he's keeping you alive as insurance.'

'Insurance? Against what?'

'Against things going wrong—more wrong than they have already.' She spoke quickly, whispering, watching the door. 'He needs time. He has to get out of the country. He's planned for that—he's had an escape route ready for years. But he wants to take as much with him as he can; he needs a couple of days to switch his accounts, clear his deposit boxes. But if anything goes wrong in those two days, he'll have you as hostages. He'll try and barter you for his freedom.'

'And you?' Alison asked. 'Where do you fit in?'

'Where do I ever fit in? I do what I'm told, I always have. And *you* would have, too, in my place.'

'I don't mean that. I mean, will he make sure of your freedom, too?'

'He's my father,' Francesca said flatly.

Tom kept his voice gentle: 'Francesca, you know, don't you, what your father and Jeremy have been doing? Kidnapping people, swindling them of their money—and then killing them.'

'No! Some people died—they were old, they just died. And then there were some accidents, some suicides. Not murder. Nobody ever proved murder.'

'These things can be faked. They say Jeremy committed suicide. Do you believe that?' Alison asked.

'Yes.' But her manner belied the word.

'Look,' Tom said, 'I know you've been part of it—I know, for instance, that you impersonated Clare Yelverton at Balmoral Creek, and at the art auction—but if you were forced to do it, if you can show that you were in fear of your life, no jury would convict you of those crimes—'

'They weren't murder.' She seemed not to be listening: the words were addressed to herself.

'If you get caught—' Tom began, but she cut in: 'I don't want to talk about it any more.' Her tone was final. Tom sensed the rising pressure of hysteria, and kept silent.

Alison asked: 'What is this place? A farm?'

Francesca relaxed a little with the change of subject. 'Used to be a training stables. Then a stud farm. Years ago. Owner went bust.'

'Who owns it now?'

'I do, on paper. I own a lot of property, on paper.' She laughed without humour.

Out in the yard a car started up with a roar that tore at their stretched nerves. Francesca ran to the door as the car drove away. 'He's gone—taken the Jag!' She stumbled out into the yard, panic-stricken, and watched as the car accelerated away. Her shoulders sagged.

'What now?' Tom shouted.

Francesca came slowly back into the room. 'We wait. He'll be back.' She was reassuring herself.

'Francesca—'

'Shut up! I don't want to hear any more! Just shut up, or I'll—' She lost interest in the threat. She sat stiff-backed on

186

one of the kitchen chairs, facing the open door. After a minute she stood up and moved a chair, so that Alison could sit down. Then she took her own chair to the far end of the room, near the stove. The light from her torch dimmed suddenly: she shook it, and after a moment's thought, switched it off. In the darkness, she began muttering to herself, but Tom couldn't make out the words. Then he did. '*In nomine* . . .' She was praying.

Tom leaned against the wall, suddenly aware of how tired he was. His instincts told him that Francesca was ready to help them, but he didn't want to scare her off by pushing too hard. Best, now, to be patient. He hoped Alison would see it that way, too.

Time passed. The air became cooler, almost chilly. Their breathing sounded louder in the silence; their ears picked up tiny mysterious sounds—dry leaves rustling in the slight breeze: the scamper of small animals. Then, in the distance, a faint throbbing, growing louder: the unmistakable sound of a car. Francesca scurried to the door. Her first reaction was unexpected, Tom thought, and illuminating: she showed not relief, but fear. Did that mean that she feared that someone other than her father might be approaching?

But in fact, it was the bald-headed man. He was bland and cheerful, and he carried supplies: sandwiches and fruit and bottled water. Tom wondered where he had got them at that hour; there had to be a sizeable township not too far away.

'Food and drink,' the plump man said. 'Don't get greedy: it may have to last you some time.' He fetched another electric torch from his car; suddenly the room seemed unnaturally bright. He moved Francesca's chair from the end of the room and handed it to Tom. 'Here's how it is,' he said. 'We have things to do. We may come back here, or we may not. If we make it, we'll tell somebody how to find you. If not—well, you'd better hope that we make it. There's food and water. It's not much, but it's better than dead, which is the alternative.' He turned to Francesca. 'Outside, kid: we've got things to do.' They closed the door and locked it, the key grating drily against the tumblers.

'What sort of thing?' Alison wondered. 'What do you suppose they're doing?'

'I think—this could be one of their kidnap hide-outs—that would explain the handcuffs. My guess is, they're destroying evidence.'

Alison shivered. 'Do you suppose other people—old people—have been chained up here, like this? It seems so unimaginably cruel. Perhaps Clare—'

'Don't think about that. Try to relax, save your strength. We've got to figure a way out of here.' Tom tried to sound more confident than he felt.

'I went to the police this morning, to tell them about Jeremy Clays,' Alison said. 'But they thought the whole story too far-fetched to be true.'

'That's why they got away with it for so long. It's a lawyer's crime, made possible by the law. I should have cottoned on earlier, when you told me that there are no death duties in this State. That law attracts old people from all over the country: people who want to be generous to their heirs. An old wealthy person, alone, living hundreds of miles away from any relative: a natural victim. But how to fleece the victim without getting caught? Jeremy, the lawyer, found a brutally simple answer: kidnap old people and manipulate their estates. In Clare's case, that meant leaving her heir—you—with a million dollars' worth of art, which Clare had apparently bought for two million. It didn't have to be art—it could be real estate, jewellery—even things like stamps or coins.'

'But in the end—' Alison choked on her anger and indignation.

'But in the end, the victim had to be murdered, yes. But that didn't pose much risk. The heir—the one with the obvious financial motive—is far away, clearly blameless; why suspect that an accident is anything but what it seems?'

Alison stood up and tried to massage some feeling into her numbed fingers. 'I've always thought of myself as a tolerant, forgiving person. But I tell you, Tom, I would kill those people without mercy, if I could.'

'I think they're already into the business of killing each

other. There's another, very nasty thread woven into this fabric that I—'

He was interrupted by the unlocking of the door. Francesca came in, followed by the bald-headed man. She made an awkward business of entering, trying to manage the flashlight and carry two large metal buckets. The man laughed, making no attempt to help her. 'The lady is concerned for your personal hygiene. You mustn't be left without a pot to piss in, she says. Ain't that considerate of her?'

Francesca put one bucket near Alison, and then crossed to Tom. Tom stood up as she approached, and she reared back in alarm, dropping the flashlight, which went out. She dived for it, letting go of the bucket, which rolled, clanging, into the wall. The plump man cackled with laughter, and switched on his own torch. Francesca struck out at Tom with her fist. 'Don't touch me!' She overbalanced and fell against him, and with a conjuror's deftness, pressed something into the palm of his hand. Then, apparently overwhelmed with panic and confusion, she ran from the room.

'She left you her torch, too,' the plump man observed drily. 'Now you can watch each other squatting.' Chuckling at his own joke, he slammed the door and locked it.

In the darkness, Alison stumbled against the bucket and swore. 'I'd still like to string that bitch up by the heels.'

Tom waited tensely, listening. Only one car drove away: the Jaguar. 'I was hoping they would take both cars,' he said.

'Why?'

'Because then I would be sure that they had both gone.' He began feeling around for the flashlight. He could just reach the floor with his free hand, but the area he could cover was limited. 'There's something strange going on: I think Francesca's just handed me a key.'

'What do you mean—you think? She either did or she didn't.'

'I'm sorry. She gave me something. It might be a key. But it's an odd shape.' Tom extended the search with his foot, very cautiously: he didn't want to kick the torch away.

'Tom! Do you think she's decided to help us?'

189

'We'll see.' Tom dragged the flashlight within reach. 'It's a key, all right. It's wrapped round and round with sticky tape.'

'Why did she do that?'

'I guess, in case she dropped it. The sound of a metal key hitting the floor would be a dead giveaway. Also—' Tom picked at the tape with his nails—'she probably wanted to delay us. She wouldn't want us dashing out of the house before Daddy got clear away.'

'But—' Alison was confused—'why were you worried about them *both* going? Who would stay behind, and why? There's no point in laying a trap for us, when we're trapped already.'

'Morbid suspicion. I just feel—ah!' He had finally unwound all the sticky tape. 'Yes, it's a key: for the handcuffs.' In seconds, he had freed them both. Alison put her arms tightly round him, breathing fast as if from hard exercise.

Tom said quietly: 'Why do I get the feeling there must be a catch somewhere? This all seems far too easy.'

'Francesca was very jumpy. She may have had a change of heart.'

'Or be taking out some insurance of her own, yes. All the same, I think we ought to be very careful.'

Locking the door had just been a symbolic gesture: the window-frame was as rotten as old cheese. Tom pulled the whole window clear, and stepped through the gap. Across the yard, the white bulk of the Mercedes showed ghost-like in the darkness. The keys were in the ignition. 'Let's go!' Alison whispered, glancing nervously around. The glow from the torch enveloped them in a bubble of yellow light.

'Wait.' Tom took the key out of the ignition. 'Where's the bonnet lock?'

'I don't know. Why?'

'There's something wrong. Look.'

It wasn't much: a small loop of wire protruding under the dashboard. 'That wasn't there before.'

It took them a few minutes to get the bonnet open, but it was worth the trouble. Untidily but effectively rigged, just in front of the steering-wheel, was an oblong slab of plastic explosive, wired up to one of the plug leads.

Tom whistled. 'So it was a trap.'

'But why? Why didn't they just shoot us while we were chained up?'

Tom pulled the detonator and its wiring clear, and clipped the lead back on to the spark-plug. 'My guess is that this is Daddy's work. Another piece of insurance, in case we got free. I don't think Francesca knew about it.'

'Tom! They're coming back!'

It was true. Although they could see nothing yet, the drone of a car engine was clearly audible. 'What shall we do? Is there another way out of here?' She pulled open the car door.

'Leave the car,' Tom snapped. 'We'll have to run for it.'

'Leave the car? But—'

'If there's one bomb, there could be another. There isn't time to check it. Let's go!'

'Which way?'

'Behind the buildings. There's no cover anywhere else. Come on—we have to stay together.'

But after a few paces Alison stopped. 'Give me the keys.'

'But—'

'Don't argue. There isn't time.' It was true: they could see the headlights now, swinging and glittering in the distance. Tom handed over the keys reluctantly and Alison ran back to the Mercedes, opened the boot, and took out her long sports bag and a small oblong box. She slammed the boot shut, leaving the keys dangling from the lock, and ran back. 'Here.' She thrust the box into Tom's hand.

'What is it?'

'It's a tool-kit. Among other things, it contains one very sharp kitchen knife. Run!'

They ran. They detoured the house by way of a long alleyway between outbuildings—barns or stables, they couldn't tell which. The ground was uneven and littered with debris: Tom had to use the flashlight, much against his will.

He tried to pick a route that would keep the farm buildings between them and the approaching car. It was easy going

191

at first, over grass or weeds that crunched drily underfoot; then the ground became harder, dustier. He became aware that they were climbing: a gentle incline, but climbing, nevertheless. Alison began to falter, winded. Tom reached for her sports bag. 'Let me carry that.'

'No.' Her tone brooked no argument. Tom wanted to know why it was so important, but neither of them had breath to spare for talking. They pushed on, Alison grimly ignoring the pain in her side.

The slope became steeper: they had to climb in earnest. Tom could hear the faint trickle of water nearby, but he couldn't tell which direction the sound came from. He looked back: they were above the farm now. The layout of the buildings was outlined in the car's headlights. Alison scrambled higher: she was hampered by the sports bag, but determined to keep it close. Tom followed. They were moving slowly now: using their hands as well as their feet to gain height.

They found the creek a few minutes later. It was wide, they thought: how wide, they couldn't tell. Skirting a large outcrop of rock, they found they were paddling through water no more than a few inches deep, trickling through the stones.

They climbed a few more feet. Alison had to rest. She doubled over for a minute, then slowly straightened up. 'It's not them,' she said obscurely.

'What?'

'Look.'

They could now see over the top of the main farm house into the yard. The car parked behind the Mercedes was tall, squarish: a Range-Rover, its headlights still blazing. There were two men, one of them slim, like a boy. The other man moved, crossed the yard in front of the headlights. At his heels, a black shadow. A dog. Alison's breath rasped in her throat, 'Now we know how Clare died,' she said.

Tom made himself look away from the light, tried to recover his night vision. 'We'd better keep moving.'

'Where to?'

'As far away from those guys as we can get.'

192

'The dog will catch up with us.'

'The stream may confuse the scent.'

'We have to fight sometime.' She was not arguing, merely stating the obvious.

'But we don't know who they are.'

'I do. They're the bastards who killed my aunt.' However, she trudged up the slope ahead of him, without further comment.

Ten minutes later, the hill defeated them. They came to a group of large, slab-like rocks, and then an almost vertical cliff wall. Water trickled down the rock-face from fissures above their heads. In the daylight, it might be climbable; but in the dark, they both knew it was impossible. Tom tried to reconnoitre along the cliff-face, slipped on the wet rock, bruising his knee. Down by the farm buildings, the dog barked, once.

'He's picked up our scent,' Alison said. She sounded unexpectedly calm. She moved away from Tom into the shelter of the large rocks. Tom remembered the box he had carried all this time: a tool-kit, she said. He opened it and rummaged inside. There were some metal things, shaped like pencil stubs; and several quill pens. And a kitchen knife with a four-inch blade, sharp as a razor. It wouldn't be much use against guns; but he didn't feel quite so defenceless.

The wind, up on the hill, was quite chilly: he wished he had a sweater with him. Or even his blazer. The wind was pushing the clouds northward: the stars appeared, gleaming coldly from a black velvet sky; but as yet, the moon was still hidden. Even without the moon, it was fractionally less dark.

Alison said quietly, 'Your white shirt shows up against the cliff.'

Startled, Tom took his shirt off. 'Is that better?'

'Yes. Is there a rock you can get behind? They may have guns.'

Tom had thought of that, too. 'I'll see if there's any cover over on this side. If you see a chance, run for it; I'll hold them as long as I can.'

193

'There's brave.' Her tone was gently mocking. It was strange, Tom thought, how often people became light-headed in the face of real danger.

Their pursuers were closer, now: their shoes scraped on hard ground. The dog led them inexorably upwards; without the dog, they wouldn't have known where to begin looking. Tom shivered as the wind raised goose bumps on his bare skin. He moved carefully along the base of the cliff. A movement far to his left caught his eye—a speck of light, a glint of metal—distracted him momentarily. Something rolled under his foot, nearly pitching him off-balance. It was part of the branch of a tree, perfectly straight, and about two feet long. Now, he had a stick and a knife: two weapons. Things were looking up.

There was a clatter on the stones, and the dog came at him out of the darkness, leaping high, teeth bared. Tom raised the stick, just in time. The jaws fastened on the wood, and the dog's weight pulled it down, pulled Tom forward. He thrust with the knife, hit bone, jarring his wrist. The dog snarled, shook its head powerfully. The stick broke in two, and the beast leaped for Tom's arm, missed and sank its teeth into his chest. The pain was fierce and frightening. Tom stabbed downwards with the knife, blindly, wildly; the brute was eating him alive. The dog, distracted, began snapping at the knife. If it gets my wrist I'm done for, Tom thought. He was pressing his free hand against the wound in his side. The blood was warm on his fingers. He was losing. The dog was too fast.

Then, without warning, it was over. There was a sound, close to his ear, that he had never heard before and was never to forget; a sound like the hissing of a snake, or like a huge wing beating the air, once. The dog lay on its side, its jaws still snapping, its feet flailing at space, but ever feebler, like a clockwork toy running down. The animal seemed to be pinned to the ground: and there was something sticking out of its side. A feather.

'Are you all right?' Alison was standing over him: he didn't even realize he had fallen down. 'What's that?' he asked stupidly.

'What does it look like? It's an arrow. Look, pull it out for me, will you? I'm not strong enough.'

Wincing with pain, Tom pulled it out. It *was* an arrow, by God, fully a yard long, with a metal pencil-like tip, and a white goose-quill flight. And Alison was carrying—

'Yes, it's a bow,' she said crisply. 'Move yourself: we've got things to do.'

To his surprise, she wrapped his shirt round the bloody corpse of the dog, tying the sleeves in a knot, to hold it in place. 'Shift that thing up here,' she said.

He dragged the body to the spot she had chosen—a slab of rock overhanging the steepest part of the creek bed. 'They're down there somewhere,' she whispered. 'They sent the dog ahead to flush us out. Now, it's going to perform the same service for us.'

'A bloody bow and arrow!' Tom said, wondering. 'Why didn't you tell me?'

'There wasn't time. It's no big deal. Tennis isn't the only sport in the world, you know. Now, I need to know where those bastards are. When I give the word, I want you to pitch that damned animal over that rock. And duck down fast.' She edged away from him in the darkness. 'Now!'

The dog was enormously heavy. It took all Tom's strength to heave it up on to the rock and push it off the other side. It thudded on to the wet scree, and rolled in its grotesque shroud down the slope, carrying an avalanche of small pebbles. There was a shout from below, and then Brumby was in the path of the sliding body, feet apart, crouched in the orthodox firing position, left hand supporting the right wrist, shooting rapidly, accurately, the slugs thumping into the thick body.

Now Alison knew where Brumby was. She shot coolly, methodically. And, against the thunder of the gun, noiselessly.

Her third arrow struck Brumby in the chest, its flight deflected upwards by the fourth rib, pushing fragments of bone into the heart muscle. He staggered for a moment, like a dazed prizefighter. He was dead before he hit the ground. Red, standing nearby, heard the fall, but didn't know the reason. He ran to his partner, and stooped, disbelievingly, over the body. Alison, not knowing she had hit, was still shooting into the darkness. Her last arrow went through Red's thigh, severing the main artery. He fell into the shallow water, and screaming, bled to death in minutes.

Tom and Alison heard the screaming, heard the silence that followed the screaming, and stayed where they were, listening hard. Alison wanted to move: she felt sure it was all over, but Tom forced her to wait. 'Not yet,' he said firmly.

'Why not? I got one of them. Maybe both.'

'Yes. But I think—' Tom paused. His attention was not directed downhill, towards the farm, but to their left, where it was just possible to make out the jagged black outline of the hill against the sky. 'I think,' he went on, whispering, 'that we've been doing other people's work for them. Francesca set us up with that act of hers.'

'Set us up? How?'

'She and her old man left us here as bait. Think about it.' He anticipated her question. 'There had to be at least four people involved in your aunt's murder. Jeremy, for the legal work; Francesca, to impersonate Clare; and at least two people to do the actual kidnapping and murder—the executive branch, as it were. You've just lopped off the executive branch.'

'What about Francesca's father? Where does he fit in to all this?'

'He's the spider at the centre of a different web. It's complicated: I'll explain later.'

'All right. But what did you mean about Francesca leaving us here as bait?'

'It's a clean-up operation. Francesca and her Daddy are systematically wiping out everyone connected with Clare's murder: that means us, and the other members of their own gang. They hired a professional to do the job—he killed Jeremy, and tried to kill me. When that went wrong, they had to improvise another scheme. They kidnapped us, and then phoned their two hit-men to come and help finish us off. They wanted all their fish in the same barrel.'

196

'But what was all that charade about letting us escape? Why not leave us chained up?'

'Because they wanted our attention focused on each other when they ambushed us all. Also, if we managed a few deaths between us—which we have—it makes their job easier.'

Alison wasn't convinced, he could tell, but he persuaded her to be patient a little longer. 'If I'm right, they'll have to make a move soon. Our only chance is to outwait them.'

'Our *only* chance? Why?'

Tom moved his head slowly, scanning the darkness. He blessed the chill in the air: it kept him alert. 'If I'm right, it means that they've come prepared. That means a long-range weapon: a rifle. And possibly an image-intensifier.'

'What's that?'

'It's a sort of telescopic sight that lets you see in the dark. It's unlikely that he'll have one, but I don't want to take any chances. The first thing we need to know is where they are.'

'If they're here at all.'

Tom was beginning to share her scepticism when the sound came, sending their pulses racing. It was a hollow, metallic click, and it came from their left, in the place where Tom thought he had seen something earlier. 'They're on the move,' he whispered.

'What was that?'

Tom grinned. 'It's almost impossible to close a car door quietly. They're parked somewhere over there, beyond the creek bed.'

'All right, you've proved your point. What now?'

'You wait here. Keep watching and listening. I'm going down to get Brumby's gun.'

'*Whose* gun?'

'Sorry, I was showing off. I *think* the bozo down there was ex-detective Ronald Kilkee, nicknamed Brumby. I'll—'

'Yes, I know. You'll explain later. You're a surprising man, General.'

That was Lewis's pet name for him, Tom remembered; and he was startled by how painful the memory was. He picked his way slowly down the slope, crouching low, trying not to make any noise. He felt frighteningly exposed: if Papa had got an image-intensifier, and if he had an L39 sniper's rifle . . . those things could put a bullet through four inches of concrete. Well, if his luck ran out, he wouldn't know much about it.

He found Brumby lying on his back, the arrow in his chest sagging like a drunken flagstick. He pulled the arrow free, felt Brumby's throat for a pulse. The man was dead as stone. A few yards away, he found the other killer, just as dead. Oddly, this one, lying on his side, had his thumb in his mouth.

It took him five minutes' careful searching to find the gun. He wanted to check the clip, but was afraid of the noise it would make. He found a few cartridges in Brumby's pocket, and crept back up the hill with his trophy.

Alison was shivering with cold. 'I don't think I can just sit here any longer.'

'All right, we'll move. How's your bushcraft?'

'I've no idea. The question's never come up before.'

'I'll wager it's better than theirs. They're city folk. They'll not go far from their car. Let's see if we can find a way round this damn hill.'

They felt their way crabwise across the slope, and after about a hundred yards they were able to climb again, threading through massive boulders and thrusting outcrops of rock. They had to rest frequently: once, Tom took time out to check the gun. It was a Walther PP automatic: a man-stopper at short range.

'Are we going anywhere in particular?' Alison asked, 'or just running away?'

'They've parked their car on the other side of this hill somewhere. That means there must be a road. I want to find it.'

It wasn't a road, just a broad path like a bridle track, and it was on a high ridge without much cover, but it ran in the right direction. They moved slowly, crouching, ready at any minute to dive for shelter. They were quite a sight, Tom thought, had anyone been there to see: a half-naked man with blood seeping out of a hole in his chest, and a pint-sized Amazon complete with bow and a quiver full of arrows. He had never thought of the bow as a serious weapon before: now, having seen what it could do, he rated it more terrifying than the pistol he was carrying.

It took them an hour to come up to the car. Tom's eyes were well accustomed to the dark by now, but even so, he didn't recognize its shiny bulk until they were almost on top of it. He tugged at Alison's sleeve, and they left the path, making a wide detour to the shelter of a thin copse of gorse and mountain ash. They watched the car for several minutes, but they could see no sign of movement, in it or near it.

'I don't think there's anyone there,' Alison whispered.

Tom didn't think so either, but he would have liked to make sure. 'Will an arrow break the side window at this distance?'

'No chance. Probably not at any distance.'

'Hell.' Tom was at a loss what to do next.

Then, faintly, out of the distance, came a cry: a shriek of agony, like the sound of an animal leaving a limb behind in a trap. Then shots—several shots, a dry, drumming noise.

The hills baffled the sounds, threw them back and forth, disguising their source. Tom started forward, changed his mind, held Alison back. They still didn't know if anyone was in the car.

Suddenly there was a commotion ahead, and they both ducked for shelter. There was no need: the car door slammed, the engine roared into life, and the headlights raked over their heads as the Jaguar turned in a tight arc, jolting over the grass. The wind blew the faint smell of its exhaust into their faces.

'Did you see who it was?' Alison asked.

'No. But I'll give odds it was Francesca.'

'So where's Papa?'

They went to look. The darkness was yielding to the first grey coaxing of dawn. From the spot where the car had been parked they could see the roofs of the farm buildings and the broad, shiny path of the creek. A blunt buttress of stone, invisible before, jutted out of the hillside to their right, masking the place where they had hid.

There was a lot of dead ground between them and the farm, still shrouded in total blackness. Papa was down there somewhere: they could hear him, even if they couldn't see him. He was grunting with effort, like a weight-lifter, and he sounded as if he was dragging something over the loose stones. As they watched, there was a flash, and a loud report that echoed, throbbing, down the valley. Now they knew where he was. He began to sing, tonelessly, and the dragging sound ceased: he had reached firmer ground. The grunting began again, slow, unrhythmical. The light was increasing every second: now they could just make him out, a squat shadow, dragging one foot, using the rifle for support.

The light revealed other things, too: a shapeless mass in a white shroud, and two sprawled bodies.

'We'd better go after him,' Alison said. But she made no effort to move. 'Was it—?'

'Francesca, yes. I think she stabbed him. After they found the bodies.'

'Her own father?'

Tom shrugged. 'I think he had become a liability.'

They watched as the plump shadow lurched a few more yards. They felt tired, curiously lethargic. Tom explained, at last: 'That man is an American named Underhill—Baz, or Boss Underhill, they called him. A Mafia godfather, operating out of Detroit. His partner was a professional killer called Joseph—"Slow Joe—" Largo. About seven years ago, Underhill and Largo were nailed by the FBI— a cast-iron case. Incredibly, they were allowed bail. They jumped bail, disappeared. Later that summer two bodies fished out of Lake Michigan were identified as Largo and Underhill.'

'How do you know all this?' Alison asked wearily. She lowered herself stiffly to the ground, and leaned her back against the cold rock.

'The background, I knew from Press reports. The rest I put together from bits and pieces. Underhill and Largo were not dead, obviously: they were smuggled into Australia by

200

a lawyer called Jeremy Clays, who paid out a hefty bribe to an immigration officer named Chiswick.'

'You know the immigration officer's name, too?'

'We met, as you might say. Chiswick was later murdered, to keep his mouth shut, and his body dumped in a remote cave in the mountains. When I was filming in those mountains, I stumbled on his skeleton.'

The bald-headed man had reached the meadow behind the farm. He was moving more slowly, having to rest between each step. They could no longer hear the sounds he was making. 'He's getting away,' Alison said listlessly.

'He can't.'

'Go on. So Jeremy's smuggled his crooked father-in-law into the country, given him a new start, a new identity. How did you find out about him?'

'Through a girl I never met—a dancer, turned hostess, turned whore, called Vicki. She met Underhill in the States —was possibly his mistress for a while—and by an unlucky accident, recognized him when she came back to this country. She also had the misfortune to fall in love with a policeman.'

'It happens,' Alison smiled. Then she stopped smiling. 'Vicki? Isn't that—?'

'The girl your aunt befriended, yes. Underhill found out about Vicki, had her killed, and then began to get neurotic about Vicki's close acquaintances. Vicki visited Clare, as we know. I don't know why Underhill thought that Clare might be a threat, but he probably told Francesca that she had to be eliminated—and the plot to murder your aunt sprang out of that. Francesca saw the chance of making a big profit on the side, and couldn't bear to pass it up.'

'And now Francesca's got away.'

'Nothing we can do about that. The police will pick her up.'

The plump, bald-headed man stumbled and fell near the farm buildings. He crawled a few yards, leaving his rifle lying in the grass, and then painfully heaved himself to his feet. He lurched into an ungainly run, tacking unsteadily

201

like a drunken man, and disappeared round the corner of the stables.

Alison sprang to her feet. 'Hell! I left the car keys down there. In the lock of the boot.' She began to run down the hill, dangerously fast. Tom jogged after her. He was feeling dizzy.

They had covered less than half the distance down the slope when the explosion stopped them in their tracks. In the retreating thunder of the echoes they heard glass breaking, masonry falling . . . 'It's the Merc,' Tom said. He was standing in the wide, shallow creek-bed: water oozed and trickled through the pebbles under his feet. The water was very shallow, but dark; the pebbles shone whitely, like eyes, like huge, luminous spawn. Everything moved, lurched. The stream was so small, but it seemed to be roaring like a water-fall: there was a noise like a tidal wave, like an express train . . .

Tom fainted.

He came to briefly, and tried to explain. 'The first bomb was there for us to find. The real one, the biggie, was—'

No one seemed to be listening. The roaring overwhelmed him again.

CHAPTER 31

The first person Tom saw, when he came to, was Julian. He groaned and shut his eyes, but Julian was still there when he opened them again. There were other people there, too: featureless faces, bobbing like pink balloons. He was in bed: in a hospital ward, by the smell of it. Then, blessedly, Alison's face shaped itself magically from one of the balloons. She held his hand, and that made him feel a lot better. There was still room for improvement, though: his whole body seemed stiff and sore, as if he had suffered some medieval torture.

Julian was still chattering excitedly, but Tom had missed

most of it: 'Every major distributor wants it. They're offering deals that would blow your mind.'

'I don't know what you're talking about,' Tom said.

'The picture. This publicity has made it the hottest property of the year. If we can get it out this winter, it'll gross a billion.'

'How's Lewis?'

'Not good,' Julian admitted indifferently. 'But he's going to pull through. In any case, we can manage without him. The script has been re-shaped to give Zee Miller more scope, and we're making a big feature of your involvement, of course. As soon as you're well, Tom, we'll have to work really fast.'

'Work at what?'

'Why—the picture. Sam and Nikos are working out the details now.' Julian laughed his high-pitched nasal bray. 'You haven't taken it in, have you? We want you to take over the part in your own right. We're going to make you a star.'

Tom pressed his head deeper into the pillow and closed his eyes again. 'Stuff it,' he said.

Alison outwaited them all—visitors, film crew, reporters, police; but when they were alone, they found little to say. They still held hands, and that seemed to be enough. Then Alison said, 'They think you'll be out of here in a week. Maybe less.'

'Good.'

'You'll need to convalesce.'

'Will I?'

'I know just the place. Orpheus Island, on the Reef. Very quiet, very exclusive. I booked us a bungalow there. It has a sunken bath.'

'Does it have a double bed?'

'It was the first thing I made sure of. I'm no fool.'

EPILOGUE

Francesca's trial lasted four weeks, and she was acquitted on all charges except one of obtaining money by false pretences. The judge ruled that her detention in custody awaiting trial was sufficient punishment for that offence, and she was released immediately; coincidentally on the same day that Lewis Goring died, after a series of operations had failed to save his life.

On New Year's Day, Tom and Alison went to see a performance at the Sydney Opera House. It was the first time Tom had been to the opera since his divorce from Maria. He enjoyed it more than he expected to, and Alison loved it. She cried non-stop through the last act.

They had come up to Sydney for a reason—to attend Brian's farewell party. He had taken a job as a hairdresser on a luxury cruise liner and was leaving the country—probably for good, he said.

After the performance they stood on the steps overlooking the Harbour, and watched the big white ship manœuvre out of Circular Quay. The tugs hooted, the ship's Tannoy blared jolly music, and a few people cheered. The liner backed, turning, until it seemed certain that its stern would collide with the piers of the Harbour Bridge. Then the tugs pulled the bow round into the channel, and cast off. The big screw began to push the boat forward, its lights gleaming on both sides. It was a moving, beautiful sight. Alison, with Tom's arm round her shoulder, cried a little more, because she felt so happy.

On board, the passengers were settling down, exploring, getting lost: some blasé, some excited as children.

Francesca was one of the blasé ones, at least outwardly. There was a month's unashamed luxury ahead of her, and she was going to enjoy it. And that was just the beginning. There was money salted away in Switzerland, Argentina,

South Africa: more money than she could possibly spend. But she would try: by God, she would try . . .

The maid came in and checked the linen; then the cabin stewards introduced themselves, and the purser brought some papers. It was always like this at the beginning of a cruise: the through-traffic was non-stop.

Then the hairdresser: a big man with a round, soft face and kind eyes. Gay, of course, but so many of the best hairdressers were. Just to say that Madame could call at the salon any time: just ask for Brian. Or Brian would style Madame's hair in the comfort of her own cabin, any time.

'Now?' Francesca asked. 'Before the First Night party?' Hardly anyone slept, the first night out.

'Of course. There's plenty of time.' Brian fetched his things: hair-dryer, aprons, box of shampoos, lotions, combs, scissors. He began to hum merrily, along with the Tannoyed music. 'If Madame would sit here—?'

There was something faintly familiar about him, Francesca thought. Had he been at the trial? In the public gallery? So many people: she couldn't possibly remember. 'Have you worked on this ship long?' she asked, making conversation.

'Oh no. In fact, Madame is Brian's first client.' His big hands closed round her neck. 'And probably his last.'

If you have enjoyed this book and would like to receive details of other Walker Mystery-Suspense novels, please write for your free subscription to:

Crime After Crime Newsletter
Walker and Company
720 Fifth Avenue
New York NY 10010